THE
VIKING
PRINCESS

ISBN 978-1-954095-59-5 (Paperback)
The Viking Princess
Copyright © 2021 Emily Martin

Yorkshire Publishing
4613 E. 91st St,
Tulsa, OK 74137
www.YorkshirePublishing.com
918.394.2665

Printed in the USA

THE
VIKING
PRINCESS

Emily Martin

TULSA

DEDICATION

To my loving mother and father for rising above impossible
odds and becoming my heroes. Also, to my sister, who never
let the expectations of others define who she became.
Lastly to God, for not only giving me life but
for giving me a life worth living.

CONTENTS

CHAPTER 1

THE CALDER

~⟡~

*Fear thou not; for I am with thee: be not
dismayed; for I am thy God: I will strengthen
thee; yea, I will help thee; yea, I will uphold thee
with the right hand of my righteousness.*

Isaiah 41: 40 K JV

~⟡~

Atlantic Ocean, A.D. 900

Aamber Rose Egil gulped down the stale bread and moldy cheese
she'd stolen from the kitchen while hiding in a dark corner of the
women's deck, hoping not to lose any to the other hungry passengers aboard the *Calder*. Even though she was the daughter of the
Calder's captain, Einar Egil, it did not guarantee her safety or access
to food and drink. This food she'd swiped from the prisoners' por-
tions. Being only 12 and small-framed, for her to set foot near the
ship's kitchen was out of the question. Vikings never share anything,
especially food or money. Sometimes she could convince her older

1

brother Elof, who was 15 years old and almost as large as her father, to sneak her food, but obtaining food was hard, even for him. As payment, she would launder his clothes or clean his weapons and armor.

The shipped rocked and Aamber braced herself against the rough wall, the sharp splinters poking through her thin dress into her back. Then, she glanced around the room. Sleeping pallets lined the walls in miserable messes. Aamber knew the women kept a slew of weapons hidden among their belongings, at least they did if they were smart. Viking women had to defend themselves not only from the men on the ship but also from other women who were jealous of them. The fifth deck was where all women on the ship slept. The lucky ones had pillows; the very lucky ones had padding to sleep on. The ones not as fortunate slept on the bare floor, clutching blankets around them to keep from freezing to death if they had even that much. Some only slept with the clothes on their back and many slept together to share body heat.

Aamber wasn't a fortunate one with the threadbare, patched, burgundy shawl she always kept with her by wrapping it around her waist during the day and using it as a blanket at night. Not to mention her gray, pitiful excuse for a dress. All the women on the ship were at least twice her age and her mother slept with her father; she was the only woman to sleep at a different location on the ship. The rest of the women aboard were either Viking wives or mistresses. Often, the women who became friends were the wife and the mistress of the same man. The wife was relieved not to have to suffer the abuse of her husband alone.

Aamber often heard stories about how land wives were cherished and loved, and left their husbands if he took a mistress. She couldn't imagine such a life. The ship was the only home she'd ever known. Having lived on the *Calder* since birth, she'd never set foot on dry land. At night she would try to imagine what it would be like not to be rocking back and forth constantly at the mercy of the angry waves, what dirt would feel like running through her fingers, and how amazingly soft it would be to sleep in the lush grass she saw growing on the banks during their brief stints near land. Aamber wondered if these dreams were what had kept her alive throughout her miserable existence.

Often the women brought flowers back from the land after a raid. They would dry them and use them to perfume anything from their hair to their laundry water. Sometimes, Aamber would eavesdrop on the other women's stories of life on land. She loved the stories of how they lived in separate houses, family by family, fistfights were rare, and people attended something called "church" on Sundays. Their stories were her only connection to the outside world. It was the world she so desperately wanted to be a part of, but never dared hope she could be.

After brushing off her skirt, she headed down to the first deck, cringing as she passed the guard to the storage deck. Odin never tried to hide his leering sneer.

"Better not be headed to the main deck. Your father will have your hide," he chuckled. Aamber shivered at the strange gleam in his eyes.

"Mind your own business Odin," she spat back, which earned her another evil chuckle from the man.

Aamber stepped from the stairway into the fresh sea air and took in a deep cleansing breath. Men scrambled around the deck, working to keep the amazing *Calder* sailing in the right direction. The ship was massive, with a mermaid on the stern holding her arms out to the sea. The wind blew her curls around her face, and only a sash covered her chest. Her mother loved mermaids. Being the adoring newlywed that her father was at the time, he'd had one carved on the prow of the ship during the first year of marriage.

Aamber walked up to the rail and looked out over the blue horizon. She stepped up onto the bottom rung and leaned over to stare into the murky green depths of the sea. The salty spray kissed her cheeks and the wind stroked her long red hair. Sometimes the sea was their best friend, sometimes it was their worst enemy. Aamber never tired of the endless blue and loved to watch for dolphins or any other marine life. Often, the ocean felt as if it was her only friend. It was strange even to Aamber that she didn't know how to swim, having lived on a ship her whole life. Some day she would teach herself to swim, being determined not to live this miserable lifestyle forever. A seagull flew overhead, its belly white against the vast blue. "If only I had wings, I could fly away from this horrendous place," she murmured to herself.

Aamber didn't much worry about the men on deck bothering her, even though she could feel their disgusting glances. If they neglected their duty stations, her father would take their heads off, literally, and she always had the trusty knife at her waist as a last resort. Watching the sunrise and sunset were the highlights of Aamber's days and she refused to let fear take that from her, having had so much already stolen from her in her young life. All the glorious colors that blended and reflected off the water were the only beautiful things in her life. So much needless pain and suffering surrounded her. Many tried to fill the void with intercourse, whiskey, or money. Only, it seemed to Aamber that, no matter how much they tried, they were never happy. Could there possibly be something more to fill the ever-present void in their hearts?

Heavy boot thuds approached Aamber's back. Inwardly cringing, she tried to make a break for the stairway. Her father grabbed her arm and wrenched her around to face him. "Why are you down here! You know I don't like you to be on the main deck!"

"I…I…I was watching the s…s…sunset. Please, father, I avoid the main deck all day, but this is the only deck where I can watch the sunset and breathe fresh air."

His eyes narrowed. It reminded Aamber of the white orca eyes she would see leap out of the water from time to time. "If you keep smarting off to me like that, I'll quit protecting you from the men."

Aamber felt steam rising above her head, and her face turned as red as the sunset. Some protection he gave! As soon she was old enough to walk, she was handed a knife and told she was now old enough to take care of herself! If it weren't for her mother sneaking her food as a toddler, she wouldn't have survived! Meeting his hateful stare with her own, before she could think, she blurted. "What protection?!" Which earned her a smack across the face so powerful it knocked her off her feet. "You're going to pay for that little snide remark and then we'll see if you're still an unappreciative little brat! Now get back to the women's chambers!"

Without looking back, she jumped up and ran up the first couple of stairs until she was out of sight, then stopped to feel her smarting face. Father's smacks always left a handprint. After gingerly touching her eye she groaned. It was going to swell. Great. Just what she needed. Impaired vision when her father would be gunning for her. Aamber climbed the rest of the way to the women's chambers, noting a strange smile on the storage deck guard's face, but shrugged it off. He probably thought the hand print she sported was funny.

When she'd settled in the far corner of the room, 20 women stumbled in with a burst of color and laughter, their toilet water engulfing the small space. Their annoying shrills always gave Aamber a headache. All of them were in different degrees of dress and all of them were in different degrees of drunkenness. Drinking was most of the women's coping mechanism, and usually the only form of drinkable liquid on the ship. They collapsed on their respective pallets, undressing as they went. Women would be in and out of the room all night, some meeting their lovers, and some wouldn't enter the sleeping chambers until morning. It was rare to find the women's sleeping chambers empty at any given time.

Most of the time, the women ignored Aamber, which suited her fine because, when they did acknowledge her, it was always with an insult or abuse. They hated her for being the captain's daughter, even though she didn't receive any special treatment. They also hated her for the fiery red hair that she kept in two Dutch braids so it wouldn't be in her face. Not to mention the fact that having two braids made it twice as hard for someone to grab all her hair and control her head, which was her father's signature move. Apparently, red-haired women were supposed to be more alluring to men and have unholy skills in the bedroom. Some believed red hair gave the woman magical powers. Therefore, every woman on the ship was either jealous of her or hated her or both.

Aamber guessed there were about 50 women and 30 men on the ship. Their clan was very small compared to others but the Egil clan had the nastiest reputation of all the Viking clans sailing the

Atlantic Ocean. They were known for their brutality to others and even to the members of their own clan. Aamber had heard many stories of other Viking clan captains killing themselves rather than being taken prisoners by her father. Their prisoners wished they were dead every waking moment. Many clan members simply enjoyed torturing them, even if they didn't have any information or money to gain from it. This was why the clan was so small. Only a very small number of men and women could survive the clan itself, let alone the raids.

There was no loyalty among the members of the clan. It wasn't uncommon to find men and women murdered in their sleep. Men fought over food, money, jewels, and anything else they could think of. Women fought over clothes, food, drink, weapons, and one another's sharp tongues. Sometimes the men killed each other in front of everybody. Nobody cared. They would enjoy the show and then return to their activities. During all the fighting, the women simply tried to stay out of the crosshairs, which was sometimes impossible. Many children and women had been killed during these fights. Aamber never forgot their gray faces and blue fingers when they were thrown overboard.

The clan made about four raids a year, never allowing anyone in the town to survive unless you counted the women who were kidnapped and either forced into marriage or into being mistresses. The rest of the time they kept to oblivion upon the large Atlantic. The only rule on the ship, known as "The Rule," was that there was no stealing another man's wife or mistress. If The Rule wasn't in place, the clan would have killed itself off completely in a day. Any who broke The Rule were castrated while fully coherent by the slighted man. Then they were placed in a wooden box filled with vipers and thrown to the bottom of the ocean.

When she was younger, Aamber had wondered why there weren't many other children aboard the ship considering the number of couples. She eventually learned most babies did not survive pregnancy because of the malnutrition, drunkenness, and the beatings the women endured. Any child who survived to parturition either starved to death, died of illness, or was killed by a member of the clan for being annoying, eating too much, or taking up too much of their woman's time. Special care had been taken to ensure Elof's and Aamber's survival through infancy. Her father wanted an heir and her mother had always wanted a daughter. Unfortunately for them, after their tenth birthday, it was up to them to survive on their own, as if their parents had protected them much before.

Throughout their lives, their father and experience had trained them in all forms of combat: archery, fencing, knives, hand-to-hand, and even slingshots. Even though Aamber was small and without much muscle, she was quick and smart. She memorized every weak spot of the body and mastered every weapon she could obtain. When she wasn't hiding in a dark corner of the ship or scavenging food and water, she was practicing some form of weaponry, though the only people she could trust to spar with were her mother, father, and brother. With anyone else, it was kill or be killed. The form of weaponry she was most proficient in was archery. Her father bragged she could split a strand of hair from 50 feet away. It was the only nice thing he ever said about her.

The only problem was that arrow-making materials were scarce. Once again, she traded with her brother, who could take part in raids. She would ask him to gather materials for her in exchange for clean clothes when he returned. For years, she'd begged her father to allow her to attend the raids. She had no interest in stealing and killing but she would love to explore what land was like and collect her own materials for making weapons. Aamber never understood why he wouldn't relent. It wasn't as if, during this stage of her life, he concerned himself about her safety. Maybe it was her mother who didn't want her to go.

Aamber tried to settle in for the night, wrapping her shawl around her shoulders. She always slept with her back against the wall in the corner of the room. The fifth deck was the highest deck of the ship, and therefore incurred the greatest portion of the biting wind chill. She tried to block out the noises of the other women shuffling, bickering, and sometimes squealing at one another's stories. Some exchanged clothes and jewelry and others bandaged each other's wounds. The noise and light from the candles didn't bother her; she had years of practice blocking it out. Strangely, though, the women quieted within the hour; it usually took at least three, but Aamber wasn't going to complain. The night was uncommonly warm, and the ocean was calm. She quickly drifted off into a deep sleep.

Thunk! A sudden noise in the darkness caused Aamber to jolt up about an hour later. Her amber-colored eyes scanned the room, illuminated by the soft moonlight streaming through the only window. Something wasn't right. Someone was missing from their pallet. She rose up on her knees, brushing her long red braid over her shoulder, and reached down to clutch her knife. The hair stood up on the back of her neck and arms, causing her to have goosebumps.

The room was pitch-black except for the trickle of moonlight. Women slept on pallets in front of her, their chests rising and falling in a smooth rhythm and their breaths making small whistling sounds. Aamber slowly rose to her feet and stepped out of her corner. The sound of her footsteps echoed in her head like gongs. Suddenly, a pair of hands grabbed each of her arms and wrenched them behind her, the long fingernails digging into the soft skin of her wrists. While she tried to scream and fight, a gag was shoved into her mouth, and something hard hit her head before she could even form a coherent thought. Aamber slipped into blessed darkness.

Abilene Adisa watched Aamber crumple into the arms of her friend, Adina. Abilene was the wife of Odin Adisa and Adina was his mistress. Some women rose from the sound bleary-eyed but quickly laid back down when they realized there was no safety threat to their own person. Besides, she'd told them to settle down to sleep when Aamber did. They'd all listened because of who her husband was. His being the second meanest Viking on the ship gave her social status.

"Are you sure about this?" Adina asked in a scared stage whisper. "If Captain Egil found out we kidnapped his daughter and set her up for rape by Odin, we would all be punished for breaking The Rule."

Abilene narrowed her eyes and hissed. "Don't be an idiot, Adina! She's not the girlfriend or wife of any man on the ship. So how would we be breaking The Rule?"

Adina rubbed the cloth of her thin dress between her fingers. "But wouldn't the captain consider her to belong to him since she's his daughter?" she ventured hesitantly, diverting her eyes from the snake-like, green-eyed gaze of her companion. "Besides, she's never done anything to harm us. Why should we do this to her? She's only a child!"

"Are you that stupid!" Abilene snapped. "To please Odin, of course! The only abuse she's ever taken is when she smarts off to her brother or father. It's only fair she takes her turn. Besides she's 12 years old, not a child. And you know how much and how long Odin has wanted her! Since she was born all he's talked about is the captain's daughter with the red hair! Do you really want to disappoint him and reap the consequences?" Adina slowly shook her head in reply. "Then help me carry her!"

Odin Adisa rubbed his hands together in anticipation, and his black teeth gleamed in the moonlight. He'd snuck down to the stairway door earlier and had witnessed the altercation between the captain and his daughter. He knew tonight would be the night he'd waited 12 long years for. Tonight, he'd have the captain's daughter, which would give him status, and maybe land her as a mistress. If he could get her as a mistress, he could train her young. He wouldn't make the mistakes he had with Abilene and Adina. To have an heir of his and the captain's blood would be worth more than gold and the boy would be unstoppable. Odin couldn't help letting an evil chuckle escape.

Abilene quickly tied Aamber's hands behind her back in case she woke. She and Adisa each grabbed one of her legs and dragged her out of the room and down the stairs to the third deck, her head making a *clump, clump, clump* sound on each step as they went. The third deck was set aside for storage of anything from food to extra weapons. Odin was responsible for guarding the room. If anything was found missing, it was he who had to replace it. Because of this, he'd become the second meanest man on the ship, after the captain. Even though he was over 50 years old, he had the physique of a 20-year-old. His skin was like leather and his hair was as white as fresh snow, which he kept tied behind his head in a greasy ponytail. He also kept a long white, yellow-stained beard caked with food.

Although all the Viking men stunk, Odin had the nickname skunk and it was said he hadn't bathed since he was ten years old. He was standing in front of the storage room door with his bulging muscled arms crossed over his chest when the women arrived with their quarry. His eyes darted toward the women when they arrived at the landing, evil sparkling in the blue irises. Both Abilene and Adina shivered. They'd seen that look many times over the years, but somehow it was even worse now.

Odin growled at them. "Well, you two actually did something right for a change, even though you took your sweet time about it. Leave her here and go back to the women's chambers. If either of you says anything about this, I'll slit your throats after letting any and every man on the ship do with you as they please! Understood?" Both women nodded their heads vigorously, unceremoniously dropped Aamber's legs with a *thunk, thunk,* and ran back up the staircases to the fifth deck. Adina tossed a short, pitying glance behind her shoulder at Aamber. Her gut clenched. Aamber looked like her younger sister laying there, who had died in the raid she was captured in. A single tear made a trail down her cheek and overwhelming shame filled her soul.

When Aamber began to wake, her head throbbed and there was enormous pressure on her pelvis. Her vision was blurry, but she knew exactly who was on top of her, Odin Adisa. There was no mistaking his smell. Inwardly, she panicked and began to struggle to get away, trying to kick her legs and push with her arms. Odin released a cruel chuckle. He leaned forward, whispering in her ear, his wretched breath burning her nostrils. "Yeah, go ahead and struggle. That makes it all the better."

His menacing laugh sent chills down her spine and she struggled not to vomit from the smell and pain. A gag was in her mouth and, if she did vomit, she would asphyxiate. Even so, she made guttural noises and tried to slam her head into his, everything in her fighting to get away from what was happening to her. Although she was only 12, she knew what he was doing to her. Aamber couldn't have grown up on a Viking ship without hearing the horrendous stories. Unfortunately for her, he outweighed her by at least 200 pounds, maybe more, and her efforts were futile.

The pain was excruciating. Aamber wanted to cry but refused to give him the satisfaction. She cried out in her heart, "Help me! Someone, please!" Then suddenly, Odin had finished with her. He grabbed her by the braids and held her up so high her feet dangled off the ground. Her eyes had started to clear, so she brought her leg up and kicked him hard in the groin as quickly and as many times as she could.

He roared and slammed her against the wall. "You little wench!" he gasped. Then he began slamming her over and over into the wall. Aamber worried he would cave in her skull or her neck would snap from the force he used.

Suddenly he stopped, heaving from exertion. "Look at me," he said in a deadly whisper. Aamber pried her eyes open as much as she could. "If you ever tell anyone about this, I'll kill you and your precious mother! Got it?!" Aamber croaked out a yes and he tossed her out the door down the stairs. She fell in a heap on the second deck landing, almost blacking out again.

Aamber lay still until she was sure he wasn't going to follow her down. Every single part of her body hurt and she was amazed she'd survived. The tears flowed freely now and her only skirt was ripped from top to bottom. The only thought running through her brain was how simple-minded she'd been. She'd let her guard down, and this was the result. "Stupid, stupid, stupid! How could you have let this happen to yourself!" she yelled over and over in her head. *Never again*, was her last thought.

Heavy, masculine footsteps on the stairs above her made Aamber freeze in fear. They stopped just above her, the toe of her father's boots just barely visible above her eyes, and she pushed herself up with her arms. She lifted her head, tear trails creating a salt crust on her cheeks. Her father stared down at her; his eyes dead. "Now you know what happens without my protection," he said simply and then continued down to his chambers. Aamber's world crashed down around her. Her father had known what Odin was doing to her and he hadn't stopped it.

Trying to pull herself up with the wall, rage coursed through her veins. Anger at the women who'd captured her, at Odin, at her father, and at the world gave her the strength she needed. Aamber didn't know how badly she was hurt but she did know that she must get away from the third deck landing where Odin was sure to be. When she'd finally made it to her knees, she leaned over and threw up the little bit of bread and cheese she'd eaten earlier, and then continued to throw up bile.

After she was through, her throat burned and she felt rippling pains tearing through her stomach like a storm through the sea. Aamber held still until the burning and pain subsided to a more tolerable level and then she continued to pull herself up, beginning to panic and worry she would never get away. When finally on her feet, she tried to take a step and managed to fall down the last flight of stairs to the first deck. Everything went black again.

Aamber awoke when the first rays of dawn were peeking over the horizon, the bright rays trying to tease her face into a smile. Chills went through her body, not only from the cold but also from the knowledge the men would be filing out onto the deck soon. Her skirt was ripped in half and she was very exposed. Looking to her right, she saw a bucket of soapy water used to swab the deck left out from the previous day. Aamber crawled her way to it, trying not to get splinters in her legs.

As she cleaned the blood off her head and the rest of her body, she considered her options. If she told her brother, he might be irritated but there was no way he would challenge Odin or their father. If she told her mother, she would shake her head at her and ask her what she'd done wrong to incur Odin's wrath. Her mother might give her some help healing but it would be all the help she'd receive. One thing was painfully clear to Aamber: She couldn't live the rest of her life like this. Now that Odin had raped her once, he would have no problems doing it again. She would have to grow eyes in the back of her head, and never sleep, and, somehow, she'd have to escape this ship.

Pushing herself up with the bucket, Aamber limped her way to a cleaning closet. Today was Friday, so nobody would be needing anything from it. She could sew her skirt with the needle and thread she kept tucked in a bag she'd sewn to the waist of her dress, which had luckily escaped Odin's greedy hands, unlike her precious knife. Aamber collapsed into the closet and pulled the door closed. The only glimmer of light was the faint line coming from under the door, and Aamber had never been so grateful for the darkness. She braced her back against the wall after scooting over a mop and broom and assessed the damage done to her skirt, blouse, and undergarments. The skirt and blouse could be salvaged, but she would have to use pieces of her shawl to patch her undergarments. As she sewed, she could hear men going about their morning activities. The musty smell of the moldy mop did nothing to help her still queasy stomach, and her throat was still raw from vomiting.

When finished, Aamber returned her sewing material to its pouch, pulled her knees up to her chest, hugging them to her, and laid her head in her lap. She was very, very bruised and she believed she might have a concussion, but didn't think anything was broken. Cuts and scrapes covered almost every inch of her body, but none were serious. Her pelvis ached and an overwhelming feeling of shame consumed her. Aamber was shocked she wasn't more seriously injured after the night she'd had. No tears made it past her eyelids.

Aamber had shed all the tears she would allow herself, but her trembling didn't cease for hours. Her heart felt numb. She felt dead.

Aamber stayed in her compact position for what seemed like years, taking deep, cleansing breaths and planning what to do next. From now on, she would sleep in cleaning supply closets and anywhere else she could hide and brace a door closed. Building a small boat of her own and escaping on it would be the only way out. Taking a lifeboat wasn't an option. They'd know she'd managed to escape the ship. If they knew she was still alive, they'd hunt her down and kill her. Her father never wanted someone to survive and give up the *Calder's* weaknesses. The motto was that, once you became a Viking, you would always be a Viking.

It also couldn't be when they'd planned a raid and they were close to land. Nothing would be left for her to build a life out of, and the people in the towns nearby would realize where she'd appeared from. Her efforts at food and liquid scavenging would have to be doubled if she were to become healthy enough to last a few days in a boat without food or water, but where could she build a boat without anyone noticing? Not only that, where would she get the supplies? And lastly, where could she settle where her family would never raid?

Wracking her brain, she could come up with only two options for a place to build her boat: in the storage deck, which obviously wasn't an option, or in the hull of the ship where the prisoners were kept. Aamber often hid stuff down there. Currently, she had a bow, several arrows, a sword, and two knives hidden there. The prisoners never saw her. It was as dark as night down there and she was as quiet as a mouse. Plus, there were stacks of crates she could hide behind, which had a tarp she could cover the boat with. Finding wood for the boat would be easy. Chairs and tables were broken all the time during drunken brawls.

But how was she going to get tar to cover the bottom of the boat so it wouldn't sink? Aamber would never be able to get the boards tight enough and smooth enough to float on their own. The extra tar was kept in the storage deck. Then it dawned on her. She had a knife that her brother had wanted for a long time. He'd tried to steal it on multiple occasions. It would be the perfect bribe for him to get her at least one whole can of tar. What could she say she wanted the tar for though? Maybe a prank on one of the other women. That would add a little icing on the cake for her brother, who would enjoy such a spectacle.

Now, if she did manage to escape, how would she keep her family from looking for her? Another idea came to her. She could leave her shawl soaked in blood where she used to sleep and leave a trail of it to the side of the ship. They would think someone killed her in her sleep and then threw her body off the ship. There was still one problem. No one had ever escaped the *Calder* before. Was she going to be able to pull it off?

CHAPTER 2

THE ESCAPE

For God hath not given us the spirit of fear; but of power, and of love, and of a sound mind.

2 Timothy 1:7 KJV

Atlantic Ocean, A.D. 901

Aamber quickly ate the food that had been set before her, wracking her brain for the reason that her parents would provide her and her brother a "family dinner." This was something they had never done before and she couldn't imagine why they would now. Her heart was frozen in fear for what they were about to say but she ate whatever she could consume of the food. It was the first time since she was ten years old she could remember having a full stomach. There were several kinds of fish and endless rolls. There were even a few vegetables.

Elof sat across from her at the small square table and her parents sat on each side of them, her father on her left and her mother on the right. Her brother, now 16, was as large as their father and had started growing a beard. Their father hadn't changed at all in the past year, at least, not that she could tell. Her mother, though, had lost weight and look sallow. Her skin had a yellowish-green tone to it. Aamber had been worried about her but hadn't asked what was wrong. If she had, she wouldn't have got an answer and maybe even a smack to the face.

Aamber had changed quite a bit over the past year. Because of her increased efforts at scavenging and the constant hunt for boat materials keeping her mind busy, she'd grown several inches and had gained weight. She no longer looked like a bag of bones but looked trim and healthy. Her red hair shone in the sun, and she often struggled to keep covered with her small gray dress. It had gained the attention of several men on the ship, unfortunately, including her father.

They were in the captain's chambers, where her parents lived. As she ate, Aamber observed the luxury surrounding her. After a year of sleeping in cleaning supply closets, just the rug in the corner of the room looked like heaven. A huge bed that took up most of the room was covered in red blankets of satin, with a golden weave. A diamond-studded chandelier hung from the ceiling. Candles in the chandelier lit the area around the table while casting eerie shadows around the sides of the room. It reminded Aamber of the interrogation tactics they used on the prisoners in the hull of the ship. They would shine a bright light on them after months of darkness and drill them for answers to their questions. Aamber had learned several techniques for extracting information from these interrogations while building her boat.

Aamber's boat was finished and she'd stored all her weapons in it along with any food she could find, having scored even a large bottle of wine. She'd made a large bag out of a piece of the tarp she used to cover her boat. That would certainly come in handy. The rest of the tarp she would use as a sail. She'd made oars, swiped a large length of rope and a compass, and had even found a small anchor. Now all that remained was waiting for the perfect time. Aamber wanted to be as close to land as possible and would have to escape in a storm. Any other time she would be caught by the watchmen. Aamber had heard a good storm was brewing tonight but she'd hoped to get a little closer to land before making her attempt.

As far as Aamber knew, they were 50 miles from land. Escaping during a storm was going to be dangerous enough, but it wasn't like she had the opportunity to see if her boat was seaworthy. Escaping was either going to be the most dangerous thing she would do in her life or the last, but it was the only option. Aamber couldn't spend the rest of her life on this ship, trying to avoid the horrors of the *Calder*. Just the thought of never leaving this ship and the nightmares it contained made her sick.

Her father pushed his plate away and wiped his mouth and hands with a rag. "All right, I think it's time we got to the point of why I invited all of you to dinner tonight," he smacked. "I have a very important announcement to make. I assume all of you know of the Uffe clan? They sail aboard the *Ukritt*."

"Who doesn't know about them? They are the largest Viking clan to sail on the Atlantic," Elof replied around a full mouth of fish.

"Yes, well, our clan is soon going to join forces with theirs," her father stated in a matter-of-fact manner after putting his elbows on the table and making a tent with his massive fingers. Aamber's eyes widened and she glanced at her mother, who'd turned even paler. *How could two clans possibly combine? And what was her mother so afraid of?* Aamber thought to herself.

Then her father turned his attention toward her. "You are going to marry Rafiq Tacitus. The captain and leader of the Uffe clan." Aamber's mouth fell open and a single tear ran down her mother's cheek.

"What?" Aamber squeaked out. A sick feeling had settled in her stomach and sweat began rolling down her back.

"You're going to marry the leader of the Uffe clan, bringing our two clans together. With our reputation and their numbers, we could rule the entire Atlantic Ocean! And what better way to ensure the union than to make the clans family? You will be the queen of the ocean."

Aamber searched her brain for any and every reason to convince her father this marriage would be a bad idea. Despite what his name meant, Rafiq Tacitus was one of the meanest men on the ocean. He already had had like five wives and the horrors they had endured at his hand made the most seasoned of all Viking wives cringe. He had them all executed when they either did something he didn't like or they became too ugly for him to endure, and many said it was the nicest thing he'd ever done for them. "But what if he kills me like he did his other wives. Wouldn't that break the union?" Aamber was surprised at how calm her voice sounded, considering her father was offering her up on the altar for sacrifice. That was at least a reasonable suggestion.

"He's assured me that no harm will come to you until you have birthed an heir. You are of childbearing age, aren't you?" he asked, tapping his chin. "Well, even if you're not yet, it won't be long until you are," he answered with a shrug. Then steel entered his eyes. "Just to be clear, there's not going to be any negotiating. Whether you want this union or not, it is going to happen. You will do this for your family and your people who are counting on you. Our clan will not last much longer without fresh blood. Your mother has already attempted every argument possible and has not succeeded. She doesn't want to lose you but I discussed with her that she's had a weak spot for you too long and needed to cure herself of it. And what better way to do that than having you marry off and start a family of your own?"

Aamber looked down at her plate and swallowed the lump that had suddenly appeared in her throat. She hadn't known her mother cared for her so much as to argue with her father for her. Maybe that was what the problem had been and why she'd been looking so sickly of late. Aamber knew there wasn't any point in arguing. It would only result in more pain for herself and her mother. She looked back up at her father after a moment, into his almost black eyes, and nodded.

"Good. I thought you would put up a fuss but you seem to have matured over the past year. Now, let's enjoy the rest of this delicious food in peace. The wedding will take place tomorrow. We are set to meet up with the *Ukritt* at Stone Pass. Prepare yourself tonight, Aamber. By tomorrow's end you will be a married woman," her father said with a sickening smile and a wink.

They continued to eat in silence. Elof kept casting furtive glances at her. Aamber almost thought she saw pity in his eyes. Her mother didn't even try to hide her tears, and only picked at her food. Aamber studied her family, knowing this would most likely be the last time she would ever see them. Her father was strong-jawed with black hair and black eyes. He kept a black beard trimmed to the shape of his face. His clothes were all faded black leather. Scars covered almost every visible piece of skin, which was tanned and rougher than burlap. He was lean, with broad shoulders. A single scar ran from his forehead to his chin on the right side of his face. He was one of the meanest men Aamber had ever known and she hoped that she wouldn't meet more men like him. The only part of him he'd given her was his weaponry skills, which were among the most cherished things in her possession.

Next, her mother. Thin as a rail with blonde hair and the same color eyes as Aamber. Picking at her food, tears trailing down her face and her bottom lip trembling as she sat beside Aamber. She was the only person who'd cared for her through her miserable childhood. Aamber's mother had never been a conventional mother who kissed her head and tucked her in at night, but Aamber was grateful for the things her mother had done for her and would never forget her because of it.

Then her brother, who was the spitting image of their father but not as rough and scarred, at least not yet. Aamber imagined he was what her father looked like when he was younger. The only physical difference between the two was that Elof had lighter hair, almost brown. She couldn't say her brother loved her but at least he respected her. Without his help, she doubted that she would be alive today. Aamber let the few good memories run through her mind as she ate all her stomach could hold and slipped as much bread into her pockets as possible. Tonight had to be the night of her escape. Time had run out.

Aamber slinked her way down the stairs into the hull of the ship, as she'd been doing for the past year. She grabbed the handrail and clenched her teeth before she fell down the last five stairs when the boat lurched to the side from the raging storm. All she could think about was that she was fixing to be out in those angry waves in her tiny boat and she screamed inwardly. She'd hoped for a storm to escape in, but not the worst storm she'd ever experienced. Lightning streaked across the sky every two seconds and waves tossed the boat back and forth like a skirt on a clothesline in the wind.

Before stepping into the room when she reached the bottom of the stairs, she scanned it for guards and threats. Something didn't seem right or smell right. It was a trap. She could feel it in her bones. This time she wasn't going to fall for it. Odin had been trying to get her again all year and, with the announcement of her coming wedding, he would be desperate. Aamber knew he'd wanted her to become pregnant the last time he'd raped her. He wanted a son with her father's blood.

Grabbing the knife concealed at her waist, Aamber took a step into the room. Someone grabbed her arm, but this time she was ready. As Odin tried to sling her around toward him, Aamber unsheathed the knife and thrust it upward into his gut, then twisted. She repeated the process two more times. Aamber felt his grip slacken and he stumbled backward, the whites of his eyes visible all around his irises. He collapsed against the wall holding his stomach. "You actually stabbed me. I didn't think you had it in you," he whispered through his black teeth with a small chuckle. "I've fought men twice my size my entire life and now have been killed by a child."

Aamber squatted down, still holding her bloody knife, and looked him straight in the eyes. "I would have done it that night if you hadn't been so cowardly as to have your wife and mistress incapacitate me for you. Now, for once, you know what it's like to be the victim. May God have mercy on your soul." She watched as the life drained from his eyes and she wiped the blood from her knife on his pants legs.

The dead feeling in her heart increased. She'd never killed anyone before and honestly hoped she would never have to but at least now Odin wouldn't ever be able to hurt anyone else ever again. Aamber knew, though, that she'd never forget watching the life leave his eyes and his dead irises would haunt her for the rest of her life. She quickly grabbed her supplies, hoisting the small boat onto her shoulder. Even though it was small, it took all her strength to carry it and Aamber had to grit her teeth not to make a noise. She'd already left her shawl in the ladies' chambers soaked in blood. Not a single woman had stirred from her sleep.

When she made it up to the deck, she checked to make sure the watchmen were still ducking for cover and she dodged a window where a couple was inside arguing. After removing the rigging from one of the lifeboats, she rigged up her small vessel. The only lighting available was the lightning, but she had studied how it worked all year. Even though she'd never tried using it before, Aamber imagined she could do it in her sleep. As an afterthought, she swiped one of the lifejackets in the lifeboat. It would come in handy if her boat sank.

Using the rig, Aamber had her boat dangling over the edge. Avoiding looking at the black, churning water, with her heart in her throat she climbed in and used the rigging to lower herself, cringing at every squeak of the ropes. When she was close to the surface of the water, she heard men yelling. The voices were muffled but she hoped they were yelling about finding either Odin's body or her blood-soaked shawl. "Please, ocean, please be my friend," Aamber whispered to herself in a trembling voice. When she was about an inch above the churning water, she released.

After the boat hit the surface of the water with a splash, it teetered dangerously back and forth, almost capsizing in the waves. Aamber crouched down and tried to distribute her weight evenly. When the boat had settled some, she tossed her small anchor over the edge, hoping it would give the poor thing a little stability. She could feel the boat being carried away from the large ship by the roaring waves but didn't feel any water seeping through the bottom. Of course, it would be hard to tell if the boat was sinking because of all the water and spray coming over the sides. Aamber was relieved no lights had been shined on her. She hoped the men would just assume the lifeboat had come loose during the storm without connecting it to her. Of course, no one on the ship knew she had another boat and they would assume that she would never try to escape in a storm of this magnitude.

The waves took the boat so high when it dropped that it felt as if Aamber's stomach remained at the top. It could even have been considered fun if her life didn't hang in the balance. She knew trying to set sail in this storm would not only be futile but would tear her sail to shreds. The best option at this point would be to try and ride out the storm without drowning. Lifting her head, she could see the *Calder* in the distance when lightning flashed. From what she could tell, nothing seemed amiss on board. It was the only home she'd ever known and she was glad to be moving on...even if that possibly meant moving on to her grave. At least maybe she could find some peace and rest there.

Aamber awoke at the first rays of dawn, not even realizing she'd fallen asleep. Lifting her arms above her head, she stretched and yawned, and then took in her surroundings. Royal blue ocean surrounded her in all directions. The sea was calm and sparkled in the sunlight. Fortunately, the *Calder* was nowhere in sight. She deeply breathed in the fresh, salty sea air, and looked to see if she'd lost anything during the night. To her surprise, all her supplies were still tucked in the bottom of the boat. It was a miracle her boat had floated, let alone hadn't capsized in the storm. A small amount of water had collected in the bottom, which Aamber quickly bailed out with her hands.

The next step would be finding land. They had been following the coast on the *Calder*, keeping it always to the east. Unfortunately, Aamber hadn't a clue if that was still the case, but what other choice did she have? She thought about eating before setting sail but wasn't very hungry yet and she needed to save the food for when she just couldn't tolerate the hunger anymore. She did allow herself a sip of wine, though. Her throat was parched and felt sandpaper had been taken to it.

Aamber removed the compass from her pocket, pulled up her anchor, and started to sail east. Sadly, there was barely any wind. After setting up the sail for the little help it would be, she started rowing. Every hour, she checked her compass to make sure she was still headed east. Sweat poured down her face from the physical strain and the sun beating down on her head. She'd debated sailing at night, but she was much better at orienting herself by the sun instead of the stars. Besides, how would she see land in the distance at night?

Aamber had been sailing all day with no breaks and the sun was starting to set. Letting go of the oars for a break, Aamber looked down at her blistered and bleeding hands. Knowing that her face and neck were burned to a crisp from the sun, she reached down and splashed some cool seawater on her face. The skin smarted, but the cold helped numb it. Throughout the day, she'd only allowed herself two more sips of wine. Growls from her stomach pierced the silence of the ocean but she'd been hungrier during her short life. Reaching down, she ripped strips of cloth off the hem of her skirt. After wrapping her hands with them, she continued rowing until the sun had set completely. After taking down her sail, she dropped the anchor back into the water and laid down in the bottom of the boat. She was asleep before her head hit the tarp bag that she was using for a pillow.

The next morning, Aamber repeated the routine she'd established the day before, but this morning she allowed herself a few bites of bread and made sure that she wrapped her exposed skin with her burlap bag. This went on for three more days. When she awoke on the fifth day, to her utter shock, Father was standing in the boat above her. A wretched scream split the air. It took a minute for Aamber to realize it was her own and she felt as if his black eyes pierced her soul. He began yelling at her, but nothing he said made any sense. He began pointing to her mother who suddenly appeared on the stern. Only her mother was dead. Her skin was gray and her eyes had calcified. Tears sprang into Aamber's eyes. "MOM!" But when she reached out to touch her, she disappeared. In her place stood Elof, beaten and bruised.

"How could you abandon me like this? How!" he begged, the accusation of betrayal in his voice.

"I'm sorry, Elof! I didn't have a choice! Father was going to force me to marry, and I simply cannot live as a Viking forever," she pleaded with him. Before she knew it, her father drew his sword. It was then that Aamber saw he wasn't her father anymore, he was Odin. And, while he was drawing his sword back to thrust it through her, she turned over and buried her face into the bottom of the boat.

After a few minutes when nothing had happened, Aamber peeked up over her shoulder. Odin was gone. Looking forward, she couldn't find her brother, either. Aamber rose up and looked over the edge of the boat, expecting to see them thrashing above the waves. Nothing. Then it hit her; she was hallucinating. Tears poured down the side of her face, stinging her sunburn. "I didn't have a choice! I had no choice!" she screamed to no one and buried her face again in the bottom of the boat.

The next thing Aamber knew, the sun had started peeking over the horizon. She raised her head and watched all the glorious colors streak across the sky, trying to forget her hallucinations. The sunrise and sunset had been the only beautiful things in her life. Aamber had often wondered how it had all came about, and why she'd been born. Was there Someone who decided how everything worked out? Or was everything random? What miserable deity would find joy in the suffering of one of such little importance as she? Shrugging off her questions, Aamber prepared for the day.

Suddenly a ship appeared on the horizon. Aamber's spine stiffened but, remembering the events of the early morning, she just shrugged her shoulders. Surely it was another hallucination. *I will have to allow myself more food and wine,* she thought, but the ship didn't disappear like the hallucination of her family and Odin. It inched closer and closer to her. Aamber was worried at first until she saw the flag they were sailing under. She'd memorized every Viking flag in her young life. This wasn't one. Aamber wondered what country it was from but didn't have the energy to spare to ponder it. Ignoring the ship, she started rowing, checking her compass periodically.

Almost having forgotten about the ship, Aamber jumped when she heard them drop a lifeboat. It looked to have two people in it and they started rowing toward her. "Hello there!" a man called out. "Are you in need of assistance?" His voice sounded kind and they certainly didn't look like any men she'd ever met. They were tall and thin. Their skin was lighter than that of any other person she'd seen. They spoke in Latin. Her mother tongue was Scandinavian but she'd picked up a few words of Latin over the years. To her surprise, they called the greeting out again in Scandinavian.

"If you could point me in the direction of the closest land, I would greatly appreciate it," she called back.

"Young lady, you're over 100 miles away from the closest land. How did you end up out here in that tiny boat? Where are you from? How old are you? Were you sailing your boat and then the current dragged you away?"

Man, he can ask questions, Aamber thought to herself. "None of that matters," she responded, shaking her head. "I just need to know what direction I should be going to reach land."

The man eyed her suspiciously and glanced at his comrade, who shrugged. "Did you run away from home? Aren't your parents looking for you?"

Aamber answered with a simple shake of her head. The less he knew the better. "I've been out here five days. Could you please tell me what direction I need to be going to find land?"

The lifeboat was close enough now to see inside her boat. His eyebrows rose. Aamber could tell he was suspicious, but he shrugged his shoulders. "I'm amazed you've made it this long. God must be looking out for you. There's no way you're going to be able to make it back to land in that boat though. You'll have to join our ship. We're a shipping vessel for the country Océan on our way back from trading with the country of Thibault. Don't worry, you'll be safe on our vessel. Many women join us on our journeys. We hire them to launder clothes, clean, and cook. Many of them are the daughters and wives of the crew. They are treated very well. Captain is very particular about the safety of the women aboard his ship."

Aamber didn't try to hide the suspicions she felt. Why would they want to help her? Did they have plans for her worse than what her father had? But what choice did she have but to trust them? She'd already escaped one ship, surely she could again if she needed to. "I don't have any money to pay for passage."

"That won't be a problem. Just helping the other women out with the chores will be enough payment."

Aamber was still suspicious, but she knew one thing: this would be her best, and maybe only, chance for survival. This strange man was right. She wouldn't last much longer in her tiny boat. Her rations were almost gone and one couldn't live on sips of wine alone. Aamber reached down, untied the rope from her anchor, and tossed it to him. "Thank you, I'd appreciate the help." Aamber hoped she hadn't just tied a noose around her neck. The man smiled at her and tied her rope to something in their boat. One of the men faced forward and rowed, while the other faced backward and rowed toward the ship.

Aamber also got her oars out and started to help but the man facing her, the one she'd been talking to, called out. "Don't bother. I can see how blistered your hands are. You're not very heavy. We can pull you the rest of the way ourselves."

Aamber pulled her oars back into her boat and breathed a sigh of relief. "Thanks!" Then she began packing her supplies into her tarp bag. Upon reaching the ship, one of the men already aboard threw a rope and the men in the lifeboat untied the one connecting theirs and tossed the end back to her. "They'll send the lifeboat rigging back down for your boat after they've hoisted ours up. Do you know how to attach it to your boat or do you need to switch with one of us?"

"I can handle it," she was quick to reply.

"All right. Hold on to that rope until they toss you the rigging so you don't drift away from the ship. Got it?"

"Yup."

When both boats were secured on the deck, the man she'd been talking to reached out his hand to help her out of her boat. "I'm First Mate Richard Sear. Everyone calls me Rich." Aamber stared down at his hand for a moment, then finally placed her smaller one in his. He was around six feet tall, with tanned muscled arms. He was intimidating but, for some reason, Aamber didn't feel threatened. His eyes were bright blue and didn't seem to be concealing any secrets. She quickly removed her hand when she was securely on the deck. "What's your name?" Aamber froze. Her name was the one thing she hadn't considered. If she told them her real name, they would know instantly who her family was. "Cat got your tongue?"

After giving a brief thought to what a cat was, she squeaked out the first name that popped into her mind. "Ruth."

He quirked an eyebrow and, with a half-smile, asked. "Ruth..........?"

Shaking her head, Aamber said. "Just Ruth."

Shrugging his shoulders, he said, "Well, follow me, Just Ruth. I'll take you to meet the captain. By the way, I don't recognize your accent. Where are you from?"

Following him to the captain's quarters, Aamber said. "Nowhere."

He didn't press. "What's your captain's name?" she asked when they stopped before a door.

Rich smiled seemingly amused at her question, opened the door, and said. "Captain George Cullard, this is Ruth. She is the young woman we saved from the scuttled rowboat." Aamber timidly took in the room. It was tidy, with a row of bookcases on the back wall. Aamber had never seen so many books. She'd always wanted to learn to read but no one ever had the patience to teach her. A man aged about 50 sat behind a huge desk strewn with papers. The papers seemed to be the only things out of place. His white hair was pulled into a neat ponytail. He was clean-shaven and had wrinkles in his cheeks and crow's feet around his eyes. His chocolate brown eyes shimmered with kindness. He had broad shoulders and rose when Rich announced her. Aamber could swear the room shrunk by several feet. He was like seven feet tall!

"Come in my dear, come in! Welcome to the *Message*! We're so glad to have you here!" his voice boomed as he came out from behind his desk and grasped both of her small hands in his huge ones. Aamber swore one of his hands was as big as her head! He was even larger than her father! He put his hand on her back and lead her to one of the large wooden chairs in front of the desk. He sat her in one and Rich took the other. "So, tell me all about yourself and how you ended up in that boat. How many days were you out there?" Captain Cullard said while settling back into his original position behind the desk.

"There's nothing really to tell, sir. Only that I'm willing to work and, once we reach land, you'll never have to hear from me again." His eyes narrowed and Aamber worried that she had angered him somehow.

"How old are you?" he asked, seeming curious.

Aamber hesitated. "Does it matter?" she whispered, refusing to meet his gaze. She didn't miss the small look of surprise that flickered in his eyes, though he covered it well.

"I suppose not. You just look very young," he said with a shrug. "Especially to be so cagy. You would think you were running from someone. Don't you have a family worrying about you?"

Aamber shook her head. "I'm alone, sir." To her shock, Aamber felt tears spring into her eyes at the statement. Aamber had always felt alone but saying it out loud somehow made it worse.

"Well, I guess we should get down to business," he said with a clap of his hands. "There aren't many rules on the *Message*, other than the commonsense ones. I'm going to put you under the care of my sweet wife Mary. She'll nurse you until you're healed. Then, if we haven't made it to port yet, Mary will tell you what chores you'll be responsible for. Sound good?"

Aamber stared at her hands, still clasped around the strap of her tarp bag. "How will I pay you back if I don't heal before we reach port? And what exactly am I healing from?"

Captain Cullard seemed surprised. "You wouldn't have to pay us anything. We're happy to help. And, as for what you're healing from, it's exposure. You're obviously suffering from a terrible sunburn. And, if I had to guess, you're very dehydrated and starved. Besides, by letting Mary fuss over you you're doing me a favor. It keeps her from worrying and fussing over me," he replied with a chuckle. Aamber looked back down at her hands. "Do we have a deal?" he asked hesitantly.

Aamber nodded. "Great! Rich, please escort Miss Ruth here to my sweet wife. It was lovely meeting you, Ruth. You're one brave young woman." Both Richard and she stood and Richard motioned her before him with his hand. When they'd made it to the door and her hand was on the handle, Captain Cullard called out. "Oh, and I forgot one more thing." She stopped and turned to look at him, inwardly cringing. Aamber knew this deal was too good to be true. "I forgot to tell you about the church services we hold on Sundays. The men on the ship take turns preaching. I believe it's Rich here's turn next." Richard nodded and the captain continued. "You're welcome to join us. We'd love to have you there."

Aamber had heard the women on the *Calder* talk about church, but only to mock it. She decided to take a risk. Looking up at the captain, she asked. "What is church?" Both men gaped at her.

"You've never been to church before?" the captain asked incredulously.

Aamber cringed. "I......I......I'm s-sorry. Of c-c-course I'll attend," she stuttered out, waiting for the blow. A slap from him would surely hurt even worse than the ones from her father.

The captain came and kneeled before her, placing his massive hand on her shoulder. "Child, look at me." Aamber slowly raised her head and looked him in the eye. Even kneeling before her, he was taller than she. "You have nothing to be sorry for and nothing to fear. Church is where people get together to praise and worship God and learn more about Him. You don't have to attend if you don't want to, but I do think that you would enjoy it. I know you're probably starving and hurting right now and just want a warm meal and a soft bed. But when you feel better, I will tell you all about Him. All right?" Aamber didn't know who "He" was or why tears sprang into her eyes. Looking down quickly, she swallowed past the lump in her throat and nodded. The captain squeezed her shoulder and returned to his desk.

"Follow me," Rich said gently, the same look in his eyes as in the captain's. He led her out onto the first deck and then into the kitchen.

It was large and many women were buzzing around the room. It felt like they all stopped and stared when they entered. A short woman with gray hair streaked with white and pulled into a neat bun at the nape of her neck came toward them. She was plump with soft gray eyes that were surrounded with crow's feet. "Ruth, this Mary Cullard, the captain's wife. Mrs. Cullard, this is Ruth."

After wiping her hands with a towel, the woman held out her hand. "Call me Mary. I'm so pleased to have you on our ship." Aamber reached out her hand and shook it, avoiding her eyes. The pity in them made her want to cry again. What was wrong with her! "Thank you, Rich, I'll take it from here."

Rich nodded respectfully and said. "Yes'm. Let me know if you need anything," then turned and headed back in the direction of the captain's office.

"I'm sure you've been through quite an ordeal. Let's head to your chambers and get you into a warm bath," Mary said with a gentle smile.

Rich made his way back to Captain Cullard's office, let himself in, and dropped into one of the wooden chairs. The captain leaned back and laced his fingers behind his head. "So, what do you think?"

Rich rubbed the back of his head. "Well, I know one thing. She's running from someone. And from her reaction to everyone around her, whoever they are, they're pretty bad."

"Hmmmmm, how old would you guess her to be?" the captain asked, leaning forward and rubbing his chin.

Rich shrugged. "I'd guess her not to be any older than 14. I had a hard time convincing her to join our ship and you could tell she'd been stranded in that tiny boat for days. As burned as she was, thin as a rail," he said with a wave of his hand.

The captain nodded. "She has all the classic signs of being abused. Suspicious of people. Not accepting anything as a gift. I just can't get over that look in her eyes. I've never seen that amount of pain in someone so young, even in all the orphanages I've visited. And where are her parents? Are they the ones she's trying to escape? Boy, would I love to give whoever put that pain in her eyes a piece of my mind," he said, his face growing red.

Rich nodded. "I agree. But I think the best way to protect her would be to take her at face value. Let her decide who she wants to become. If someone from her past comes looking for her, they'll ask for her by name. If we don't know her real name, we could tell them honestly that we have a young woman named Ruth on our ship and not whoever they ask for. I don't know what situation she came from but obviously it was very bad. The best way to protect her is to help her build a new life as Ruth."

"But if we don't know what situation she came from, how are we ever going to know what she needs? We're going to have to pray about this. God will show us what to do. I could feel her spirit searching for Him. Someone she can trust completely and count on never to abuse or abandon her. I think He's got something very special planned for this girl," the captain said. The intensity in his eyes spoke volumes.

"I agree," Rich nodded and almost felt excited, hoping he would see what it was the Lord had planned for her.

Mary led Aamber to one of the cabins on the second deck. "All the cabins aboard are on the second and third decks. This is the main stairway. To the left are the women's cabins, to the right are the men's cabins, and up the stairs are the married couple's cabins. Each cabin has two occupants, so you'll be sharing a room with a girl named Megan, we all call her Meg. I'll introduce the two of you later. Do you have any other clothes? If not, it isn't a problem. We keep a stack of clothes that women on the ship have outgrown, or this or that," she said with a flick of her hand. "I don't know though, you're so small we might have trouble finding something that won't swallow you," she chuckled.

"That won't be necessary. I've never had more than one dress. This one will be fine. I wouldn't want to put you out any more than I already have," Aamber replied, while trying to memorize the direction they went and the turns they made.

Mary paused mid-stride and eyed her skeptically. Surprised, Aamber glanced at her and then stared at her own worn leather boots, studying the hole in the top. "Dear, please don't take this the wrong way, but that dress is worn out. Please let me offer you the clothes, otherwise they'll just go to waste." Because of the kind look in her eyes, Aamber could not refuse her. She nodded. "Wonderful! Now let's get you in a hot bath."

They arrived at a cabin door and Mary brought out a large key ring. "I'll go right away and tell Smithy to bring in a washtub and tell the women to start heating up some water. It'll give you a chance to unpack. Don't worry, your belongings will be safe in here. The cabin doors lock and the only people who have a key are their occupants. Well, the captain and I have a copy of each key, of course, in case of emergencies." With that, she handed Aamber a copper key and bustled out the door. Aamber had almost the same feeling she got after a light summer storm. Refreshed but tired.

Aamber took in the room. It was simple but neat. There were two beds with the headboards against the back wall. A window was between them and the sunlight gave the cabin an airy feeling. Both beds were covered in colorful quilts and had soft-looking pillows. There was a small chest at the foot of each bed, with two drawers apiece. Aamber knew all the pieces of furniture were nailed to the floor, otherwise they would slip and slide with the rocking of the ship. Could one of the beds and chests possibly be for her? Mary said only two people lived in the cabins, so one of them must be.

Aamber opened one of the drawers and saw clothes in it. This must be Meg's side of the room. She tried the other chest; it was empty. Aamber quickly stashed what she could fit into the bottom drawer and wedged a small sliver of wood into the track at the bottom to prevent anyone from opening it. She still had some dried food left, and the rest of the wine. She hid her bow and arrows with her sword under the bed. There was only one small knife left and she put it in the top drawer with her sewing supplies. Mary hadn't taken her visible weapons but Aamber didn't want to risk it. Of course, she probably should give them to her for payment anyway.

Aamber glanced around the room again. She'd never known such luxury and honestly wondered if she was dreaming, still floating on her little boat, or even if she had died. Running her hand across the quilt, she sat on the edge of the bed. It was heavenly soft. The quilt was made of yellow, white, and pink squares. Some of the squares were floral-patterned. Aamber loved flowers and wondered if she would ever get the opportunity to touch a real one. Aamber looked at her hand upon the quilt and cringed at the sight of her dried skin and dirty nails against the beauty.

Suddenly the door burst open and Mary floated in carrying an armload of stuff. A young boy, no older than 12 and carrying a huge metal tub, followed her. "Ah, looks like you're settling in," Mary said with a smile. "Just set the washtub down there, Smithy, and start bringing us the water the women are heating up in the kitchen. Make sure you knock before coming in though," she said pointing her finger at him and wagging it.

With a small salute, he said. "Yes Ma'am!" and hurried out the door.

Mary turned to her. "Smithy is Rich's son. He's a good boy, but we must keep him busy. Otherwise, he'll be into some kind of mischief or another. Now let's get you out of that dress. I brought some cream to put on your burn after your bath and a dress that I think will almost fit you. We might have to shorten the hem a little." Mary talked as she undid the back of Aamber's dress. Aamber was nervous. She'd never undressed with anyone else in the room before, at least not since she was a baby, but her instincts told her that it wasn't optional, and her instincts had always served her well. "My gracious, you poor girl. You're nothing but bones, and you're so sunburned you've blistered! That must hurt like the blazes! How long were you out in that boat?"

"Five days," Aamber said, her eyes on the floor.

Mary clucked her tongue and shook her head. "Well, while you're here, we're going to fatten you right up and not let you out into the sun again until you're all healed! Yes sir!" At this point, Aamber was completely undressed. "Go ahead and set down in the washtub. I'll be sure to take the water from Smithy when he gets here." Aamber did as she was told. Mary suddenly stopped and looked at her dress, and then looked at her patched underwear. "What happened here?" she asked pointing at the rip Aamber had sewn up that horrible night.

Her already flaming face turned even redder. "I tripped down the stairs and it tore." It wasn't a total lie. She had tripped and fallen down the stairs that night, causing the tear to worsen. Aamber could tell Mary didn't believe her, but she let it go.

"Honestly, dear, I don't think this dress is worth salvaging. Would it be all right if I put it in the rag pile? All unwearable clothes we turn into rags," Aamber looked up at the dress. She'd been ashamed to wear it for the past year, feeling as if the stitching gave away the secret of what'd happened to her, even though everyone on the *Calder* already knew. Aamber had been the fodder for gossip since that night but she hadn't had any other choice but to wear the dress. Now she did have a choice. Not having to wear it would make her feel as if she were starting a new life. It would make her finally feel free.

"That would be fine with me, I'm not attached to it." An almost blinding smile came over Mary's face.

"Sounds like a plan." There was a knock on the door and Mary went to answer it. She brought back a steaming bucket of water. "Here test this water and see if it is too hot for you. If so, we'll wait a minute and let it cool."

Aamber hesitantly tested the water with her fingers. It was hot, but not so hot that she couldn't stand it. "'Tis perfect," she said, which gained her another sunny smile from Mary. Mary poured it into the tub and handed her a bar of soap. The water burned her sunburn but she didn't say anything. Aamber was working on scrubbing the past off her skin when Mary suddenly put something in the water that smelled lovely. "What was that?" she asked, surprised.

"Why, it was lavender, my dear. Do you not like the smell?" she asked, sounding apologetic.

"No, no! It smells wonderful. I've just never had the luxury of using such a thing before," Aamber tried to reassure her. Mary cocked her head to one side. Aamber knew she wasn't acting like a normal thirteen-year-old girl would act in this society but she didn't know how such a girl was supposed to act. In her world, things like baths and beds and perfume were for only the highest-ranking woman on the ship, not some pitiful, stupid, broken wench like her. Looking her straight in the eye for the first time, Aamber said. "Thank you, Mary. I will never forget the kindnesses you've showed me today."

Mary studied her quizzically but smiled. "It's been my pleasure, dear." After a few more buckets of warm water and thorough scrubbing by both Aamber and Mary, Aamber was cleaner than she'd ever been in her life. Mary massaged cream into her sunburn and put her hair in a simple braid. Then, to Aamber's surprise, instead of grabbing the dress she'd fetched, Mary pulled out a much simpler white gown. It had a pink bow at the neck and seemed looser than any dress she'd ever seen. "Here, my dear. Let's go ahead and slip you into this nightgown to give those blisters some room to breathe. You can try on your new dress tomorrow. I'll bring your and my suppers up here and eat with you tonight. In the morning, when you wake, I'll come and put some more cream on that burn. Then we'll try out your new dress, I'll take you on a proper tour of the ship to show it off, if you feel up to it. For now, I'll go fetch you some water, bread, and cheese. Then I want you to take a nap before dinner. Now I expect you to be curled up in that bed when I return, understand?" Aamber promptly nodded, and Mary bustled out of the room. Before Aamber could even take a step, Mary opened the door again. "I forgot to tell you that I will have Smithy come remove the washtub after we've left the cabin in the morning," and then, as quickly as she had appeared, she disappeared again, closing the door behind her.

Aamber crawled under the quilt, snuggling in and pulling it up to her chin, once again wondering if she was dreaming. Everything was so soft and warm. She was starving and dehydrated but had no problem falling asleep. Aamber awoke to a gentle nudge from Mary who helped her rise up, pulping the pillows behind her back. Then she helped Aamber take a long drink of cold water. After she'd set the water on the chest at the end of the bed, she handed Aamber a large hunk of cheese and bread. Aamber couldn't keep tears from rolling down her cheeks. "Thank you," she whispered and then ate the bread and cheese as fast as she could.

"Slow down, dear, I don't want you to choke," Mary exclaimed. Aamber slowed a little. "I asked Meg to have supper with us so you two can get acquainted. I think you'll get along well. She's a very sweet girl, and very mature." Aamber just nodded in response. The food tasted heavenly. As she continued to eat, she realized that Mary was studying her again and looked up, her cheeks full of food.

She quickly chewed and swallowed. "Is something wrong?"

"Where are you from?" Aamber stared down at the quilt. She hated denying this sweet woman who'd given her so much, but she really was from nowhere. "Nowhere, ma'am. I've lived on a ship most of my life and have never had a country to call home." Mary pursed her lips but nodded. Aamber finished her food. It was taking all her strength to keep her eyes open.

"Rest now, dear. We can talk more later. I'll be back this evening with Meg and our dinner." Aamber didn't have to be told twice and fell quickly back to sleep after hearing the soft click of the door after Mary's exit.

A few hours later, Aamber awoke to a knock on the door and Mary entered. carrying three plates of food on a tray. A thin girl with brown hair and eyes was on her heels. Each had a glass of water and a fork. Aamber pushed herself up on her elbow.

"Wakey, wakey, eggs and bakey!" Mary practically sang. Aamber pushed herself up and out of the bed as fast as she could. "No, no, dear. Sit back down. I'll join you. Meg can sit on her bed. Meg, this is Ruth. She's the new roommate I've been telling you about. Ruth, this is Meg."

Meg held out her slender hand. "It's so nice to meet you. I look forward to being your roommate and getting to know you better."

Aamber shook her hand and said. "Same." The three women settled into the beds with their dinners of chicken and rice. Aamber took a bite, savoring it and wondering what type of meat it was. "I don't know if I've had as much food in the past year as I've had today," she whispered. After setting her plate aside, she hopped off the bed and removed the food she'd stored in the bottom drawer of her chest earlier as Mary and Meg watched her with interest. "Mary, I don't know if you could use this, but I would like to offer it to you. It's what I had left of food supplies." Aamber scooped the food up in her hands from the drawer and set it on the bed. Then she climbed back up and continued to eat, avoiding Mary and Meg's eyes.

"Thank you, Ruth, but that's not necessary. You don't owe us anything," Mary replied gently.

Aamber looked her in the eyes. After brushing a hunk of hair aside that had come loose from her braid while she slept, she said. "Please. I want you to have it."

"All right, dear. I'm sure we can use it. Thank you."

After a few moments, Aamber surprised the women by saying. "Tell me about yourself, Meg."

Meg swallowed her last bite of food and replied. "Well, I'm a Christian. I'm 14 years old. A born and bred Océan girl. My mother's the head cook on the ship. My father is a lookout. I don't have any siblings, and I help in the kitchen. What about you Ruth? What's your story?"

Aamber took a sip of her water, coming up with a distraction. "What's a Christian? I don't think I've ever heard of that before." Both Meg and Mary's eyes widened and once again Aamber knew she'd said something wrong.

Meg was the first one to speak. "A Christian means I am a follower of Christ. Christ is God's son. God sent his one and only Son into the world to die for all our sins. He was the only person who's ever existed that never made a mistake. But he loved us so much he was willing to come to earth and die for us."

Aamber diverted her eyes from the look in Meg's. Her head was swimming with what she'd just said. God sending His Son to die for sins? But not just His Son, His only Son? Who'd never made a mistake in His life? Did they think she was an idiot and would believe a story like that? But the look in Meg's eyes…It was the same look the captain had in his eyes when talking about church. It was the same look Mary had in her eyes almost every time she looked at her. A certain glow almost. Like they were complete in their hearts. Like they had someone they could always count on, who loved them no matter what. What Aamber wouldn't give to feel that way.

Later that night, both girls slept soundly in their beds, the moonlight lighting up the cabin. "No, no, no! Leave me alone! NO, NO, NOOOOOO!" screamed Aamber while fighting with her covers.

Meg leaped out of bed and ran to her. While shaking Aamber's shoulder she said. "Ruth! Ruth! Wake up!" Aamber's eyes popped open and, still in a daze and confused about where she was, she shoved Meg so hard she fell straight backward hard. Meg sat there staring up at Aamber on the bed, eyes as big as quarters. Then Aamber realized where she was and what she'd done.

"Oh Meg, Meg, I'm so sorry. I didn't mean to. I was having a bad dream and forgot where I was. Oh, please forgive me, Meg! I would never hurt you on purpose!" Tears rolled down Aamber's checks. She'd leaped off the bed and helped Meg to her feet.

"Oh, Ruth, it's all right. I know you didn't mean to. But that's the last time I wake you up from a nightmare," she replied with a chuckle. Ruth just stared at the floor, trying to stop the flow of tears. "Hey, Ruth. Look at me." Slowly Ruth raised her head. "It's all right. I promise. What were you dreaming about anyway?"

Once again Aamber diverted her eyes. "I'd rather not talk about it if that's all right."

Meg shrugged. "Sure. I understand. I have nightmares sometimes I don't want to relive. But I want you to know I'm always here if you need to talk. You can trust me."

Looking into Meg's eyes, so full of care, made Aamber's heart hurt. She looked away and nodded, tearing up. Aamber didn't think

Mary or Meg would look at her that way if they knew who and what she truly was. With that, both girls climbed back into bed. Aamber could tell when Meg dropped off to sleep. Her breathing became soft and even. Aamber couldn't get back to sleep and tears continued to roll down her cheeks. She had been dreaming about Odin and her heart was still pounding. *Will I ever be free of this fear in my heart?* she thought to herself, drifting off into a fitful sleep.

The next morning, Meg quietly slipped out of the room while Aamber was still asleep. When Aamber woke, after realizing where she was, she rose and looked around the peaceful cabin. *Is all this luxury lulling me into a false sense of security?* she wondered to herself. She guessed it was yet to be seen whether or not it was.

Aamber pulled the soft pink dress out of the top drawer of her dresser. Little white flowers sprinkled the skirt and the blouse was a simple pink. There was even a white sash she could tie around her waist. Aamber had never seen anything so pretty. After trying the dress on, and shortening the hem a little, Aamber made her way to the kitchen where Mary might be, or at least Meg. When she arrived, women buzzed around the kitchen. Aamber stood back, watching the activities. Four of the women worked on cooking. One was peeling potatoes, one was chopping vegetables, one was shredding cheese, and the last was seasoning a boiling pot of something. The other two were washing dishes; one washed while the other dried and put away. The cooks would often use the freshly washed dishes immediately. Meg was the one peeling potatoes. The woman seasoning the pot could have been Meg's twin.

When Meg glanced up, a large smile spread across her face. She said something to the woman seasoning the pot that Aamber couldn't hear, which then caused the woman to look over her shoulder at her. Meg waved her in. Aamber approached the small table. The woman chopping vegetables sat to her left and the woman shredding cheese sat to her right. Both stared at her as she entered.

"Miley (the woman chopping vegetables), Riley (the woman shredding cheese), this is my new roommate Ruth. And Ruth, this is Miley and Riley. They're twins. The two women washing dishes over there are Lacy (the one washing dishes) and Macy (the one drying dishes). They are also twins," Meg said with a chuckle. "And this is my mother Margret, the best cook in the world!"

Margret held out her hand and rolled her eyes while shaking her head. "My daughter is a little biased. It's nice to meet you, Ruth. I've heard a lot about you."

Aamber shook her hand. "Same here. Your daughter is very proud and, if you're the one who cooked dinner last night, she has every right to be," which brought a smile to Margret's face. Aamber knew what Meg would look like in 20 years, she thought to herself. "Is there anything I can do to help you?"

Margret shook her head. "Mary wants you to rest today. She's also planning on taking you on a tour of the ship. I believe she's in the captain's office right now but will be back soon. Why don't you take a seat?"

"If you don't mind, I think I'll wait out on deck. I think some fresh air would do me good."

"Of course, dear. I'll tell Mary you're waiting on her when she comes back."

"Thank you, Ma'am," Aamber said with a nod.

"You can call me Margret."

"Thank you, Margret."

Mary sat across from her husband at his desk. "So, what do you think?" she asked after telling him the story Meg had told her this morning about trying to wake Ruth from a nightmare. "I don't think she would ever hurt Meg and Meg feels the same way. I'm more worried she'll end up hurting herself. Did she tell you anything about her past?"

The captain shook his head. "No. I very seriously doubt even the name she's given us is real. For some reason though, I can't shake the feeling we shouldn't press her for details. Obviously, whatever she went through was very bad. Like you said, I don't think she'd ever intentionally hurt anyone on the ship. I'm sure if Meg thinks there's something you need to know, she'll tell you like she did this morning. All we can do is pray for her and show her the love of God."

Mary nodded. "I'm worried about her, though. I told you how yesterday she was so grateful for food and a bed. And all the weapons she was carrying!" Mary shook her head. "The poor thing. I just wish there were more I could do."

George leaned across the desk to take his wife's hands. "Sweetheart, I believe you're doing exactly what God wants you to do. I think the best thing for that girl right now is for her to have a mother figure guiding her and taking care of her as she begins this new chapter in her life. Just keep doing what you're doing. God will reveal all things in due time. We must be patient. Here, let's pray." They both bowed their heads in silent prayer for Ruth.

Aamber made her way out to the deck and watched the ship slice through the waves. She couldn't stop thinking about what Meg had said last night at dinner, about God's only Son. Could that really be the case? Why in the world would God care so much about her? He had certainly never done anything for her before. Not only had he let her be born the daughter of a Viking but he'd also let her be raped. If that was what God was about, then she wanted nothing to do with Him.

Mary soon met Aamber and took her on a tour of the *Message*. It was a medium-sized ship with only four decks. Aamber was surprised at how clean the ship was and how well organized. There wasn't even a guard at the entrance to the storage deck! The sailors seemed happy and joked with each other constantly. Aamber couldn't stop watching them. She'd never seen men be friends without being partners in crime.

"Will you be joining us for church services on Sunday?"

Aamber could tell Mary was trying to hide the hope in her voice. She'd been so kind to her, Aamber couldn't disappoint her. Besides, despite her musings earlier, she wanted to know more about this God everyone kept talking about. "If you want me there, I'd be happy to come."

"Of course we want you there!" Aamber couldn't help smiling at the joy in Mary's voice.

Aamber sat beside the Cullards out on deck before church services began, taking out her nervousness on the small cloth in her hand. The entire week she'd studied how Meg behaved and tried to imitate her. By the end of the week, the women seemed comfortable in her presence. It didn't take Aamber long to learn to follow their Latin conversations, even though they sometimes talked so fast it made her head spin. Aamber had also tried to figure out anything she could about church from the conversations she'd overheard. She'd never been to church before and was scared to death she would do something wrong. If she did, would the Cullards not like her anymore? They not only believed in their God, but they lived out their faith in their daily lives.

Rich got up on the small stage the men had assembled out of crates. He held a thick book that looked well-worn. "Good morning, everyone! Let's start this meeting off with a prayer. George, would you please lead us?"

Captain Cullard stood up. "I'd be happy to!" The captain bowed his head and the rest of the congregation followed suit. Aamber tried to watch Mary and do as she did. "Dear Lord, thank You for letting us gather here together to hear Your word, praise You, and learn from each other. You are an amazing God and none of us deserve the love you heap on us every day. Please help us to keep you in our foremost thoughts and bring praise to you in everything we think, say, or do. Please forgive us when we fall short of your glory. And lastly, I want to thank you for the unexpected blessing you brought to us this week. Please be with Ruth and show her the love you have for her. Amen"

It wasn't until Rich started talking that Aamber realized everyone had raised their heads. Aamber couldn't help wondering to herself how the Cullards could possibly see her as a blessing. She'd cost them so much time and money and she wouldn't blame them if they kept her as an indentured servant for the rest of her life! Wait, she needed to pay attention to what Rich was saying in case the Cullards asked her about it.

"Good morning again, everyone! I hope you all are doing well. Thank you for coming today. I'm not the best public speaker or very articulate but hopefully, the Lord takes over and uses my pitiful attempt," he began with a chuckle and opened the book in his hand.

"Today we're going to be in John, Chapter 3. I know you're probably thinking this is the most known chapter in the Bible and you've heard it about a million times. But I've noticed, the longer you are a Christian, the more complacent you can become. We often take for granted the amazing gift we've received and forget the joy we had when we first were saved. So, as I read these verses, I want you to consider the words and try to imagine it's like you're hearing them for the first time. Who knows? Maybe you are hearing them for the first time.

"So, let's begin. John 3. *"There was a man of the Pharisees, named Nicodemus, a ruler of the Jews: ²The same came to Jesus by night, and said unto him, Rabbi, we know that thou art a teacher come from God: for no man can do these miracles that thou doest, except God be with him. ³Jesus answered and said unto him, Verily, verily, I say unto thee, Except a man be born again, he cannot see the kingdom of God. ⁴Nicodemus saith unto him, How can a man be born when he is old? can he enter the second time into his mother's womb, and be born? ⁵Jesus answered, Verily, verily, I say unto thee, Except a man be born of water and of the Spirit, he cannot enter into the kingdom of God. ⁶That which is born of the flesh is flesh; and that which is born of the Spirit is spirit. ⁷Marvel not that I said unto thee, Ye must be born again. ⁸The wind bloweth where it listeth, and thou hearest the sound thereof, but canst not tell whence it cometh, and whither it goeth: so is every one that is born of the Spirit. 9 Nicodemus answered and said unto him, How can these things be? ¹⁰Jesus answered and said unto him, Art thou a master of Israel, and knowest not these things? ¹¹Verily, verily, I say unto thee, We speak that we do know, and testify that we have seen; and ye receive not our witness. ¹²If I have told you earthly things, and ye believe not, how shall ye believe, if I tell you of heavenly things? ¹³And no man hath ascended up to heaven, but he that came down from heaven, even the Son of man which is in heaven. ¹⁴And as Moses lifted up the serpent in the wilderness, even so must the Son of man be lifted up: ¹⁵That whosoever believeth in him should not perish, but have eternal life. ¹⁶For God so loved the world, that he gave his only begotten Son, that whosoever believeth in him should not perish, but have everlasting life. ¹⁷For God sent not his Son into the world to condemn the world; but that the world through him might be saved. ¹⁸He that believeth on him is not condemned: but he that believeth not is condemned already, because he hath not believed in the name of the only begotten Son of God. ¹⁹And this is the condemnation, that light is come into the world, and men loved darkness rather than light, because their deeds were evil. ²⁰For every one that doeth evil hateth the light, neither cometh to the light, lest his deeds should be reproved. ²¹But he that doeth truth cometh to the light, that his deeds may be made manifest, that they are wrought in God.*

"So, let's look at this verse by verse. Let's start in Verse 3. It basically boils down to you will not go to heaven unless you are saved by Christ and baptized with water into the family of God. That's pretty cut and dry but is also very important, and is the basic principle behind Verses 3 through 5. Verse 6 basically boils down to a bird cannot be a chicken and a duck at the same time. Either you're of the spirit or of the world. There's no middle ground. We've all seen people who try to live in the middle, but it's not possible. The Bible says if you are lukewarm water, God will spit you out of His mouth. Nobody likes anything lukewarm.

"Verse 7 is making an analogy to the wind and the spirit of those who are saved by the Holy Spirit. You don't see the Holy Spirit. Even though we know the Holy Spirit is God and lives in us, we don't know exactly how He lives in us. The exact mechanisms behind it. But that doesn't mean He doesn't exist.

"Verses 8 through 16 talk about how Jesus was crucified. Now I can't say it any better than the actual verses. God loved us so much, He sent His only Son into the world to suffer the worst kind of death possible. He was the only man that ever existed who never sinned. He never made one mistake. But he loved us so much he took our sins upon him and took the punishment we deserve.

"And Jesus is the only way to Heaven which is the subject of the next verses. Many have tried different paths. The path to Heaven is narrow and the path to Hell is wide. And the verses after that discuss how you cannot be associated with the light and the darkness at the same time. Like I said, there's no middle ground.

"And lastly, we will be able to be identified as Christians by our works and our attitudes. We represent Jesus on earth. So, we need to make every effort possible to show non-Christians the glory of God. Remember, it's not about us. It's about Him.

"Well. That's all I have for the day. Let's sing our praises to God and give all glory to Him after a prayer." Everyone bowed their heads again as Richard prayed. Then the whole group began to sing. Aamber tried to follow along as best she could but she'd never heard these songs before. They were all about God and his love for his people, His power, glory, and goodness." Then the services ended.

Aamber held back tears and anger burned within her chest. If God really loved her that much, why did he allow so many bad things to happen to her, or to anybody for that matter! God had never shown His love for her before. Obviously, all this stuff was hokey pokey and worth nothing. But Aamber knew in her gut that that wasn't true. The look in all these people's eyes. The way they treated her. The kindnesses they had shown proved it. She'd seen people's true nature at its worst and truly believed there was nothing decent in any man on his own. The only thing she could find different from the Vikings she'd known and these people was these people believed in this God. But then why had He not ever protected her? Had He?

It was then Aamber remembered her inner cry for help and how shocked she was that she wasn't more injured after her horrific experience at Odin's hands. There were over a dozen other instances she could remember escaping dangerous situations by the skin of her teeth. Was that God protecting her all this time? But why did he allow her to be in that position in the first place? What was the purpose of it all?

Later that night, Aamber woke up from another nightmare of Odin. The sheets on her bed were soaked with sweat despite the chill and her blankets were tangled from her struggling. Luckily, this time she had not awakened Meg. Aamber plopped back down on her bed and sighed. Every nightmare seemed worse than the last. Why must fear follow her to a place that seemed safe? Was her subconscious telling her that she wasn't safe?

Aamber wrapped a blanket around her shoulders and made her way to the cleaning closet. Cleaning closets had become the only place where she felt safe and could clear her mind ever since that fateful day and she'd had to visit one every night since arriving on the *Message*. When she was safely tucked behind the cleaning supplies, she pulled her knees to her chest, laid her head on them, and sobbed. Her anxiety and shame overwhelmed her. She didn't deserve to be among these people. They were too good for a pitiful wench like herself.

To Aamber's surprise, about an hour later the door slowly opened. Mary stood before her wrapped in a shawl in a nightgown. She didn't say anything, just looked at her. Her eyes were full of questions and pity, but also something else. Respect. Then she held out her hand. It almost felt as if she was reaching out to Aamber's soul. Trying to give her a second chance at life. Aamber didn't have to think twice; she reached out and took it.

Mary led her down the hall to the captain's office and sat her down in one of the wooden chairs. She squeezed her shoulders and said. "Wait here, my dear. I'll be back in just a minute. I need to fetch the captain and make us all a cup of tea."

Fear shot through Aamber's heart, and she twisted around, grabbing Mary's hand. "Am I in trouble? Did I do something wrong? Please, Mary! Tell me and I'll never do it again! Please, I'm begging you." Her eyes were as large as saucers shining with panic, and Mary's heart squeezed in response.

"No, no. Of course not, my dear. You've done nothing wrong. I just think that it's time for us three to have a serious conversation."

Aamber nodded and twisted back around in her chair after Mary exited. What did she want to talk about? What could she possibly say if they wanted to know where she was truly from or what her nightmares were about? All her secrets had weighed on her like the entire ocean since she'd arrived. If only she could tell someone, anyone, where she was from and what she was up against! Aamber worried the small cloth she carried around until Mary returned with three steaming cups of tea on a tray with the captain on her heels.

Mary sat in the chair beside Aamber's and handed her one of the cups, then gave one to the captain after adding two lumps of sugar to it. "Would you like some sugar with your tea, Ruth?" Mary asked her as she stirred two lumps of sugar into her own cup.

Aamber shook her head and sipped her tea. "No thank you, Ma'am."

Mary nodded and stared into her lap. The captain leaned back in his chair and made a tent out of his fingers across his stomach. Dark circles surrounded his eyes and Aamber felt bad for being the reason he'd been awakened. Aamber's stomach clenched and she worried her lower lip. She couldn't meet the captain's eyes. He cleared his throat and began. "Ruth, we know that you are running from something or someone and strongly suspect the situation you came from was very bad. We want to help you. But we can't help you unless you tell us who you are and what you're trying to escape. You have my word you won't receive any punishment for anything you told us before and we will not lose any respect for you because of the situation you were in. Also, nothing you tell us will leave this room." He leaned forward. "Ruth, look at me, please." Slowly Aamber raised her eyes. "I believe that God sent you to us and......"

Before he could continue or Aamber could stop herself she blurted. "God! God! What has God ever done for me! I have had to endure things no person on this planet should ever have to even hear about let alone experience! I have been beaten, raped, starved, and almost killed! Where was God then? Where? How could you possibly say that God loves me when He let me be born the daughter of a Viking? And not only a Viking, but to the meanest Viking who ever sailed the Atlantic Ocean? Where was He then? Tell me, Captain! Where? Why couldn't you have been my parents? Or someone like you? Why?" she screamed and then buried her face in her hands and sobbed, her fiery red hair falling around her face in cascades.

Mary reached out and took one of Aamber's hands in hers but, strangely, neither she nor the captain said anything. When Aamber had gained some measure of control, she finally unloaded all the secrets she'd been carrying. She told them things she'd never told another human being before. About her father, her mother, her brother. She told them about her fear, her hunger, her pain, and her loneliness. About Odin, about her shame from that night, and how she had to kill him. And finally, about the shame she felt because of who she was.

When she'd finished, Aamber took in a deep shaky breath and wiped her eyes with her cloth. The room was dead silent for a moment with only the wind whistling outside. Then Aamber heard the captain rise from behind his desk and come and kneel before her. He gently brushed her hair out of her face and raised her chin to face him. "Aamber, I don't know why God allowed you to experience all of that pain, but what I do know is He loves you and has a very special plan for you. The moment I met you I felt the Holy Spirit tell me you were His child, even if you didn't know it yet, and that He had something very important planned for your life. Child, you are so very loved. God has been there for you through it all. It's why you survived. Many men could not survive what you have. Please, do not turn your back on Him." His eyes were full of hope.

Aamber could barely see through the tears pouring down her cheeks. "But I've done so much wrong, Captain. How could God possibly want something to do with me? I'm a thief, a killer, a liar, a...." she couldn't continue.

Captain Cullard gently shook his head. "Child, everyone has sinned and fallen short of the glory of God. One of His own apostles was a murderer. You'll never be good enough to accept the grace He has freely given you. None of us will. But that's what the cross was for. He loved us so much, He was willing to die for us and take the punishment we deserved."

"Now that's something I don't understand, either. Sometimes you say Jesus died for our sins and sometimes you say it was God. And then sometimes you talk about this Holy Spirit. Are they three gods? Are those all just different names for God? But didn't Meg say Jesus was God's Son? So, which one of them actually died for us?"

The rest of the night was spent explaining the answers to all Aamber's questions. It wasn't until the sun started streaming through the windowpanes that the small group realized the time. They'd been sitting in silence for a few minutes, soaking in the events of the last few hours. Looking out at the glorious sunrise, Aamber said. "I want to have God in my heart like you do. Everything about you is different and good. You have this joy that radiates from you. But more importantly, you have peace. I want that. I want to be a true child of God. How can I do that?"

Tears began streaming down Mary's face and they shone in the captain's eyes, as well. Both were beaming from ear to ear. Captain reached out for her hand. "Are you sure, my dear? This isn't a decision to be taken lightly. Being a Christian doesn't mean nothing bad will ever happen to you, it just means that you will always have Someone to trust and turn to when things get hard. And you have the promise of a life in Heaven with Him after this one."

Aamber looked him straight in the eye. "Captain, I have never been surer of a decision in my life. This is what I've been looking for since I was born. God is everything I have ever wanted." After having said this, for the first time since she could remember, Aamber felt light enter her soul and, for the first time in her life, she felt truly alive.

The captain nodded. "Then repeat after me in prayer. 'Dear Heavenly Father, I confess that I am a sinner, and I repent of those sins. I believe that Jesus is the Christ, the Son of the living God, and I accept him as my Lord and Savior.'" Aamber bowed her head and repeated the prayer, feeling the light and life grow inside her heart.

When she'd finished, the captain and Mary wrapped her in huge hugs. "Welcome to the family!" Mary said, wiping the tears from her wrinkled cheeks.

When they all could talk without crying again, they returned to their seats. They spent the next half-hour planning her baptism. The captain's eyes grew sad. "Aamber, Mary and I have never been able to have children of our own. If we could, we'd take you as our adopted daughter in a second. But I fear the possibility of running into your old family is very high if you were to continue to live on the ship with us. But there's an older woman in Océan. She's a very quiet Christian woman who's been looking for someone to live with her and help her with chores around the house. She would treat you well and I truly believe she would become like a grandmother to you. Another reason she's a great candidate is because she is a retired schoolteacher. Mary will start your education immediately but I'm sure Ellen would be more than willing to continue it after you go to live with her. You could maybe even attend school. We have a home in Océan but we're only there a few weeks out of the year and maybe three months in the winter. You need more stability and support than that. But even then, we'd always be there for you and you could come to us if you needed anything. Do you understand?"

Aamber smiled gently and nodded. She understood completely. Besides, even with how wonderful it would be to have the Cullards as adoptive parents, more than anything she wanted to live on land in a place of stability. Besides, Océan was an unlikely place for Vikings to ever hit. The main exports from Océan were wheat and rice. The country was known for its successful agriculture. Wheat and rice weren't coveted by Vikings.

"As far as your name, it's painfully obvious where you come from when you hear it. And now that you've been reborn and are starting a new life, I believe it's only proper we give you a new name. I think the name you've chosen fits you well. And since we'd like for you to be our adoptive daughter, you could say your name was Ruth Cullard and not be lying. It wasn't a lie when you said you're not really from anywhere. If anyone ever asks, you can just say you've lived on a ship most of your life. Your father was the captain and your mother and brother also lived with you, and leave it at that. Or, if you want, you can say Mary and I are your parents, which again technically wouldn't be a lie because we consider ourselves your adoptive parents. But, ultimately, you were wise not to tell anyone where you are really from, except for us, of course. The less people that know, the better. Even people who you trust could unintention-ally tell someone who knows your father and they could tell him where you are. Are you sure you got away with them thinking you'd been killed?"

Aamber shook her head. "No, not completely certain. But surely that's what they think. No one has ever escaped that ship alive before. And they would probably think it was just one of the Vikings on the ship who didn't want our clans to combine and killed me. To their minds, it should be the only reasonable conclusion."

Mary and the captain nodded. "In situations like this, I always think of the prostitute Rahab in the Bible. She saved her family by lying to the authorities and sending them in the opposite direction to protect the Israelite spies. I hate the idea of you having to hide your history and tell incomplete truths but I can't think of any other choice in the matter other than you just keeping your history a secret. Like I said, you can say things like you lived on a ship and such, but I would keep talking about your childhood to a minimum."

"I agree. Don't worry. No one will ever find out but you two. I didn't even plan on telling you but, obviously, circumstances changed," Aamber replied with a small smile. Both Mary and the captain smiled back. She reached out and took the captain's and Mary's hand in each of hers. "Thank you for everything. Especially for saving my life. Twice!"

The last couple of weeks spent on the ship were the best days Aamber could ever remember living. She grew close to Mary, who had become like a mother to her. Mary taught her a lot about reading and, by the time the couple of weeks were up, she could read simple sentences. Margaret had become an aunt and Meg a sister. The other women in the kitchen became like cousins and even the men on the ship became friends, especially Rich, who'd become like an uncle to her, as had Meg's father.

The day before they made port, they had a dinner celebrating the fact that they had completed the trip safely. There was lots of laughter and even some tears. Lots of promises to write letters were exchanged and even a few toasts. Aamber had never laughed, eaten, or drunk so much in her life. She had a feeling there would be many more days like this in her future and knew the best decision she'd ever made was running away from the *Calder*. The only regret she had was she couldn't share her newfound faith with her blood family, but that could never be.

"Oh, Ruth! I'm going to miss you so much! You've become the sister I never had. Promise me that you'll write," Meg said, throwing her arms around Aamber. It still always surprised Aamber a little bit when someone touched her. She hadn't been touched consistently since she was a baby.

Squeezing Meg to her, she replied. "Of course I'll write! You've become like a sister to me, too! But you'll have to be patient. My letters will probably be pretty short until I learn how to write more," she said with a chuckle.

Meg waved one of her hands dismissively. "Not a problem. Worse comes to worse, just draw me a picture. Just having something from you would be enough."

Mary walked up to the two girls. Aamber couldn't help noticing the look of sadness that had entered her eyes the last two days. It mirrored the look in her own. "You girls having fun?"

Both girls nodded. "Mary, why can't Ruth go with us on the next trip? She won't tell me a thing. I know you would love to have her here with you. It's no secret you think of her as a daughter."

The look of pain that flashed in Mary's eyes wasn't missed by Aamber. "I'm sorry Meg. I would love to have her on the next trip, but it's impossible."

"But why?"

"Ruth is going to live with a lady in our church that needs her."

"Who?"

"Miss Ellen. She's having trouble getting around and taking care of her house. Besides, I believe she is very lonely. Not to mention, she could teach Ruth here how to read and write so much better than I could. She could also teach her about other subjects too. The only other thing I could teach her would be simple math." Ruth could tell that Mary wasn't only trying to convince Meg but was also trying to convince herself.

The next morning, there was another round of hugging, and many, many tears. Aamber had to say goodbye to the captain at the dock, he had to oversee the unloading of the ship, decide what maintenance needed to be done, give the workers who were leaving their final pay, and figure out exactly who was going to come back for the next run in two months and how many he would need to hire. Mary was going to take her to Miss Ellen's house. Aamber's heart ached. The captain had been much more of a father to her than her own had been. Not only that, but they'd spent many, many hours talking about Jesus. They'd walked the deck for hours talking and Aamber never once felt like she needed to look over her shoulder or fear that he would harm her. He'd helped her work through so much anger and fear. Aamber had learned so much in the few weeks she'd been aboard the *Message*. Her whole life had been changed and she knew God had led her to these amazing people.

Aamber followed Mary and the captain down the gangplank but paused before she touched the ground. This would be her first step onto solid ground and she was almost afraid. Captain held out his hand, showing her a small smile of understanding. Aamber's hand trembled when she took it. She would never forget the feeling. The ground was so hard and solid but it was also soft. It felt strange not to have to brace herself against the rocking of the ship and her first few steps were awkward. Aamber couldn't keep a small giggle that was a mixture of happiness and nerves from escaping.

When they were safely away from the ship, the good captain flagged what Mary said was a taxi carriage and then kneeled before her. "Look at me Aamber," he whispered. As she looked up, a single tear made a trail down her cheek. "You've begun a new life. But I'm not going to lie to you. You can never change who you are or your past. Even if you call yourself Ruth, you will always be Aamber on the inside. It wasn't Ruth who was reborn. It was Aamber. I want you to remember who you are and I want you to be proud. You've survived things that no human should have to. Believe in yourself and live the life God planned for you."

The tears flowed freely now but Aamber didn't look away as she nodded. "Now, do you remember our emergency signal?" She nodded again. "Good. I love you, dear. I will always be here for you. Never forget you're my daughter. But more importantly, now you are a daughter of God. He will never leave you nor forsake you." With that, he kissed her forehead and both women climbed into the taxi carriage waiting for them. Aamber watched the captain grow smaller as the carriage pulled away.

A carriage ride was another first in Aamber's life. She distracted herself from her sadness and anxiety on the way by looking out the window at the horses. The only horse she'd ever seen was the head of one carved on the stern of a ship they had rendezvoused with when she was nine. They were so much more beautiful in person. At times, when Aamber couldn't sleep at night on the *Calder*, she'd tried to imagine what the rest of their bodies looked like. It was nothing like she'd expected. Aamber was glad she could almost see the ocean through the entire ride. The thought of being far from it made her heart pound. Unfortunately, though, the sky was covered with clouds and mud stained everything from their skirts to the carriage wheels. Aamber hoped it wasn't a sign of how her future would be.

After only a few minutes, the carriage stopped before a little cottage. "This is our house, dear. We don't stay here very often but it's our little home base. I need to grab a few things before we get to Ellen's. If you'd like to come in with me, you're more than welcome to. But I don't blame you if you don't want to brave the mud again," she told Aamber with a small smile. Leaning toward Aamber she whispered. "I'll only be a couple of minutes and, don't worry, you'd be safe here."

"Are you sure you won't need help carrying anything?" Aamber replied.

"No, no, dear. I can get it. You just wait here and I'll be back in a jiffy!" The driver helped Mary out of the carriage, gave Aamber a small smile, and climbed back into his seat. True to her word, Mary was back in about five minutes carrying a small bundle. Soon they were off again.

The carriage stopped about a mile outside of town. When the taxi driver opened the door, Aamber looked at Mary, who avoided her eyes. The taxi driver helped Mary out of the carriage and then reached out to help Aamber down. She looked at Mary for a sign about what to do. Mary nodded, letting her know that he wouldn't hurt her. Aamber gingerly climbed down, being sure not to step on her new skirt or in a mud puddle. The women on the ship had been so generous. She now had three blouse-skirt sets, four sets of stockings, two pairs of shoes, and even a soft brown shawl. Mary had also given her a Bible, a notebook, and some pencils.

After seeing her safely to the ground, the taxi driver handed her tarp bag to her and looked up at Mary. "I'll wait for ya here, Mrs. Cullard."

"Thank you, sir."

Aamber's heart squeezed. She had hoped Mary would stay a while. They turned in unison to look at the small house. It was a soft white with blue trim, a small porch, and symmetrical windows. The door was bright red and red rose bushes surrounded the house. A white picket fence completed the picture. They walked up the short path to the house and up the two steps to the porch. Mary used the large brass knocker. Aamber almost felt as if the thuds were nails in her coffin. The Cullards were the most amazing parents she'd ever known. Who knew what this Ellen would be like? Aamber had the sudden urge to bolt back to the *Message* but, no matter what, she couldn't put the Cullards in danger, which would be exactly what she was doing if she asked to live on the *Message* with them.

The oldest woman Aamber had ever seen answered the door. She walked with a cane, her shoulders hunched, and her white hair in a ponytail. She was so thin her dark blue dress hung on her frame. "Hi, Ellen! How are you?"

The woman's eyes lit up at the sight of Mrs. Cullard. "Mary! Oh, it's so nice to see you! Come in! Come in! It's been much too long! And who is this young lady?" As she spoke, she ushered them into her small, neat cottage and onto two comfortable chairs.

"Ellen, this is Ruth…" and as Mary told Ellen her story, Aamber studied Ellen and the house. It was small and it was obvious that Ellen didn't have much money, but the home was comfortable and clean. The chairs were cushioned, the wooden floors swept clean, and rag rugs gave a homey feeling to the room.

"Well my, my, my. You've had quite an adventure for someone so young," Mary said, leaning back in her overstuffed chair. Aamber smiled at the woman and stared down at her hands clenched in her lap. It wasn't until then that she noticed she was clenching them so tight her knuckles were white.

Mary took a sip of the tea Ellen had served them. "You see, Ellen, Ruth doesn't have any parents. And while Mr. Cullard and I would be thrilled to have her as our daughter, living on a ship with no stability is no life for a young lady her age. Then I remembered, during our last stay at home, you mentioned you were looking for someone who could help you around your house. It seemed to me like a match made in heaven. Ruth is one of the sweetest young ladies I've ever met. She's also one of the hardest-working. I figured maybe she could live with you. You need help around your house and Ruth needs stability and could attend school. Of course, Mr. Cullard and I would pay for anything she needed and would come and visit her as often as possible. What do you think?"

Ellen was quiet for a minute but a slow smile made its way across her face. "I think it's a wonderful idea. It would be so nice to have someone to talk to. And, besides, this house could use some young blood in it. I honestly don't know what kind of rules I'd have, having never raised a child of my own. The only ones I can think of are that she attends church and school. But I think Ruth and I could figure the rest out together. What do you say, Ruth? Do you want to be roommates?"

Aamber gave her another small smile. "I would love to, Ms. Ellen."

After a long visit, Mary said goodbye. She handed Aamber the bundle she'd gathered from her house. "These are a few things I thought you might need. Now, remember, Ruth, you're still our daughter and can come to us if you ever need anything. We will come and visit you as much as we possibly can." She reached into her pocket and pulled out a small silver cross. It had an amber rose in its center. It was the most beautiful thing Aamber had ever seen. After tying it around Aamber's neck, she leaned forward and whispered. "Let this represent who you are. You're still Aamber Rose but now you're a child of God. You are brave, beautiful, and loved. Never forget that." Mary kissed Aamber on the cheek and left, trying to wipe the tears from her cheek. As Aamber watched the taxi pull away, Ellen came up behind her and squeezed her shoulders.

"Don't worry, dear, she'll come and visit. I know it's hard but I also know you and the Cullards love each other. I think we'll grow to love each other, too, and I think someday soon it'll seem like we're one big family. Aamber turned around and embraced the older woman, holding her to her as if she were her only friend in the world.

"I pray so, Ms. Ellen."

CHAPTER 3

THE BETRAYAL

When thou passest through the waters, I will be with thee; and through the rivers, they shall not overflow thee: when thou walkest through the fire, thou shalt not be burned; neither shall the flame kindle upon thee.

Isaiah 43:2 KJV

Océan, A.D. 906

Prince Michal Moore of the great country of Océan looked up the winding staircase his beautiful fiancé Princess Cheryle Hernandez was descending. She wore a dark green dress and her chocolate brown eyes were only for him. Her long black hair was twisted up into elaborate braids that begged him to release them. Tonight, at the Valentine's Day ball, they would announce their engagement to the world. His heart felt as if it were bursting with love! When she was only a few steps above him, he reached out his hand to hers and she laid her delicate dark one in his. "My love, you take my breath away."

"Oh Michal, stop it. You're embarrassing me!" She giggled and blushed.

"I can't help it. I've loved you for so long, my dear Cheryle, and tonight I will announce to the world you're mine. I cannot imagine a more perfect day or a more perfect woman." He quickly glanced around and, seeing no one, gave her a light kiss on the lips.

"Oh, Michal, you mustn't do that! Not until we're married. It's not proper!" she said in a teasing tone.

Taking one last look around, he turned her toward him and pulled her into his arms. He whispered into her ear. "I don't care." Then he gave her the longest kiss he ever had. When he pulled back, her cheeks were flushed and she avoided his eyes.

"I love you, my dear Cheryle."

"And I love you, my darling angel," she crooned.

Michel spent the rest of the evening staring into Cheryle's eyes, dancing with her, and ignoring everyone else at the ball. At one point when they were dancing, he saw his mother wave him over. "My apologies, my dear, I think my mother needs me for something."

Cheryle gave him a seductive grin. "Don't worry, sweetheart, I'll mingle with the other guests and you can find me later." The minute he stepped away, a tall man with dark features swooped in and finished the dance with her. Michal had to check his jealousy. He had to remind himself that Cheryle's heart belonged to him—but then why did she look at the man like that? Why did she dance so close to him and whisper in his ear? He kept his eye on the couple all the way over to his mother.

"You needed me, mother?" His mother stood beside his sister Chrystal in a soft gray dress. Michal couldn't help noticing how lovely the pair was. Chrystal was really growing up. Her blond hair was twisted in elaborate curls and her blue eyes shone with innocence. Her dress was a soft pink that highlighted the blush in her cheeks. Men were already buzzing around his younger sister like flies, but it seemed she'd yet to notice. Both Chrystal and he had got their father's blue eyes and their mother's hair. Many people had remarked that the siblings could be twins. His mother's eyes were a soft gray, which matched her dress, and were full of worry at the moment, which was very strange for her. She leaned forward and whispered to him. "I need to speak with you alone."

"Is everything all right?" Michal said with a crease forming in his brow.

"Yes, yes. There's just something important I want to discuss with you."

It was then that father walked up to the trio. His light brown hair was slicked back and his dark blue suit brought out the color of his midnight blue eyes. He bowed to Chrystal and elaborately asked her to dance, making her giggle and respond just as elaborately. Michal smiled and inwardly hoped he would be as good as a father to Cheryle and his children as his father was to them.

Michal offered his mother his arm and subtly made his way through the crowd to one of the private sitting rooms just off the ballroom. Of course, Michal never understood why women insisted on calling them sitting rooms. They weren't much bigger than closets. They were created to offer couples a respite from dancing and a little bit of privacy to talk, without so much privacy that it could ruin the young ladies' reputations. Two chairs sat in each, with a small table between. There were no doors, allowing the occupants a good view of the dance floor. They were also on the other side of the ballroom from the musicians, so the music would not drown out the conversations.

After seating his mother, he took his seat and reached for her hand, leaning forward to show he was listening to what she had to say. "Michal, I have struggled about whether to say this for a long time and I beg of you not to become angry with me. Please know what I'm about to ask you comes from the love of a mother and not anything malicious. Also, I ask you not to say anything until I have finished. Do you understand?"

"Of course, mother." His mind was spinning. Mother only started conversations like this when it was bad. What could possibly be wrong on this most wonderful of nights?

"Son, I know you believe you love Cheryle. And I of course believe you are sincere but, before you announce your engagement, I think it is important for a parent to sit down with their child and ask them to seriously consider this question. If there is any hesitation the announcement should be postponed until there isn't any. Also, I believe it is important to ask their child if they sincerely believe the one they're intending to become engaged to is truly in love with them. Do they believe them to be the person who will stand by them through all the trials of life? Who will always love them, and who they will always love? So now I ask you, my son, do you truly love Cheryle and will you be willing to care for her the rest of your lives, and do you believe she truly loves you? But, more importantly, have you each asked God if the other is the one they believe He made for them?"

Michal was stunned. If anyone but his mother had asked him this question, his immediate response would have been "Yes," but the worry he could read in her eyes made him pause. Mother had always been one to allow her children to make their own decisions. The only time she had conversations like this with them was when she was truly worried. Michal felt a sickening feeling in the pit of his stomach and stared down at his hands holding his mother's small ones.

He truly believed he loved Cheryle but were her feelings as strong as his? He couldn't get the image of her dancing with the other man out of his mind. But that was just Cheryle's way, wasn't it? She was bubbly and she flirted and teased with everyone. He knew he would do anything to take care of her but would she be willing to take care of him if worse came to worst?

He'd prayed to God about Cheryle for years. He'd begged God to turn her heart to him. She was so beautiful and wonderful. Surely God wouldn't have allowed him to grow such strong feelings for her and then she not really love him! He refused to believe otherwise. Looking into his mother's eyes, despite the feeling in his stomach, he said. "Yes, mother. I believe we do, and we have."

Michal could see a little of the worry leave his mother's eyes but knew she'd read the worry in his own. "All right son, may God bless you and your union."

He led his mother to his father and started searching for Cheryle. After looking through the entire ballroom, he decided to check the garden. He couldn't imagine why she would be in the garden. Cheryle hated the outdoors but he figured he would check, just in case. He was walking past his favorite fountain when he heard her giggle and froze in place. He could tell she was behind the hedge to his right. They couldn't see each other but Michal could hear everything she said perfectly. "Oh, Chuck. We shouldn't be doing this. Michal is supposed to announce our engagement tonight."

"Oh, my sweet, what does it matter? We have no intention of stopping our courtship after you're married, anyway. You're only marrying him to bail out your country. You might ultimately have his name, but you will always have my heart!"

There was a long pause. Michal could only imagine that Chuck was sealing his declaration with a kiss. Michal's heart fell to his feet and anger filled every fiber of his being. He stepped around the hedge separating him. Cheryle saw him over Chuck's shoulder and turned as white as a ghost. "Michal!"

Aamber Rose sat astride her chestnut horse, looking out over the horizon at the sunset. Cinnamon munched on the lush, green, summer grass. Aamber Rose reached down and stroked the horse's neck, then looked back toward the horizon at a passing carriage. Océan was such a beautiful country. Ever since she'd escaped the *Calder*, her life had been full of many beautiful things. It amused Aamber that she'd lived on the ocean her whole life and then moved to a country called Océan to live the rest of her life. But she wouldn't trade this country for any other the world had to offer. It had beautiful forests full of mystery and lush green meadows the deer played in all day. The people were kind and knew each other by name. Océan was a very large island and Aamber loved every speck of dirt it contained.

However, despite her vastly improved circumstances, Aamber's heart was full of sadness. *Thank you, Lord, for the time I had with them. Please let me someday be half the person they were,* she prayed silently. Today was the first anniversary of Ellen's death and the second anniversary of *Messenger's* death. Ellen. The sweet lady who'd taken Aamber in, no questions asked. She'd fed her, clothed her, and became a grandmother to her. Mrs. Cullard was true to her word and she and Mr. Cullard had come and visited her every day until the *Messenger* set sail again. They lived in harmony as a family for three years, until the fateful day the *Messenger* sank in a storm. There were no survivors. The Cullards, Meg, Margret, Rich, and everyone else were gone. Aamber had been inconsolable for days. Then, exactly one year later, Ellen died of old age. Once again, Aamber was alone in the world...but not completely.

Aamber had made it her life's mission to try to help people the way she'd been helped. After Ellen died, she'd built herself a cottage in the thieves' forest. Aamber soon discovered she had a talent for surviving in the woods and she taught others how to, as well. It allowed them to feed their families while they got back on their feet without stealing. Aamber not only taught them how to honorably feed their families but also how to defend them by offering self-defense lessons.

Because Aamber was known and respected in the town and the forest, she let the men she worked with use her name as a reference, which would help them get jobs. That also gave her the opportunity to witness to these desperate men, who, because she gave them their pride back, were willing to listen. The people of the town and of the forest became her family, and she was never lacking for love. Aamber had made enemies, but her friends were true ones who would be in her life forever.

Aamber reached up and touched the cross with the flower around her neck. She'd never taken it off and, as long as she had a say, she never would. Not only did the necklace remind her of the parents she'd lost but it also represented her faith, which had only grown stronger over the years. Ellen had taken her to church every Sunday and, through it and Bible study, she'd learned how to face the challenges of life with God and how to live a Christian life. Her silver cross truly represented who she was.

After she shifted on Cinnamon, the horse gave a little knicker. Aamber reached down and patted her neck again. Cinnamon was the daughter of Ellen's old horse, who had died not long after Ellen did. Since Cinnamon was born, she and Aamber had been inseparable. Aamber never rode her with a saddle and she let her roam free. Any time Aamber needed her, she would whistle, and Cinnamon was there in a blink. Cinnamon was the first horse Aamber ever rode and was named not only for her coat color but also for Aamber. Ellen nicknamed Aamber Cinnamon because of Aamber's temper, which Aamber had to work hard to rein in during the days she'd attended school. But Ellen seemed always to know what to say to make her feel better. The two women never fought and they thoroughly enjoyed each other's company. It turned out Ellen had been just as lonely as Aamber.

Oh, how Aamber missed her family. Ultimately, though, she wouldn't trade her experience for the world. Even though her family had died, she knew what it was like to never have had a family who loved her. Having a family who loved her, even if only for a short while, made a world of difference and was one of the biggest blessings God had ever given her. Aamber would spend the rest of her life thanking Him for that.

Suddenly, a scream rang out, destroying the peaceful scene, and Cinnamon jumped. Aamber scanned the area, trying to figure out where the scream came from. In the distance, Aamber could see the carriage that had passed earlier was stopped. "Come on, girl. Let's go."

The carriage had stopped when circling a hill, which would give Aamber the perfect vantage point. Aamber got as close to the road as she could on Cinnamon but jumped off and climbed the hill the rest of the way on her stomach. From the top, she could look down at the carriage and have a bird's-eye view of what was happening. Three men with cloths covering their faces held bows and arrows pointed at the carriage. It wasn't long before Aamber realized it was the queen's carriage. The men had overpowered the guards. One lay further up the road unconscious or dead. Another was tied to the wheel of the carriage with blood running down his face.

A young man with light blonde hair stood before the queen, shielding her with his body. Aamber figured it was probably the prince, but she'd never seen the royal family close enough to be sure. Aamber knew exactly who it was holding up the carriage. Bobby

Rupert and his two brothers. They'd been a thorn in her side the past year. They were violent and caused problems for the good and the bad people. Aamber carefully strung her bow, careful not to move too fast and draw their attention.

"Give us all your gold! Any jewelry and money toss on the ground before us! Or you'll get what your soldiers got!" Aamber could see the prince clinching his jaw even from her distance. From what little she'd heard of the prince, she knew he was a strong warrior and fought for his men. But, unfortunately, he was outnumbered three to one, and wouldn't be able to protect his mother on his own.

To her surprise, they began to comply with the thieves' request. Aamber had thought rich people were stuck-up snobs who would rather keep their jewelry than their lives. Maybe she had them pegged wrong. One thing was for sure, Aamber wasn't going to let these jerks get away with hurting soldiers and disrespecting the queen. Aamber knew they would hurt them even if they complied. These thieves were just that brutal.

"Put down your weapons, Ruperts!" Aamber called out. One of them turned his bow on her and she let her arrow fly. It hit its mark right in the man's heart, and he collapsed to the ground clutching his chest. The prince tackled the one nearest him, wrestling away the man's weapon, and pinned him under his knee. He strung the bow and pointed it at Bobby. Bobby turned and looked up at Aamber.

"Well, well, well. If it isn't Miss Ruth. You're smarter than this Ruth. I thought you knew better than to mess with me. But not only have you been poaching my men, now you've killed one of my brothers. I guess I'm just going to have to teach you a lesson the next time we meet." As he talked, he slowly set down his weapon and backed away. Aamber climbed down the hill and kicked his bow away.

Aamber untied the rope she kept around her waist and tossed it to the prince. After he had tied up the man he'd pinned, he untied his soldier. Aamber kept her bow pointed at Bobby. When the prince headed toward him, she knew what he was going to try. Before she could warn the prince though, Bobby lunged at him. Once again, the prince surprised her by dodging the attack and wrestling the man to the ground.

Turning toward the carriage, Aamber saw the queen. She was in shock, her mouth half-open as she watched the spectacle. Aamber bowed the best curtsey she knew how. "I pray you're not hurt, my queen." Her pale visage contrasted with her dark brown dress. Aamber noticed a delicate gold cross necklace on the ground sparkling in the sunlight. Aamber reached down and picked it up; slowly she walked toward the queen and handed it to her. "I believe this belongs to you."

The soldier who'd been tied up had already gone to check on his fallen comrade while the prince took care of the prisoners. Turning back to the prince, Aamber said. "Make sure you check his waist in the back. He likes to hide a knife there, as well as in his boots." The prince followed her directions and finally looked up at her. His blue eyes startled her. She'd never seen them up close before.

Before a word was said the soldier came back laboring under the limp body of the dead soldier. All three turned to him, but he just shook his head and refused to look at them. Blood was dried and caked on the side of his face, and tears made trails through the dirt on his cheeks. Aamber went to him, as did the prince to help him carry his load.

Aamber turned back toward the prince and saw his jaw clench again. "Put him in the carriage. You can ride with him and make sure he's not jostled around while guarding the prisoners. I'll drive the horses and the queen can ride with me," the prince finally managed to say. His voice was tense and full of anger. Then he turned to Aamber. "Turn around and put your hands behind your back. You're under arrest."

Aamber couldn't close her mouth and thought she probably looked like a fish standing there gaping and trying to form words. "Excuse me?!"

His startling blue eyes narrowed into slits. "You heard me."

"Michal! What are you doing!" the queen exclaimed.

He didn't even glance at his mother when he explained. "She put you in danger, mother. If we'd handed over the jewelry, they would have left. Her actions only put your life more at risk and, because of her, you could have been killed."

Aamber felt fire spitting out of her eyes, while steam rose above her head. It took everything in her to control her tone. "I know these thieves. If you'd complied, they would have hurt you and your mother anyway. They maybe even would've done horrible things to your mother while they forced you to watch," she said, surprised at herself and how steady and low her voice was. Aamber saw the surprise flicker in his eyes but he continued to stare her down. Aamber wouldn't budge.

"And how exactly do you know these men. He said you poached his men. Are you the leader of a gang, too?" he sneered.

Aamber could hardly hold back her chuckle. "I teach his men how to live off the land, so they don't have to steal anymore. Then I let them use me as a recommendation for jobs. I'm well-known in town and my name goes a long way toward getting businessmen to trust them. If you ever condescended to go into town you might have known this."

His face flushed redder. "How dare you talk to me like this!" he roared.

"How dare you try to arrest the woman who saved you and your mother's life!" she shot back.

"That's enough, both of you," the queen said in a firm voice but Aamber had to turn and look at her because it seemed almost as if the queen was holding back a laugh. Aamber studied her as she seemed to be struggling to hold back a smile. "Michal, she will not be arrested, she should be rewarded. And as far as I'm concerned, you deserved to be talked to like that after the way you've treated her. Now we need to get back to the palace and give the soldier who gave his life to protect us a proper burial and console his family. Ruth, I would like you to accompany us." Without waiting for a response, she climbed onto the carriage stoop and waited for Michal to join.

Aamber turned back to face the prince. His eyes were still narrowed, his jaw still clenched, and he'd crossed his arms. "You heard my mother. Get in the carriage."

Aamber gave him the meanest stare she could. "I'll ride my own horse and follow, thank you very much." Aamber whistled and mounted Cinnamon, wondering what exactly her mouth had got her into this time.

When they arrived at the palace, Aamber tried to stay out of the way. They gingerly handed out the dead soldier first and he was immediately carried to be prepared for burial. A messenger and carriage were sent to pick up his family. The overall mood was somber and a current of tension underlined everything. The queen got out of the carriage with the help of her son. Aamber swung down before he had the chance to offer her assistance and she hadn't missed him rolling his eyes. "Follow me, Ruth," the queen said over her shoulder. Aamber curtseyed to the prince, making her gaze ice-cold, and followed the queen with her head down.

Michal gritted his teeth as he watched the fiery redhead follow his mother. How dare she speak to him that way! And then his mother backed her up! Was the world upside down? But even though he wouldn't admit it to anyone, he admired the girl's guts. Most women would have fainted at taking on robbers, let alone facing the queen of the land and the prince at the same time. He could tell she didn't know how to handle herself around royalty. She tried to curtsey and show the respect as well as she could, though, so it didn't offend him.

He knew he shouldn't have tried to arrest her but it seemed as if, since Cheryle's betrayal, he wanted to lash out at any beautiful young woman his age and this Ruth girl made a perfect sparring partner. After ensuring the injured soldier went to the doctor and making arrangements for the dead soldier's burial and family, he headed into the palace. One thing he would be willing to admit, though, the woman had skills with a bow. He rolled his eyes. And she had a temper that made her amber-colored eyes glitter like a tiger's.

Michal arrived while mother was telling father and Chrystal all about their misadventure. Father's dark blue eyes snapped with anger. One understood rule in his country was that no one messed with the royal family. He sent Michal an angry glance when his mother told him about how he'd tried to arrest Ruth and he laughed out loud when he heard Ruth's response. When she'd finished, his father turned to Ruth, who'd been quietly standing with her hands clasped in front of her, staring at her feet. "Ruth, I want to personally thank you for your service. It will not be forgotten. I have many questions for you and would like for you to stay at the castle tonight if you have no other obligations you must attend to. That way, tomorrow we can have a long conversation. If you do have other obligations, I will send a carriage at your convenience to pick you up from your home. Regrettably, tonight I must comfort the fallen soldier's family."

"Thank you, your highness. Your generosity is greatly appreciated but there's no need for me to be in your way tonight or to put your people out tomorrow. Just name the time and I'll be here. I am at your service." Father nodded. Michal could tell he was impressed by her answer.

"Very well. We will enjoy a leisurely supper at noon tomorrow. You are dismissed." Ruth bowed and slowly started to back out of the room. "But I would like for my son to escort you home tonight to ensure your safety." Ruth's head snapped up, and her eyes were wide.

"Ummm....uhhhh I don't think that would be wise, sir. I don't mean to argue, but I live in the thieves' forest and many of my neighbors are not fans of soldiers. I would never want to put your son in danger." To Michal's surprise, Ruth cringed as if she was expecting father to hit her. His father saw it, too. "And, uhhh, besides that, sir, your wife and son themselves can attest I can take care of myself," she said with an uneasy chuckle.

Father shrugged. "As you wish." This time, Ruth made her escape. A few minutes later, Michal could hear a faint whistle and then the pounding of a horse's hooves. The family turned to go meet the fallen soldier's family. As they filed out of the room, father whispered to Michal on the way by. "We're going to have a discussion later."

Michal inwardly groaned. He knew he was going to get chewed out for the way he'd treated Ruth. His father had always told his kids that no matter how old they were, he'd always get after them if they needed it. Michal had so many questions, though. Why did the girl think his father would strike her? Why did she seem so brave one minute and scared to death the next? How had she become such a good archer? Based on how she'd handled the situation with the robbers, did she have other weaponry talents? He tried to think of these questions instead of the dreaded task his family was facing.

Aamber rode Cinnamon to the gate of the palace the next day. "Who goes there?" the guard called.

"Ruth. The king summoned me here to meet him today," she called back. Ruth looked down into the creek dug around the palace grounds. It was wide and deep and made a good defense. It was too dark by the time they'd arrived at the castle the day before for her to admire the defenses they'd installed up close. Aamber had explored extensively around the castle, but never in an obvious way that would raise the guards' suspicions. Through her searches, she'd found many of the secrets the castle held.

The castle was large and made of gray stone, but it was not as ornate as others Aamber had seen from a distance while aboard the *Calder*. It had four watchtowers, one on each of its corners, with a fifth one higher than all the others directly in the center. Guards patrolled the tops of the walls and there was only one way in or out of the castle, at least that's what everyone thought. Overall, the castle looked solid, well cared for, but simple. The more Aamber learned about this royal family, the more impressed she became. They seemed to know what was important in life. She wondered what other surprises awaited her and whether she'd get a chance to spar with Prince Blue Eyes again. Aamber chuckled to herself, picturing his reaction to such a nickname.

After a few seconds' pause, she heard the guard shout. "Lower the bridge!" The large bridge began to lower slowly through the rope-and-pulley system they'd created. Aamber believed the design was quite brilliant in its simplicity. After dismounting and releasing Cinnamon, she crossed the bridge, her boots making a *thump, thump* sound all the way across. The guards eyed her suspiciously and Aamber wondered if a visit from one such as her was strange for the king. She certainly thought it strange.

After she entered the courtyard, the bridge was immediately raised again behind her. Aamber looked around, wondering if one simply walked up and knocked on a palace door. Oh, why not? This whole situation was ridiculous, anyway. The irony that a king wanted to speak with her, the daughter of a Viking, had kept her tossing and turning all night. What could he possibly want to speak with her about? Not even the sounds of the forest could calm her as they always had and last night was the first night in years she'd dreamed about Odin. Would she ever be able to get the chain of fear from her heart Odin had locked? It had taken hours of repeating memorized verses to herself before she could fall back asleep again.

She slowly ascended the palace steps. Two soldiers stood guard in their shiny, silver armor. *Lord give me strength*, she prayed silently. When she approached, one guard barked. "State your business here."

Aamber mustered her courage, repeating her plea to the Lord. "I am Ruth. The king asked me to meet him here today." The guards looked at each other and nodded. It was then she realized that one of the security protocols the king had installed was that the guards of the doors weren't told as a group whom to expect each day. If they both had to be told independently, it would help ensure that no unwanted guests made it through the gates because of a disloyal guard who could convince their comrade they'd simply forgotten. Aamber was impressed.

They opened the massive stone doors for her. They creaked all the way, the sound echoing off the massive stone walls. "Thank you, gentlemen," Aamber said as she walked through the doors, hoping the fear didn't show on her face or in her stance. A huge staircase greeted Aamber in the foyer, showing balconies above with doors that led to other rooms and other staircases. The size was intimidating. An older woman in a gray dress, crisp white apron, and crisp white hat entered the foyer when the doors closed behind Aamber.

"You must be Ruth. Please follow me. I'll take you to the king." They curtseyed to each other and Aamber followed the woman back through the doorway she'd entered from. The walls were covered in paintings and tapestries and huge rugs ran the length of the hallway. But, even with all the decorations, it was still almost simple and practical. The whole palace seemed to be decorated simply but beautifully. Windows lined the walls, allowing the sunlight to stream through, lighting up the hall and giving it an airy feeling.

They exited the hall through a curved doorway into a room that contained a large table. Two place settings were ready and waiting at one end. The king entered the room from another door and both women immediately bowed. "Here she is! I hope you brought your appetite, Ruth! We have a lot to discuss today!" To Aamber's amazement, he held out her chair for her. Her shock must have shown on her face. "What's wrong?" he asked, looking confused.

Aamber shook her head, trying to get out of the daze she was in. "Nothing, sir, I just couldn't help thinking you are the very embodiment of the leader the Bible describes you should be. I mean, you just held out a chair for someone who's lower than a commoner," Aamber said gesturing to the chair. She was rewarded with a brilliant smile.

Aamber allowed him to push in her chair and he took his to her left. "So, you're a believer. That's a relief. I suspected as much yesterday but we didn't really have much time to talk. I also didn't get a chance to apologize for my son's behavior. He's normally not like that. I don't understand what has gotten into the boy these days."

Aamber shook her head, inwardly marveling at how close the king's blue eyes were to his son's. "No need to apologize. He was just scared for his mother and he overreacted. I understand."

The king nodded. "I also apologize for the fact that none of the other members of my family can join us. Unfortunately, this lunch was so last-minute they'd already had previous engagements. Dinner is usually the meal where all of us can eat together. I was hoping you'd be willing to join us if we haven't finished our business by then."

"I'd be honored sir but I feel compelled to ask—What is our business?" she asked hesitantly.

"Well, there's much I want to discuss and, if I begin now, our food will get cold and Cookie will have my hide," he replied with a chuckle. "Don't worry, all will make sense very soon."

Aamber returned his contagious smile. He reminded her of Captain Cullard and her heart squeezed at the memory. "Oh, by the way, one of our traditions at this table is to pray together before the meal. Would you be willing to pray with me?"

"I'd be honored, sir." To her surprise, he reached for her hand. She clasped his and they both bowed their heads.

The next 45 minutes was filled with great food and great jokes. The king was delightful company and he made Aamber comfortable enough that she even forgot the difference in their stations. Aamber was almost sorry when it was over. "All right, the reason I wanted to talk to you: My wife told me of your amazing archery skills. I was wondering if you have skills in any other types of weaponry as well?"

Aamber nodded. "Yes sir. I am proficient in archery, fencing, hand-to-hand, knives, and even slingshots."

The king nodded, looking thoughtful. "I believe you but I want to see your skills in person. Would you mind giving me a demonstration?"

Aamber smiled. "I thought you'd never ask, sir."

Within the next ten minutes, Aamber was outside with the king preparing to show him her weaponry skills. He handed her the nicest bow and the straightest arrows she'd ever seen. "How far would you like the target to be?"

"As far as you please, sir," Aamber replied.

The king raised his eyebrows. "Challenge accepted." He whispered to the soldier who was assisting them and the target was moved 356 yards away.

Aamber strung her bow when the soldier was at a safe distance from the target and let the arrow fly. When it had hit its mark, the soldier started to bring the target back. "To be honest with you, I'm impressed you hit the target at all my dear." Aamber only smiled in response and stared down at her hand holding the bow. After the soldier had walked the distance back, he held up the target, his eyes wide. It was a perfect bullseye.

Michal watched his father with Ruth from the balcony at his chambers. His father had had a discussion with Michal last night but it hadn't been the one Michal expected or the whole one he'd expected. The king had told him that he was disappointed in him for the way he'd treated Ruth but did understand he'd been scared for his mother. "It's a learning experience son. And I know you'll do better next time. Now, for what I really wanted to discuss with you…" From then on, he'd described the crazy plan he'd come up with. The next day he wanted to test Ruth and see if she was truly as talented as the rumors suggested. The royal family had been hearing the rumors of a young woman making a drastic change in the lives of their people who were the most down on their luck but they had never heard a name before. That was why Michal hadn't made the connection the previous day but, of course, his mother had.

His father was going to test Ruth today and, if she was as good as her reputation, he wanted to hire her to train their army. The fighting methods Ruth used were different from any other's they'd seen and more effective. If she could train their army to fight the way she did, and with God on their side, nothing could destroy them.

His father had even told them all to have previous engagements for lunch that day. He wanted to size Ruth up himself, so Michal had decided to spend lunch working in his room. It was quiet and private, so he often preferred working there. But today he couldn't help watching his father and Ruth in the exercise yard below. Her reputation didn't describe even half of her talent. She was the best fighter he'd ever seen, which was bad for him. He'd hoped she would fall on her face so he would never have to see her again. Now he was going to have to work with her every day and the last thing he needed was such a large irritant in his life. Maybe she wouldn't agree. Maybe at dinner tonight he would give her every reason not to agree. Michal smiled to himself, formulating a plan.

Later that evening at dinner, Michal couldn't help being irritated. He'd planned all day what he would say to Ruth to persuade her not to agree to his father's proposal. He'd scripted exactly how it would go. First Michal would convince her that she'd never earn the respect of the troops, her being a woman and all, and he would describe all the horrors they'd inflict upon her with their hazing. Also, she had never taught such a large crowd and didn't seem comfortable in the company of strangers. He would go on to say that they didn't need her help and their old methods worked just fine. Lastly, he would tell her that he believed they could never work together closely, since he was the commander of the army. But, unfortunately, Michal knew he couldn't do it. If she could train his soldiers and give them the skills they need to protect themselves and their country, how could he not want that? Even if it meant putting up with someone he couldn't stand, his soldiers' safety came first, so he had ultimately decided to keep his mouth shut. His father had said he would make his offer during dinner. Michal couldn't help wondering what Ruth's answer would be. Everything Ruth did managed to surprise Michal, so he didn't even try to guess the outcome of tonight's meal.

The family laughed and chatted. Ruth charmed them all with her witty answers. She was smart, that much was obvious, but it was as if she didn't even realize it. Ruth had an honesty about her that he'd not seen in anyone for a very long time, except maybe his sister. Ruth's faith was as strong as her weaponry skills. Michal couldn't help asking himself, *Where did this woman come from?* She was unlike any woman he'd ever met. Even her clothes were different. Her dress was a simple burgundy, fitted with no frills, sleeves coming just past her elbows. Her outfit spoke no-nonsense, but her red braids and sparkling laughter spoke of the joy which radiated from her. But joy of the Lord wasn't the only thing she radiated. Michal couldn't put his finger on it but he almost thought it was fear. What had happened to her to make her so afraid?

"Now, Ruth. I'm sure you're wondering why I invited you here today and had you show off your amazing weaponry skills to me. Well, to be honest with you, I was testing you. I made my family have other obligations during lunch so I could size you up on my own. We'd been hearing rumors about a young woman who was making a difference in the lives of our people. We've considered inviting you to the palace for a while. You coming along and saving my wife and son yesterday sealed the deal. You have abilities with weapons and fighting techniques we have never seen or even imagined possible. If you are willing to train our army in these techniques of yours, they would be unstoppable. We could defeat any enemy. You see, we'd have you train our training officers and then they would train their men. So, you would be responsible for training about 100 men total. And also, I would love it if you would then give lessons to both my wife and daughter. I would love to have the peace of mind knowing that they'd be able to defend themselves if push came to shove. We would pay you handsomely, of course, and, after you've finished the training courses, I would love to hire you as my wife and daughter's personal bodyguard, but only for when they leave the palace. You see, because you're a woman, you are able to accompany them to places our men aren't allowed to go, such as dress fittings and the like. What do you say, Ruth? Would you like to join the palace family?" Everyone in the room turned to Aamber, wide-eyed as they waited for her answer.

Ruth stared down at her plate. Michal almost thought she turned pale. Why would his father's offer scare her? "Sir, I am honored you think so highly of me. And please don't take this the wrong way but, if I might ask, why do you want your soldiers trained as such? Do you intend on taking over another country? Or is someone threatening you?" This time, it was Michal who felt like a fish with his mouth hanging open. How dare she suggest such a thing of his father! Surely now they'd give her what she was due.

A small smile crept over his father's face. "No Ruth, I assure you. I have no want for the power to take over other countries. Greed is a sin. The only reason I ask this of you is because it is my responsibility to ensure the safety of my people and we are only as strong as our weakest soldier. And no, no one is threatening Océan, but I am not unaware that other countries see us as an easy target. If another greedy king or a Viking clan did decide they wanted our land, I don't want it to be easy for them to take it. I believe Océan is one of the strongest lands there is. Not because of the size of our army or their skills with weapons, but because we have faith in God. But I also believe you must meet God halfway and I believe God has sent you to us. To prove to you our motives are honorable, I want to assure you that, after the delightful day we have spent in your company we would like to keep you in our lives as a friend whether you work for us or not. People like you are rare in this world. So, when I meet someone like you, I'm willing to do everything I can to keep them in my life." Michal could almost see Ruth's visible sigh of relief. How could she even think that of her father? And how didn't he become angry at her blatant insult!

"I would be honored to train your army, sir. But I couldn't offer more than three days a week, and one of those days could not be Sunday. I also wouldn't want you to pay me. I have no need for money. I hunt for my food and can make my clothes and shoes. Truly it would be my honor to train your army. And if you feel that you must pay me, just donate the money to the church. Do we have a deal?"

Father immediately reached his hand across the table, and they shook.

Later that evening Michal sat with father by the crackling fire. Father rocked back and forth in his chair as if he didn't have a care in the world. Mother and Chrystal were taking a walk in the garden in the cool evening air. Michal was sure they often used their walks to discuss woman things, which Father and he were glad not to be subjected to. "Father, are you sure about this whole Ruth thing? I mean, the girl basically asked you if you wanted to become a cruel king and conquer other lands. I mean is she daft? Has she not lived here long?"

Father continued to rock, staring up at the ceiling. Michal was starting to wonder if he'd even heard him and collapsed back into his seat with a sigh. It seemed as if anything he'd said since Valentine's Day was wrong. Why did it seem like his whole personality was falling apart after what had happened with Cheryle? Why was he letting his anger affect everything he said and did? He was better than that. But the reality was that his anger consumed him and he didn't know how he would ever get it out of his system. *Please God, I can't rid myself of this anger on my own. I need your help!* He silently prayed.

His father finally leaned forward and looked at him. "Son, I know Ruth's background. Everything she's said and done that seems so offensive to you stems from it. She doesn't mean any harm or to insult us in any way. Her life was hard when she was young, which is why she struggles to trust people, especially those she's just met. I'm only telling you this much because I think you need to know if you are going to work with her. But that is all you need to know. The truth is she is taking a great risk training our army. If certain people were ever to find out it was her who trained them, they would kill her. That is why I'm not going to tell you who she really is. It's not a matter of trust, because I trust you with every fiber of my being son. But for her safety, and your own, only your mother and I can ever know who Ruth truly is. She has overcome impossible odds in her short life and I respect her greatly."

"But how can you just take her word for it, father?" Michal asked, splaying his hands.

"She didn't tell me who she was, son. The truth is I've known all along. I've had people watching her since she showed up in our country five years ago. I wanted to see what she would make of herself. And she is one of the bravest and strongest young women you will ever meet."

Michal leaned back into his chair and tried to digest all his father had said. It filled in a lot of pieces to the puzzle Ruth was but the puzzle was still incomplete. Maybe someday he would have the rest of the pieces but today he would trust his father's judgment. His father had resumed his gentle rocking. "Father, there's something I need to talk to you about." His father looked at him but continued rocking with his fingered laced behind his head. "Ever since what happened with Cheryle, I have been so angry. This rage consumes me, father, and I find it turning me into someone I don't want to be. You know me. I am not an angry man. But it's like, no matter what I try, it won't go away. It's like a poison eating me from the inside out and I don't know what to do anymore."

His father stared into the fireplace for several long moments. Michal knew he was weighing his next words, so he leaned back into his chair to wait patiently, exhausted by the toll that admitting this to his father had taken. Michal had never been one to discuss his problems with another but he was at his wit's end. His father sighed, then began. "Son, you experienced a very significant betrayal. You loved Cheryle and trusted her. It is natural for you to be angry, and the wound will take a long time to heal.

"But I have never experienced a betrayal such as yours and know I can't imagine what it feels like. But Jesus did experience this kind of pain. He knows a betrayal so horrible no human could fathom it. You need to spend time in prayer and ask God to give you the grace to forgive Cheryle, just as He's forgiven you each time you've betrayed him. And, son, I know you're not going to like hearing this, but I also believe God brought Ruth into our lives not only to help train our army but to help you work through this anger. If anyone on this planet has a right to feel betrayed and become bitter, it's her. But as you have seen, she doesn't let her anger eat her from the inside out.

"I wish I could take your pain from you son. I would bear it myself in a heartbeat. But I can't and I know these words I've said probably won't help you much. But the truth is, I don't have an answer to help you with your anger other than to turn to the One who holds all the secrets of the universe. I will be praying for you, my son, and am willing to talk with you, pray with you, and even just sit with you any time you need. I will always be here for you. And even if someday I can't be here for you, I have the comfort knowing that your Heavenly Father will never fail you in that way. Now let's pray together, my son, and ask God to lead you on the path to healing."

Michal clasped his father's hands like a lifeline and bowed his head. A single tear ran down his cheek by the time the prayer was over.

CHAPTER 4

THE TRAINER

No weapon that is formed against thee shall prosper; and every tongue that shall rise against thee in judgment thou shalt condemn. This is the heritage of the servants of the Lord, and their righteousness is of me, saith the Lord.

Isaiah 54:17 KJV

Océan, A.D. 906

Aamber stood on a balcony, looking out at the hundred men she was supposed to train. They seemed able-bodied to her, but oblivious to the dangers that could be surrounding them. The castle was in the middle of a clearing, with forests beyond. Who knew what secrets the forests held? Obviously, they didn't. Michal came to stand beside her. "What are you thinking?"

Aamber looked at him sideways, surprised he'd asked. "They look strong but we have a lot of work to do," she replied after a moment.

There was a long pause, but for some reason the tension between them seemed to Aamber less than before. There was an unmistakable cloak of sadness and distance Michal kept around himself. She knew the walls surrounding his heart were strong, as were hers. "I believe almost every member of my family has apologized for my behavior the other day except for me. To be honest with you, I thought you were a simpleton who didn't know what she was up against. But I was wrong. You knew exactly what you were doing. I just have one question, though. You could have easily killed all three of the Ruperts within a minute. Why didn't you?" His blue eyes shown with such intensity Aamber had to look away. How could one man have such a penetrating gaze? She never felt this way when talking to his father or sister who had the same eyes.

Ruth looked away toward the horizon and Michal once again was left wondering what she was thinking. He used to think he was good at reading people, at least before Cheryle. But Michal had a feeling this woman wouldn't let anyone know what was going on behind her beautiful eyes unless she told them. It seemed almost as if she wore a cloak around herself and would allow people to see only so much. He couldn't help wondering what had happened to her to make her so suspicious of everyone she met. "I don't believe in killing unless there's absolutely no choice. My job isn't to punish those men. It's only to make sure their actions don't hurt others. The Lord says vengeance is His. Besides, the death they're facing is much worse than anything I could have done," she finally replied.

Michal nodded and turned back toward the men. He wanted to ask her so many things but knew it would be futile. The enormous gorge between their two souls was wide and he didn't have the strength to try and build the bridge. "You think you can handle this group?" he asked unsurely.

"I'll manage," she was quick to reply.

"I guess we should get started," he said with a sigh.

When the commander saw Ruth and Michal approaching the soldiers, he gave the command and the men stood at attention. "At ease, soldiers," Michal commanded. Their poster relaxed but their attention was still solely focused on him.

"You were told to report here today to receive specialized training, which you will be required to teach your troops. Miss Ruth here is going to be the one to provide this training. I expect you to give her the same respect you show me. Understood?"

One brave soldier commented. "We are to be trained by a scrawny woman who couldn't lift a 50-pound sack of feed if she tried? Is this a joke?"

Michal went and stood before the young soldier, who he believed was named Jasper. He couldn't be much older than 17 and Michal stood so close their noses almost touched. "I have never been more serious about anything in my life, soldier. If you start making a habit of smarting off to your superiors and questioning the king's decisions your career in this army will be very short. Do I make myself clear?" Michal said in the deadliest voice he could muster.

"Yes sir," was the young man's reply, but Michal could read his skepticism.

Turning to the rest of his troops, Michal said, "I expect every soldier in this army to give her the same respect they give me. Do I make myself clear?"

"Yes sir!" rang out among the men in unison but Michal knew Ruth had an uphill battle ahead of her. These men were not going to appreciate having to follow a woman's orders, and Michal had no idea how they were going to change that.

Ruth took a step forward and spoke in a strong, clear voice. "Good afternoon, gentlemen. I know being trained by a woman is unorthodox and I can easily understand how you could resent me for coming in and telling you how to do your jobs. So let me make one thing clear. I'm here to teach you methods that could potentially save your men's lives. This is all that should matter to you. But I know you're not going to listen to anything I say if I don't earn your respect. Therefore, this is my challenge to you today. I will fight or compete with any of you in any form of weaponry one on one. Hand-to-hand, archery, knife-throwing, or fencing, take your pick. If I win, we've taken a step in the right direction. If you win, I'll surrender the class to you and you never have to see my face again. But also, because we have limited time, I'll give you 10 minutes to discuss amongst yourselves which of you will challenge me in what. Only five men can challenge me. After that, you must agree you'll be willing to let me teach you. Do we have a deal?"

Michal had been watching the men's faces during this speech. They had gone from surprised to incredulous to amused. The men's voices made a low hum as they discussed who would challenge Ruth in each form of weaponry. One of the soldiers turned to him. "What about you, sir? Do you wish to be one of the men?" he asked with a smile on his face.

"Well, I think the point is for Miss Ruth to gain your respect. She already has mine or she wouldn't be here. If you don't believe me participating will interfere with that, I'd be willing to," Michal replied with a shrug.

Michal caught Ruth's look of surprise out of the corner of his eye. *I guess she is human,* he thought to himself. *I didn't think anything could surprise her.*

The men continued to discuss amongst themselves. When the 10 minutes was over, they'd chosen Michal to challenge Ruth in fencing, Gregory Arnold to challenge her in archery, Joseph Burges to challenge her in knife-throwing, Jacob Smith for slingshots, and Jaxson Baily for hand-to-hand combat. These men were the best in the army at those competitions. Michal hoped Ruth hadn't got in over her head.

Within an hour Ruth had thoroughly bested all four of the soldiers and it was down to her and Michal. If he was being honest with himself, Michal didn't think the match between Ruth and him was necessary. He could see the respect for her grow in the men's eyes the past hour but, of course, he wouldn't back down. It might even be fun. Practicing fencing was Michal's favorite pastime and he planned on giving Ruth a run for her money.

They stood facing each other and drew their swords. Ruth made a small curtsey and asked. "Are you ready, Prince Blue Eyes?" Michal almost stopped short at hearing the ridiculous nickname and the teasing glint in her eyes made him smile.

"I see you've noticed my good looks, my lady. Let us begin." The soldiers roared with laughter and Ruth even chuckled. They circled each other, each trying to determine the other's weak spot. The soldiers circled them, enjoying every moment of the spectacle.

"Come on, boss, you can take her!" cried one of the soldiers. Several whoops and hollers followed. The sun was hot and had been beating down on their heads. Michal knew he had the advantage. Ruth had been working and fighting for an hour in the heat now. Surly she was tired.

Ruth suddenly lunged at him but he managed to block her blow with his sword. "Is that all you got?" he threw at her, enjoying the look of defiance in her eyes.

"Oh, your highness, I've yet to begin to fight." Ruth tossed back.

Ruth lunged at him again and they went back and forth at each other several times, each playing defense or offense as required. The circle of soldiers parted as they moved. As Ruth ducked to avoid Michal's next slash, she made one of her own at his legs, causing him to jump and lose his balance. His sword went flying but he ran to get it before she could pin him. He had to slide the last part of the distance and immediately twisted onto his back to block her next blow.

Ruth slid her sword down his, making a screeching sound. He stared into her amber-colored eyes, enjoying the sport as much as she was. It was then that he glanced over her shoulder at the balcony of the castle and saw someone he'd hoped to never see again. Ruth used his distraction to knock the sword from his hand. After disarming him, she looked over her shoulder to see what had distracted him while trying to catch her breath. There was no one there, and she looked back at him with a question in her eyes. He looked away and shook his head; then she offered him her hand to help him stand back up.

"Well done, Prince Blue Eyes. You're a worthy opponent, as the rest of your men were." Ruth sheathed her sword and turned toward the soldiers. "Have I at least earned your respect?"

The soldiers answered in unison. "Yes ma'am!" Ruth nodded and, glancing again at Michal, she said. "Let's all take a 15-minute break. Drink some water and prepare yourselves for your first lesson. We still have three prime hours before dinner."

The men began to stretch and drink from their canteens, their conversations once again creating a low hum. Ruth walked over to the tree under which she kept her tarp bag and sat in its shade to rest. After retrieving his sword, Michal walked over to join her and she offered him a drink. After watching the soldiers for a few minutes, he said, "Thank you for not saying it."

Without even sparing him a glance, she replied. "Saying what?" as if she didn't already know.

"I know I screwed up out there. Letting myself get distracted like that. It's an amateur mistake. I know better than it," he said wanting to beat himself over the head.

This time she looked him in the eye. "Mistakes like that aren't amateur, they're human. No matter how much training we put ourselves through, we cannot always account for the unpredictability of life. It is where we have to trust God to make up for our shortcomings." After a few minutes' pause, she asked. "Who was it, anyway, who distracted you so on the balcony?"

He stared straight ahead for a few minutes, debating whether or not to tell her. He'd not spoken about Cheryle or what had happened to anyone outside of his immediate family since that fateful night but, if father were right and she was the one God meant to help him through his anger, she had to know the whole story. Besides, everyone seemed to know it anyway. "I don't know if you know this or not, but for the past two years I'd been courting Princess Cheryle Hernandez." She nodded, her amber eyes showing that she was listening intently. "Well, we were supposed to announce our engagement during the Valentine Day's ball last February but, before we could, I caught Cheryle in the garden with another man. I overheard him say they'd been courting the entire time Cheryle and I had and they had no intentions of stopping their courtship after we'd married. Apparently, she was only allowing me to court her and leading me on because her country was struggling and they wanted us to marry so Océan would bail them out. Her country was struggling because of the debts the royal family had accrued. Needless to say, it didn't end well for us."

Ruth nodded solemnly. "So, what is she doing back at your castle?"

"I have no idea," he shook his head. "No one in my family would have invited her. Maybe her family is here on business. Either way, I have no intentions of seeing her."

Looking into his eyes for the first time since they'd begun their conversation, Ruth said. "I'm sorry she hurt you so badly. She was stupid for not realizing what a rare treasure it is for a good Christian man like you to love her. Maybe Cheryle's finally realized the magnitude of the mistake she made and she has come to ask your forgiveness. Maybe she even wants you back."

Michal rolled his eyes. "She can have my forgiveness but I will never give her my heart again. I could never trust her."

Ruth smiled. "You're not as stupid as I thought." Michal couldn't help chuckling. He'd never in his life met a man or woman who was more frank.

They left the shade and headed toward the soldiers, who immediately gave them their attention. The moment they were in earshot, the soldier who had asked if her training them was a joke turned to her. "Hey Ruth, are you sure you're not doing this just to catch a man? I mean, it's a great way to see if one of us could handle a woman like you."

All murmurs in the crowd ceased. Michal started toward the young soldier but Ruth put up her arm to stop him. He looked down at her, surprised, and she hoped he could read the message in her eyes. This soldier was obviously never going to respect her until she stood up to him herself. Michal couldn't help thinking she had the same look as when she'd taken on Bobby Rupert.

Ruth started walking toward Jasper and the soldiers behind him began to back up, leaving their comrade standing alone. When she stood toe-to-toe with the soldier, she said, "Tell me, soldier. Do you think you could handle me? If so, I dare you to kiss me right here, right now."

Aamber would never forget the shock in the young soldier's eyes. He couldn't be much older than she and was maybe even younger. His Adam's apple bobbed. But, not to be seen as a coward, he began to lean toward her. Aamber immediately dropped him to the ground and had him pinned with a knife at his throat. He struggled against her hold to no avail. "If you ever disrespect me or make such insin-uations again, I will castrate you myself. No real man, let alone a soldier, would make such accusations against a woman. They're sup-posed to be better than that! Am I clear?"

Aamber had to let up some pressure off his throat so he could answer. He squeaked out "Yes ma'am," and Aamber finally released him. He lay panting, trying to catch his breath in the dirt.

Aamber turned to the rest of the soldiers. "All right, gentlemen. I hope you're ready for your first lesson. Now, it's going to come as a bit of a shock for you and we're going to have to take a field trip to get there. So, leave your weapons here. You will not be needing them. Follow me."

Michal watched the soldiers as they started to follow Ruth. One of them finally reached down and helped the young soldier out of the dirt. Michal could tell his pride was severely bruised, but maybe now he had learned his lesson. One thing was for sure, he couldn't have reprimanded the soldier any better himself. Now he only had himself to reprimand for how impressed he was by Ruth. She'd given the soldiers the chance to let her prove herself to them and didn't expect them to just take Michal's word. That took guts and humility.

They followed Ruth out of the exercise yard and, to Michal's surprise, out of the castle gate. When they had reached the edge of the clearing surrounding the castle, they came upon four commoners, who almost seemed to be waiting for them. One was a scrawny kid who couldn't be more than 12. The next was an old man who looked as if a strong wind would blow him away. Beside him stood a man in about his mid-thirties who looked strong. The fourth was a mid-dle-aged woman who was mostly skin and bones. Ruth approached them and talked to them a few minutes, and then they disappeared into the woods. When she rejoined the group, Michal asked. "Who was that?" All he got in response was a knowing grin.

"All right, gentlemen, listen up. Your first lesson today is going to be on the art of subterfuge. I have asked four friends of mine whom I've trained to hide in the forest within a five-mile radius of here. Your job is to find them and bring them to me. Now, mind you, they will not come willingly and you have to catch them. But let me make myself clear: You are not to harm them in any way. You have exactly two hours to complete this task. Good luck!"

Michal and his men entered the woods. They'd decided to do a grid pattern search. At one point he saw a young man sitting on a doc fishing and asked him if he'd seen anyone suspicious. It crossed his mind that this might be the kid he was looking for, but it couldn't be. That kid was skin and bones. This one was heavyset and looked older. The kid shook his head and returned to fishing.

Next, he came upon a woman hanging clothes on the line near her small cottage. Once again, he wondered if she might be the woman he was looking for...but she couldn't be. She, he remembered, had thin brown hair. This woman's hair was stringy blond. He asked her if she'd seen anyone go by, but she smiled and shook her head. At one point he came to a clearing in the woods and saw a man was in the middle, plowing the field. Michal wondered if it could be one of the men he had seen but, as he approached, he realized the body type was all wrong, and once again the gentleman said he'd not seen anyone pass.

It wasn't long before he heard the whistle signaling the end of their hunt. He was hoping his men had had better luck as they made their way to where Ruth was waiting for them. But, upon arrival, it was obvious that not one of his men had been able to find and capture Ruth's friends. After all the men were accounted for, Ruth blew another hard whistle, and it wasn't long before her four friends appeared again out of the forest. "Well, my friends, how'd they do?"

"Terrible," the kid piped up. "I spoke to several of them and none of them realized it was me." The woman and the older man had the same stories. The middle-aged gentleman said not one soldier had found or spoken to him despite how many had gone past him. Ruth seemed quite pleased.

Turning back toward the soldiers, she said, "Gentlemen, let me introduce you to the young man who was fishing, the woman who was hanging clothes on the line, the gentleman plowing, and the one who was right above your heads the entire time." Michal hoped he wasn't the only one with a stunned look on his face.

The rest of their training time was spent with Ruth's four comrades describing how they had disguised themselves and the techniques they had used. When they finished, Ruth thanked them and once again they disappeared into the woods. Turning back toward the soldiers, she said, "On Wednesday, I'm going to teach you the different techniques described to you today and a few more. It'll be up to you to practice these skills and find the combinations that work the best for you. Then, on Friday, we're going to have another test. This time you'll be doing the hiding and I'll be the one searching for you. We'll see how far you've come. This is how our training will go. I won't just show you my techniques. I'm going to make you teach yourself. Otherwise, you will never fully learn. Good luck to you all, be safe, and I'll see you Wednesday."

The large group headed back to the castle and dispersed once they reached the courtyards. Michal walked beside Ruth. "You sure you're up for training my mother and sister tonight? We've had a long day."

"Aww, your highness. I didn't think you cared," she said with a teasing wink. "Of course, I'll be fine. I've had days a lot more arduous than this one. Besides, your father insisted I stay for dinner the days I'm at the palace. I wouldn't feel right eating your delicious food without earning it."

This made Michal laugh out loud. "Oh please, my family would have you for dinner for free every night, if they could. You've done pulled the wool over their eyes. I've yet to figure out how you managed to put blinders on them so thoroughly. And, by the way, you can call me Michal. I daresay we're going to be working together closely for the next few weeks. This whole 'your highness' business will get old."

She raised her eyebrows. "I don't think I could do that. To me, you will always be Prince Blue Eyes."

Michal laughed out loud. "All right, Carrots." Ruth punched him in the arm. "Hey, hey, hey. No need for violence. Let's just agree to call each other by our given names. Do we have a deal, Ruth?"

She considered him for a minute and finally replied "All right, Michal. But no promises about never calling you Prince Blue Eyes. It fits you too well." He smiled. His name seemed nice when she said it. The guards opened the castle doors for them and they entered the large foyer. "Is there a place I could clean up a little before dinner?" Ruth asked, nervously smoothing the hair that had escaped her tight braids.

"Cookie always leaves me a washbowl by the entrance to the dining room on my training days. But don't worry, my family isn't big on formality at the dinner table. My father believes it should be a place for genuine conversation and formality should be saved for meetings and the ballroom," Michal tried to reassure her.

Ruth nodded her head, once again staring at her feet. Why did she barely ever meet his gaze? "I just wouldn't want to offend any-one," she almost whispered. Would this woman ever stop surprising him?

They were the first to arrive at the dining room. Cookie had been kind enough to leave each of them a separate washstand and towel. They washed their faces and arms, getting the grit from the forest off. Out of the corner of his eye, he watched Ruth use the water to smooth the frizz in her hair. He shook his head. She would learn soon enough that his family were just people too. It wasn't long before the rest of the family joined them. Father sat at the head of the table, his mother to his right, and Chrystal beside her. Michal sat to his left and Ruth beside him. Once again, they spent a delightful evening. Michal and Ruth regaled them with the stories of their first day of training.

"Is that what you're going to be teaching Mother and me this evening?" Chrystal asked with a small laugh.

Ruth smiled. "No. The soldiers already know basic self-defense and weaponry. I intend to start you and your mother with those. But don't worry. Your lessons will not be near as strenuous as the ones I've planned for the soldiers. At least, not at first. When you've gained some experience, I will increase the difficulty level. It's up to you and the king as to how far you would like to go." Chrystal nodded. If Michal knew his sister at all, he knew she'd want to learn everything she could. Who knew? Maybe someday his sister would be a worthy sparring opponent. Goodness knows she outsmarted him daily.

"I am afraid I will not be able to join you in our first lesson tonight, Chrystal. Some last-minute business came up this afternoon I must attend to. You do understand, don't you, Ruth?" the queen asked reluctantly.

"Of course, my lady. The country's business is more important," Ruth was quick to reply. Michal looked to make sure she wasn't being sarcastic but only sincerity showed on her face. Michal knew what the business was that kept his mother away from the lesson. His mother wanted to be there when his father told him why Cheryle was here. It surprised Michal that he hadn't even thought of Cheryle since he'd seen her on the balcony. Maybe the hold she'd had on his heart for so long was finally beginning to loosen.

Aamber followed Chrystal to the ballroom. It was where they would begin their self-defense training. Chrystal had changed into a simple blue cotton dress and black boots. The dress brought out the blue of her eyes. To Aamber, Chrystal's eyes were more of a sky-blue and Michal's were closer to the color of the ocean on a sunny day. Their father's eyes were such a dark blue that Aamber sometimes thought they were a deep violet. The ballroom was spacious and large with marble floors. Their footsteps echoed off the massive stone pillars and walls as they entered.

Chrystal walked to the middle of the ballroom and spun around to face Aamber, flinging her braid over her shoulder in the process. Aamber had been genuinely impressed by Chrystal. She could immediately tell the young woman had a very generous heart. Aamber was also impressed by her lack of pretension. Many princesses would have shown up for their lesson in a fancy dress and hairdo. Also, many princesses would have resented having to learn to fight, but not Chrystal. She seemed eager to learn and had a bubbly personality that made her fun to be around. Aamber felt quite dull and taciturn next to her.

"All right, teacher! What do you have for me to learn first?"

Aamber spent the next hour teaching Chrystal basic self-defense moves. She was impressed with how fast the young woman learned. Chrystal was quick and didn't make the same mistake twice. When they had finished, Chrystal turned around with a secret smile on her face. Strands of blond curls that had escaped her braid framed her face and she was winded from their exertions.

"Ruth, do you know how to dance?" she asked breathlessly.

The question caught Aamber off guard. "Uh, no, ma'am. I've never had the opportunity to learn. And come to think of it, I've never attended a function that had dancing," she replied with a shrug.

"Well, I'm going to let you in on a little secret. Even though I just celebrated my fifteenth birthday, I'm already planning my sweet 16 birthday ball. I've been looking forward to it pretty much my entire life because it'll be my official introduction to society. Mother and I talked it over and we decided we would love for you to be our family's honored guest. With the ball being a year away, it'll give us the chance to get to know each other better and I'll teach you how to dance. What do you say, Ruth?"

Aamber was shocked. Why would they want someone as lowly in status as her at their ball? Then before she could recover, Chrystal grabbed her hands. "Oh please, Ruth! It would be so much fun. You could help me plan the whole night and we could help each other pick out our dresses and get ready. Oh, please, please, please!"

"Of...of course, my lady. I am at your service," Aamber was finally able to reply.

"No, no, no. None of that 'my lady' stuff. I command you only address me as Chrystal. And I don't want you to come because you feel you must. If you don't want to go, all you have to do is say so. But I want you to know I would love to have you there," Chrystal said.

Aamber couldn't resist the pleading look in her eyes. "I'll come if you wish me to be there, my lady. I just don't like the thoughts of potentially embarrassing you with me having never attended such a function before."

Chrystal released one of her hands and waved her own as she said. "Oh pish posh. Don't be silly. You could never embarrass me. I learned a long time ago not to care what the 'elite' in society think.

They're just a bunch of stuck-up busybodies who I'm shocked don't run into stuff more often with how far they've got their noses stuck in the air. Besides, there's a first time for everything. Now, let's start by teaching you the most popular dances."

The two girls spent another hour teaching Aamber some of the most popular dances. Chrystal hummed and led, while Aamber followed as close as she could. Aamber couldn't stop watching her feet and she kept stepping on Chrystal's toes. Chrystal would only laugh and encourage her new friend to keep trying. Suddenly they heard a man chuckle behind them when Chrystal once again had to remind Aamber not to watch her feet.

Chrystal turned to her brother and put her hands on her hips, her brows furrowed. "Oh, be quiet, Michal. Mother practically had to put a stick under your chin to stop you from looking down when you first started to learn." Aamber froze and also turned. The last person she wanted to see her pitiful attempts at dancing was Prince Blue Eyes.

Michal stood leaned against one of the ballroom doorways. His arms were crossed and one of his legs was tucked behind the other. He had a huge smile on his face. Aamber crossed her arms and met his amused grin with an angry stare. "I think you've found Big Bad Ruth's only weak spot. The soldiers today should have challenged her with dancing instead of weaponry. They always like to keep up on the latest dance moves to impress the young ladies. Who knows, maybe Ruth would have found a beau herself," he said with a wink.

"Now you sound like Jasper and who's to say I don't already have a beau," Aamber shot back while rolling her eyes.

"Oh really." Michal left his relaxed position and came to stand toe-to-toe with her. "And who is this mystery man?"

Aamber gave him a secretive smile. "Like I'd ever tell you."

Michal cocked his head to the side. "Oh, come on, Ruth, if you're going to be a part of this family, you're going to have to give a little."

Aamber raised one eyebrow. "Doesn't seem like it to me. Didn't your mother just bail out on her first self-defense class so she could discuss with you in private what your ex-fiancé was doing here?"

Chrystal doubled over laughing. "Oh, brother, it seems we've finally found a woman who can match you wit for wit." Before Aamber could blink, Michal was chasing Chrystal around the ballroom like they were kids, threatening to tickle her when he caught her.

When he had her cornered, Chrystal called out. "Ruth, help!"

Before Michal could brace himself, Aamber had him in a lock and Chrystal was tickling him and making him laugh so hard that tears were rolling down his face. When he finally escaped, Chrystal said. "Where have you been my whole life, Ruth? I've never been able to get him like that!"

Michal made a move as if he was going to grab Chrystal and she squealed, jumping behind Aamber. Michal then smiled and wagged his eyebrows at Aamber as if he were going to grab her next. Aamber just crossed her arms and rolled her eyes. Michal groaned. "It's two against one!"

Chrystal shook her head in response while laughing. "Now, enough teasing. Michal, maybe Ruth would benefit to have you as a partner. I'm not accustomed to leading and I can play the piano why you dance."

"That's not necessary, Chrystal," Ruth was quick to exclaim inwardly panicking. She wasn't sure she wanted to spend time in Prince Blue Eye's arms.

Michal turned another teasing grin toward Aamber. "What's the matter? You scared you'll fall in love with me, little Miss Ruth?"

Aamber scrunched her eyebrows, irritated. "No, of course not!"

He walked toward her and held out his hand. "Then may I have this dance?"

Aamber rolled her eyes as if exasperated but placed her hand in his, not understanding why it trembled or why she had a hard time meeting his piercing blue gaze. Chrystal began playing the tune she'd hummed earlier and Michal led Aamber out onto the dance floor. Almost immediately, she tried to watch her feet but Michal pulled her chin up so she had to meet his eyes. Then he placed his hand on her side.

Aamber didn't understand why his touch sent tingles up her spine and she reminded herself to breathe. From that moment on, Aamber stared only into his eyes and trusted Michal to lead. He was a strong leader and Aamber soon forgot her uneasiness. *Good grief,* she thought to herself. She was going to have to do a better job at guarding her heart. But she couldn't seem to keep herself from drowning in Michal's sea-blue eyes, from inhaling his earthy, masculine scent, and reveling in his gentle touch on her back. Aamber had long ago accepted the idea that she'd never be able to have a romantic relationship because she could never tell another about her past and it hadn't bothered her much until that moment in Michal's arms.

Unbeknownst to Aamber, Michal was having as much trouble guarding his heart as she was her own. To him, she seemed so vulnerable and brave. Ruth was the most beautiful woman he'd ever met in face and in spirit. She always smelled of pine trees and lilacs, a strange but alluring combination. In the few days he'd known Ruth, she'd demonstrated her indomitable spirit but there always seemed to be something in her heart that kept her from truly showing others who she was. Michal couldn't be sure but it almost seemed as if she was ashamed. These questions consumed his attention until he heard the voice behind him, causing him to visibly cringe.

"Well, well, well. Isn't this a pretty picture?" The voice cut through the congenial atmosphere like a knife. Chrystal stopped playing, Aamber's eyes widened in shock, and Michal refused to turn around.

Then Michal turned and looked at Chrystal. "Why did you stop playing? The dance isn't over."

Chrystal hesitated but began playing the music again. Aamber could hear Chrystal's uncertainty in the music that she had played so gaily before. Michal stared only at Aamber but a guarded look had filled his eyes. Aamber could feel Cheryle's eyes boring a hole in her skull and Aamber wished a hole would open and swallow her up. After the song was over, Michal gracefully bowed to Aamber and she gave him her best curtsey.

"You were a wonderful dance partner, Ruth. I hope to have the chance again in the future. Now, if you ladies will excuse me, I'm tired. It's been a long day. I think I will retire for the evening." Then he exited at the opposite end of the ballroom without ever giving Cheryle a single glance.

Aamber looked to Chrystal for guidance, hoping Cheryle didn't try to rip out her hair, which Aamber thought was a strong possibility, based on the look Cheryle was currently giving her. Chrystal rose from the piano seat, glided over to Aamber, and took Aamber's hands in her own. "That was beautiful, Ruth. You and Michal make an adorable couple and dance together like you were made for each other!" Aamber didn't miss the subtle jab Chrystal had sent Cheryle and Chrystal smiled at Aamber's surprised face. Then linking their arms together, the two women turned and faced Cheryle. Aamber felt like she was a fawn turning to face a wolf.

Cheryle sized Aamber up and Aamber did the same. Cheryle was beautiful, with long dark hair that hung past her waist in curls. Her fitted dress was midnight blue and she wore a diamond necklace and earrings. Her dark brown eyes matched her dark, olive skin. The two women curtseyed in unison and Cheryle curtseyed back.

"Hello, Cheryle. Lovely to see you again," Chrystal started in a cool voice. "I trust you're having a comfortable stay."

Cheryle's eyes never left Aamber's as she began saying in an irritated voice. "Actually Chrystal, there's something I need to discuss with you. I've yet to get an audience with your parents and I need to speak with a member of your family tonight so we can fix my little problem. I would prefer to be speaking with one of the adults, but as you've seen that doesn't seem to be an option."

Aamber felt Chrystal's grip tighten and her own eyes narrowed. The woman had the nerve to try and demean Chrystal's status in the palace. Even though she was young, Chrystal was very mature and well regarded. She was given as much respect as any member of the royal family and her word carried as much weight. With a flick of her hand, Cheryle continued. "You see, I tried to join you at dinner, but the guards wouldn't allow me past the door. I suppose they're new and don't know who I am."

Chrystal sighed and looked up to the ceiling. Aamber wondered if she was praying for patience. "No, Cheryle, they're not new. We only allow people we consider to be close friends or family at our dinners. And you must understand my parents cannot give a private audience to everyone who visits the castle on *business* no matter their station. I trust the servants took care of you in the guest dining room?" Aamber had to smile at her young friend's reply.

"Oh, come on, Chrissy! Don't be like that," Cheryle whined with a pouty mouth and doe eyes. Aamber felt Chrystal's fingers tighten around her arm again. Note to self: Don't call Chrystal Chrissy.

Chrystal seemed to be struggling to control her voice as she began. "Be like what, Cheryle? I'm treating you as I would treat any guest in our palace. Now, if you'll excuse us," Chrystal said leading Aamber toward the door.

"Chrissy, wait!" Cheryle sounded panicked. "You never introduced me to your friend."

Both women stopped and turned around. Aamber didn't miss Cheryle's snake-like smile as Chrystal said. "My apologies Cheryle. This is my friend Ruth. Ruth this is Cheryle Hernandez, Princess of the Country Forêt."

Cheryle and Aamber curtseyed to each other. "So, you're not a princess. What is your station?"

Aamber didn't miss the haughty glint in Cheryle's eyes and almost wanted to snap back that she was a princess, in a manner of speaking. "Ruth's an executive here at the palace and a close family friend. Now, if you'll excuse us, Cheryle. You have my sincerest apologies, but Ruth and I have some important business we need to discuss," Chrystal was quick to respond. The three women bowed to each other and the two friends made their escape.

After they were a safe distance away, both women sighed in relief. "Where are we going?" Aamber asked, curious. She'd never been in this wing of the castle before.

"To my chambers. I have a sitting area where we can speak privately. That is, unless you're in a hurry to get home," Chrystal replied as she led the way.

"No, no. I'm in no hurry." Aamber's response earned her a brilliant smile from Chrystal. Aamber couldn't help thinking she got her smile from her father.

They entered Chrystal's chambers. The fabrics were soft blues, pinks, yellows, and greens. The room had a fresh and airy atmosphere that matched Chrystal's personality well. A medium-sized bed was on the back wall and an exit to a balcony was beside it. At the foot of the bed was a small sitting or reading area with two chairs facing a fireplace and a small table in between. Each chair was cushioned and had a small footstool. Aamber and Chrystal settled into their chairs and stared into the cheery fireplace.

After a few minutes, Chrystal led with. "So, who's this mystery beau of yours."

Aamber laughed. "I don't actually have one. Your brother just irritated me by insinuating I didn't, so I wanted to get under his skin."

Instead of being disappointed as a young girl would be, Chrystal chuckled. "I'd say you managed that."

They sat in comfortable silence for a few moments. "I hope you don't mind the way I introduced you to Cheryle. She's a member of the 'elite' society I told you about earlier. I didn't want her to look down on you and make you feel bad. I don't believe there's any difference between kings and servants. People are people. They were just born into different situations and have different responsibilities. Do you understand?" Chrystal asked, seeming concerned she'd hurt her new friend's feelings.

Aamber leaned forward and squeezed Chrystal's hand. "Of course. I appreciate you looking out for me, but you don't need to worry. Cheryle can't do anything that'll hurt me because I don't care what she thinks."

Chrystal smiled in response. "I have a feeling we're going to be great friends, Ruth."

"Me too."

Later that evening, Aamber was heading out of the castle to go home. It was already dark but a bright moon lighted her path. She and Chrystal had talked for hours. Aamber could tell Chrystal was lonely, being different from the other princesses she knew, but she was different in the best of ways. Chrystal didn't follow the social norms, as Aamber didn't, and each had found a kindred spirit in the other.

When Aamber rounded a corner, she almost smacked headfirst into Cheryle. "Oh, my goodness, I'm sorry, my lady," she said with a quick curtsey. Then, trying to avoid an awkward conversation, Aamber tried to step around Cheryle and make a quick getaway but Cheryle stepped into her path.

Cheryle's brown eyes glimmered in the moonlight and Aamber was once again feeling as if she was a fawn facing a wolf. "I've been asking around about you. As it turns out, you're training Océan's army. I've never heard of such a thing before. A woman training the army. Where'd you get your weaponry skills anyway, commoner," Cheryle spat.

Cheryle crossed her arms and stared at Aamber through half-closed lids. Aamber stared straight back. "Well?" Aamber refused to answer. She wasn't going to give this woman any information. To her surprise, Cheryle gave a soft chuckle, which sounded like the evil meow of a cat who'd caught a mouse in her claws. "I see. The quiet type. Well, let me tell you something, commoner. Not even kings are brave enough to give me the silent treatment. And no one steals a man from me. No. One. I'm gunning for you and will ruin your reputation if you don't stay away from Michal. He's mine. And if you don't start showing me the respect my station deserves I'll make sure your little friend Chrystal is the one to suffer. You've already attacked me in the castle tonight. Do you really want to make it worse?"

Aamber refused to break eye contact. She saw a flicker of fear in the evil woman's eyes and had to smile. The princess had surely heard of Aamber's weaponry abilities if she'd been asking around about her and was beginning to realize she'd challenged her in a dark hallway of the castle at night. Not the smartest move the princess had ever made and, if Aamber had been less of a woman, she would have used it against her. But Aamber also pitied the princess. Cheryle obviously didn't have much confidence in herself and needed the Lord to show her how much she was truly worth. Aamber once again made her way around Cheryle and this time she didn't try to stop her.

Aamber made her way down the hall with the events of the last few minutes churning in her mind. Something told her that she needed to tell the king about her chance meeting with Cheryle immediately, but surely this wasn't anything worth bothering the king over. He'd be asleep by now and, besides, nothing had happened. Worry gnawed at her the entire ride home.

From his balcony, Michal watched Ruth leave on her sorrel mare. He'd finished some paperwork and had been standing outside to get some fresh air before bed. Michal felt bad about ditching Ruth and his sister instead of facing Cheryle earlier but knew they would understand. Michal had felt a weight lift off his shoulders when he'd told Ruth about how badly Cheryle had hurt him but felt the weight fall right back on when he'd heard Cheryle's voice.

He'd never told anyone the full story of that dreadful night. When he'd shown himself to Cheryle and her lover, Cheryle had cried and made a big scene. Michal had never liked having his personal business aired out for the world to hear but Cheryle had no qualms about drawing others' attention. She'd apologized and begged him to forgive her as if her boyfriend weren't standing right behind, her smiling at him smugly.

When Michal rejected her, Cheryle had screamed and cried while following him back into the ballroom. The horrible things she'd said he'd never be able to forget. "You never loved me! I hate you! I'll never forgive you for humiliating me like this, Michal! You're going to regret this day for the rest of your life! You're not a man, you're a boy under his father's thumb!" Cheryle screamed at his back as the entire ballroom watched in horror. Michal didn't acknowledge her and went to his chambers while two guards escorted Cheryle to her own.

Michal had cried for hours that night, not allowing even his mother to see him, he was so ashamed. He'd cried out to God in anger, asking Him why He'd allowed him to fall in love with Cheryle. But Michal already knew the answer. It wasn't God's fault; it was his own. The next day, Michal wiped his face and refused to discuss the event with anyone, trying to pretend it never happened. His family gave him his space to work through it on his own but made sure he knew they were there for him.

Michal was angry but knew he only had himself to blame. The Holy Spirit had tried to warn him when he talked with his mother the night before and during several instances of their courtship, but he'd refused to listen. Through his tears, Michal recalled several times when Cheryle had seemed aloof from him and from God. She attended church but Michal had never seen her praying on her own and she had never discussed a Bible passage with him. It had troubled him but he was certain she was just modest.

Michal now realized he'd been so in love that he'd looked past all her flaws. He had no right to judge her relationship with God but the fruits of her spirit weren't good. Not only had Cheryle never loved him but she'd crushed him by kissing another man on their engagement night. Then, as if that weren't humiliating enough, she'd disgraced him in front of the entire country.

When Michal looked at Cheryle with fresh eyes, he realized he'd fallen in love with the idea of what he wanted Cheryle to be and the person she had tried to portray to him. He had believed he was the only one of his family who understood her. There had been several occasions when he'd noticed animosity between Cheryle and his family but Michal refused to acknowledge it. He'd even convinced himself that her vanity was the product of her young age and would disappear as she matured. How had he been so blind?

Now he found himself attracted to another woman who was Cheryle's polar opposite. A woman who loved the outdoors as much as he did, who wasn't ashamed of letting others see her deep and sincere faith, and who cared more about others than herself. A woman whose sweet smile made him go weak in the knees and whose gentle nature made him want to wrap her into his embrace and protect her forever.

Michal had to ask himself if he was attracted to Ruth only because she was so different from Cheryle or did he truly admire her for herself? He also had to consider the secrets Ruth hid and the emotional traumas she'd surely endured. Did he have the strength to stand by her as she worked through these emotional problems? Surely, though, his father wouldn't encourage a relationship between her and the family if Ruth weren't worthy.

Michal groaned and ran his fingers through his hair. For goodness' sake! He hadn't known the woman longer than a week! How could he be so attracted to someone he'd just met? Besides, there was no guarantee Ruth would welcome his suit anyway. These questions stole his sleep and kept him on his knees most of the night. Michal begged God to show him if Ruth was the woman for him. He refused to make the same mistakes again.

The next morning, the royal family was gathered around the breakfast table, discussing what they'd be doing that day and how each of them had slept the previous night. Chrystal was in the process of describing Ruth's first dance lesson when a soldier entered the room and saluted King Richard. "At ease, soldier. What message do you have for me?" the king asked in his booming voice.

"My king, you have my sincerest apologies for disturbing your family time but the Princess Cheryle Hernandez insists it is of utmost importance she have an audience with you immediately."

His father shot Michal a worried glance and he shrugged. The queen looked concerned and Chrystal began picking at her food, avoiding eye contact. Michal had no idea what Cheryle would want to discuss with his father and was suspicious of his sister's curious reaction. "Send her in," the king commanded.

Cheryle entered the dining room wearing her finest gown. Michal had to keep himself from rolling his eyes. He'd always wondered why Cheryle insisted on dressing as if she was going to the ball every day. Most days, his mother and sister wore simple but good-quality gowns. He honestly liked their plain dresses better because they didn't have to worry all the time about destroying them and they seemed more relaxed. A picture of Ruth in her simple dresses formed in his mind. Where'd that come from?

"Good morning your majesty," Cheryle crooned in her sweetest voice. "I am so sorry to be bothering you but, if it were not an emergency, I would never disturb the king."

Once again Michal had to keep himself from rolling his eyes. Cheryle's "emergencies" often consisted of a tea stain on her best dress. Cheryle pretended to look humble and fluttered her eyes at his father. "Speak your piece," Father said gruffly. Father had never liked Cheryle and Michal knew she was working on Father's patience.

"You see, your majesty, I took a walk in the garden last night. You have such a lovely garden and I love to smell the blooms in the night air." Needles prickled Michal's skin.

"How could we forget," he snapped.

Cheryle looked down, seemingly ashamed, but Michal knew it was all an act. The only thing she regretted was getting caught. "Well, when I was heading back to my room last night, I was in the corridor and...and...and that Ruth woman attacked me!" she said, thrusting her hands out as if pleading for mercy. Her large doe eyes screamed sincerity and fat tears began rolling down her perfect cheeks but Michal knew the veils that lied in their chocolate depths.

"That's a lie!" Chrystal burst out.

"I swear it's the truth," Cheryle cried and covered her face with her hands. "Chrystal just doesn't want to believe it because they're friends!"

King Richard held up his hand for silence. Every member of his family eyed Cheryle. Not a single bruise showed on her olive skin and they knew that, if Ruth had attacked her, Cheryle probably wouldn't be able to walk. "Did she give a reason for this attack?" his father finally asked.

Michal turned to his father, surprised. He wasn't really buying this, was he? A bright pink blush infused Cheryle's cheeks as she excitedly exclaimed. "She said Michal was hers, and she wasn't going to let me steal him from her!"

Michal burst out laughing. Obviously, Cheryle had decided that Ruth was her competition in winning him back and had concocted this plan for getting rid of her. Of all things she could have come up with, she'd come up with him and Ruth dating. He laughed so hard that tears began spurting out of his eyes. Chrystal kicked him hard under the table. "Ow, hey! What was that for?"

"Hush, Michal," his mother warned.

Michal could tell his father was trying to hide an amused smile. "This is a very serious accusation, Cheryle. Are you certain it was Ruth?" Cheryle nodded emphatically. "Then today at one o'clock we'll have a hearing. We'll question both parties and I will decide if there should be any action taken. Do you have any other complaints?"

Cheryle nodded again. The tears had begun to dry as she began. "My king, if I may. Ever since I returned to the castle, the guards haven't allowed me to sup with you as I always have. I spoke with Chrystal last night on the subject but they still must be confused or they dismissed her because of her youth. Could you please discuss this matter with them? I still consider you my family and wish very greatly to right the wrong I have done."

His father's eyebrows rose and he made a tent with his hands on the table. Michal wanted to catch his father's gaze, to warn him not to let her sup with them, but he wouldn't look in his direction. Chrystal's face turned red and Michal knew Cheryle had irritated his sweet sister something fierce, only heightening his own anger. Father was quick to say. "Cheryle, we have forgiven you and you are welcome at our home any time. But we can never have the relationship we had with you before. You broke our trust and there's no changing that. We only allow our closest family and friends to sup with us and I'm afraid our relationship now is more business than anything. Now, I bid you good day." And with that, his father began eating his breakfast again.

Michal would never forget Cheryle's look of shock. A guard came up to her to escort her out. Cheryle curtseyed, carrying the weight of her bruised pride, and exited the room. The moment she was out of earshot, Michal turned to his father. "You don't honestly believe Ruth attacked her, do you?"

Father laughed. "No. If Ruth wanted to hurt Cheryle, she'd be smart enough about it that Cheryle would be too scared to say anything. Besides, there was no evidence of injury. But to keep peace between our countries, I must act as if I'm taking Cheryle seriously. I wouldn't want a war to break out over Cheryle's theatrics."

Chrystal's blue eyes snapped. "How dare she accuse Ruth of such a thing! She just got jealous when she saw Michal and Ruth dancing yesterday! I told Ruth they made a beautiful couple and danced like they were made for each other, so Cheryle decided to try to get rid of her!" Michal's jaw fell open at his sister's confession.

Mother nodded solemnly. "I agree, but you shouldn't have laughed at her, Michal, and you shouldn't have taunted her, Chrystal." Mother sighed. "But, given the circumstances, I understand. Next time, though, I expect more of you both."

Michal nodded at the rebuke. "Of course, mother, I'm sorry. I wasn't really laughing at her. I was laughing at the idea of Ruth and me courting. We'd kill each other with our tempers!"

Laughter echoed around the table. "I don't think it's such a crazy idea. Watching you two dance together last night, it was like you'd known each other all your lives!" Chrystal piped up.

To his utter shock, his mother nodded in agreement. "Yes, I do believe Miss Ruth would actually be able to tame our wild mustang if she took a notion to."

"Oh please," Michal groaned. "Father, please talk some sense into them."

His father smiled at him. "Father?"

"Sorry, son. You're on your own. I've already begun to see the signs you two like each other. It's been obvious from the day you met." Michal stared around the table at his family and rolled his eyes while shaking his head.

Aamber rode Cinnamon to the castle, chewing on her bottom lip the entire way. She'd had a foreboding feeling since running into Cheryle the night before and it had only intensified when the messenger fetched her to the castle at one o'clock today. When Aamber reached the palace gate, the soldiers immediately lowered the bridge. Apparently, they were expecting her. The messenger led her through the doors of the palace. "This way, please, my lady." Aamber followed.

"Could you please tell me what this is all about?" she asked, her anxiety growing by the second.

The messenger shook his head and opened the door to the court room. Aamber's stomach was in knots. The king sat on his throne, the queen on her throne to the left, Chrystal standing behind her shoulder, and Michal standing behind the king's shoulder on the right. The faces of the royal family were grim. Princess Cheryle Hernandez stood before the throne, her hands clasped before her and a cocky look on her face.

Aamber went before the throne and did her best curtsey. "Your majesties. How can I be of service?"

"Ruth, Princess Hernandez claims you attacked her in the castle corridor last night. Is this true?"

Aamber was shocked. She remembered Cheryle saying she'd "attacked" her, but had believed it was theatrics. "No, sir! I would never do such a thing! I bumped into her when rounding a corner but I swear I never laid a hand on her!"

The royal family's faces didn't change the entire time she spoke. "Liar!" Cheryle shrieked, sending piercing pains through Aamber's head. "She attacked me and said if I didn't stay away from Michal, she'd kill me!" Cheryle said, pointing at Aamber.

Looking back at the king, Aamber held out her hands. "Sir, you've seen my abilities! If I'd wanted to hurt her, she would be black and blue!"

"See, see! She admits it! She admits it! Don't you think someone with her abilities would be able to hurt someone without leaving a mark?!"

The king looked back at Aamber. "Sir, I know we haven't known each other long," she said. "But surely you know I would never hurt someone without cause like that."

The king looked down, avoiding her eyes. "Because you have no proof otherwise, I'm afraid I must punish you, Ruth. Cheryle, please leave the room." Cheryle stared at Aamber the entire time she left, a smug smile on her face.

When she was gone, Aamber said, "Please, sir! You've got to believe me!" but the king held up his hand, stopping her.

"I'm sorry, Ruth, I have no choice." He lowered his hand and motioned to the scribe to write down his decree. Aamber felt her stomach drop to the floor and struggled to keep the tears at bay. "Your punishment will be that you are required to spend one day with my son Michal. You two will take a horseback ride together, and then have a picnic lunch." Aamber blinked. Did she hear that right?

Within the hour, Aamber and Michal were riding their horses across the green countryside, both pondering the strange turn of events in the court room this afternoon. Aamber asked herself, *What had the king been thinking? What was the reasoning behind such a punishment? Was it really a punishment?* Michal wasn't as confused as Aamber. He was more suspicious of his father's motives. Ultimately, the pair independently decided that they enjoyed a good horseback ride, so they would enjoy the sunny afternoon.

When Cinnamon pulled ahead of his large buckskin, Michal dug his heels in. Aamber glanced at him, raised her eyebrows, and urged Cinnamon to go faster. Soon they were racing to the picnic site, their laughter streaming behind them in the wind. They were neck-and-neck by the time they made it to the stream and the horses were panting, sweat running down their sides.

They swung down and Michal tethered his horse to a tree after giving him a long drink. "Well, I'd say Buck and I showed you and your little pony who is boss when it comes to racing."

Aamber raised her eyebrow. "Pl…lease," she dragged out. "You ate our dust!"

Michal laughed, letting it go for the moment, and pulled the sack of apples, bread, and cheese out of his saddlebag. They settled by the stream, eating in comfortable silence. The trickle of the stream, compounded with the birdsong and rustling of the grass, made for a perfect setting. "Why do you think your father did this? I don't understand. He knows I didn't attack the princess," Aamber suddenly asked and popped an apple slice into her mouth.

Michal leaned back, enjoying the warm sun on his face. "Cheryle barged into our breakfast this morning and made the accusation. Father knows you wouldn't do such a thing but, if it seems like he let his army consultant attack the princess, it would put a strain between our countries. This way, he can honestly say he punished you without actually doing you any harm. The fact that he chose to send you on a picnic with me is probably to tease us about what this is all really about."

Aamber cocked her head to the side. "What is this about?"

Michal raised his eyebrows when he looked at her confused face and laughed. "Cheryle being jealous and thinking you and I are courting."

Aamber choked on the bread, then began laughing and coughing at the same time. When she'd finally recovered, she had tears running down her eyes as she said with a raspy voice. "To think of us courting. We'd kill each other with our tempers!"

Michal was surprised she'd basically repeated exactly what he'd said that same morning. She'd even had the same hysterical reaction. Maybe they were more alike than he thought. "That's exactly what I said. But I think my family is trying to play matchmaker. They probably believe me having a new girl would help me with Cheryle being here. Goodness knows, my family never liked her. They're probably scared I would take her back." To Aamber's surprise, he suddenly jumped up and took off his shoes. "Let's go swimming." Aamber was shocked and began chewing her bottom lip. "What's wrong?" Michal asked confused.

Ruth had suddenly looked like a scared rabbit. "Um, I don't think I will today. But you go ahead."

Michal wondered at her strange reaction. "Oh, come on! Loosen up a little. It would be fun. Especially on a sunny day such as this!"

Michal made his way into the water and motioned for Aamber to join. When she refused, he ran up the bank, picked her up off the ground, and pretended he was going to throw her into the stream. Aamber panicked. "NOOOOO, NOOOO please don't!" she begged hysterically.

"Hey, hey, hey calm down. I was just teasing." He sat her down gently, and Aamber shoved him. He fell backward into the stream. After he sat up, the water flowed around him. It wasn't even a foot deep where he'd fallen and a lily pad had landed on his head.

Aamber turned to go but Michal stood up and grabbed her. "Come on, don't be like that. I didn't mean to scare you. What's wrong?"

Tears continued to flow. Aamber tried to pull away, humiliated by her reaction, but Michal wouldn't release her. Hiccupping, she said, "I…I can't swim." She lowered her head in shame and twisted a cloth in her hand. "I almost drowned once and since then I'm scared to death to be in deep water."

Michal was surprised. This woman who took on men three times her weight was afraid of something as common as swimming. "I can teach you to swim if you'd like. That way you wouldn't have to be afraid anymore."

Aamber jerked her head up, surprised. Her eyes were red, and Michal felt his heart melt at the innocence in them. "W-what?"

His smile was blinding. "I can teach you how to swim."

"Really?" The hope in her eyes was almost childish. It was more joy than he'd ever seen on her face.

"Of course. Learning to swim isn't hard," he shrugged.

Her eyes grew as big as saucers and she looked back and forth between him and the water. "Now?"

"Why not?" he challenged.

Aamber once again looked down at the stream. It was gentle and deep, perfect for teaching someone to swim. Michal gave her a gentle smile and grabbed both her hands. "Do you trust me?" he asked. As he had when they were dancing, he had to pull her chin up to meet his gaze.

Aamber considered his question. To her shock, she did trust him, despite having known him for only a few days. She sighed. "You know I do."

He gently pulled her into the water and led her to the deeper part until it reached their waists. Releasing her hand, he said. "Here, watch me. All you do is move your arms like this and kick your legs back and forth." He demonstrated, enjoying how hard she was concentrating. He stood back up and Aamber looked away. His light linen shirt clung to him, showing off his muscular chest. She knew that she was blushing and chewed on her lip. Michal chuckled and teased. "If you keep chewing on your lip like that, you'll make it bleed. Now you try."

Aamber looked at the shore as if she was thinking about bolting. Michal swept her off her feet, and she grabbed his neck with a gasp. "Nope, I'm not letting you run. You can do this. A woman as brave as you can handle learning how to swim." He squatted down to let her float in the water. Her grip on his neck tightened and he couldn't help admitting that he liked having her that close. She smelled like sunshine and lilacs.

After getting accustomed to the water, Aamber took a deep breath and slipped off his lap, trying it herself. It took a few attempts but she soon found her rhythm. Michal wasn't surprised how easily she took to it. Given how gracefully she handled her weapons, it seemed that she and water should be best friends. He watched her swim for a few minutes making sure she'd got the hang of it.

A laugh seemed to bubble up out of her. "You were right! This is fun! I can't believe this is what I've been missing my whole life!"

Michal laughed at her childish joy. "Can I get that in writing?" She tossed him a saucy grin and continued swimming. He jumped in and swam to the other side of the creek. When Chrystal and he were small, their father had tied a rope to a tree for them to swing off into the stream.

Ruth watched him with curiosity as he untied the rope from around the trunk. "Watch out!" he called and swung in.

When he resurfaced Ruth was laughing. He spat water into the air in an arch onto her head and she splashed him back. "You try now."

She looked up at the rope, then back at him. The challenge in her eyes made him laugh. After climbing off the bank, she held the rope and stared off the rock into the water. "This is the perfect test to see if you're over your fear," he shouted up to her.

Still looking unsure, she took a running leap off the rock and let go just above the water. Michal held his breath, worrying she might panic at being so suddenly submerged in water. After a few moments, when she'd not come up, he swam down after her, panic rising in his chest.

Ruth was on the bottom of the stream, using a rock to hold her down smiling up at him. After releasing the rock, she swam up to the surface, sputtering and laughing. Michal took in a deep breath. "Hey, that wasn't nice," he growled, giving her a good splash.

"Payback for you threatening to throw me in earlier," she said as she splashed back.

Michal ducked under the water. Aamber searched for where he'd gone but couldn't see through the murky depths. Suddenly, he came up behind her tickling her sides. She fought to free herself but he was too strong. It was strange to her she didn't feel threatened. Since Odin, she'd never let a man get near her.

When he finally released her, she threatened "I'm going to get you back for that." To her shock, he held up the two ties that she used on her braids. "Hey, give those back." She reached for them but he dodged her. He swam around her in a circle like a shark, reaching up and undoing her braids partially and dodging her when she reached for him. By the time he'd finished, her long hair floated in the water around her.

When they'd tired of swimming, they lay on the bank in the sun, letting their clothes dry. Aamber had picked a bunch of wildflowers and was making a chain of them for a flower crown. Michal turned over on his side and admired her red hair, now hanging in damp waves down her back. He still had the hair ties in his pocket. He once again noticed the silver cross around her neck with the copper-colored rose in the middle. It suited her. "Where'd you get the necklace."

Aamber glanced at him. "My mother gave it to me," she said with a shrug.

Michal raised into a sitting position. "I never knew you had a mother," he teased.

Aamber rolled her eyes. "Everyone has a mother."

"You don't talk about family."

Looking out of the corner of her eye, she said, "By choice."

Michal took the hint. He couldn't help wondering about her past and how she had learned to fight the way she could. Aamber had a strange way of being able to connect to people. It was as if she met them where they were and refused to let them stay that way by trying to help them better their lives but they never learned anything about her.

He still believed she was beautiful when irritated, so he decided to press. "Do you have any siblings? Not everyone has siblings."

She sighed. "A brother."

His interest was piqued. "Where is he now?"

Aamber shrugged. Michal pondered for a minute. "Who taught you how to fight?"

"You know, you're nosy," she shot at him. It made him laugh, which irritated her even more.

"Come on, Ruth. Answer this last question and I'll leave you alone."

She chewed on her lip, considering whether to answer or not. Finally, she said, "My father."

Michal smiled, winked at her, and then lay back down on the bank. "Just so you know, I didn't say I wouldn't ever bother you again. I'll just stop for the moment." She threw the flower chain on his nose, causing him to sneeze.

Aamber laughed and Michal couldn't help thinking he liked the sound as she said. "Karma."

He looked back at her. She had started braiding her damp hair and, when she finished one side, she held out her hand for the tie. Michal cocked his head, as if he didn't know what she wanted. Ruth rolled her eyes and kept her hand out. Finally, he surrendered the tie, and she began on the other side.

"You know my sister wears her hair in all kinds of different styles. Why do you only do two braids?"

Aamber sighed. "I thought you said you weren't going to pester me anymore."

He shrugged. "Sorry, I didn't realize it was such a personal question."

Once again, he turned on his side and propped his head up with his hand. "Let's make a deal. Once a week you and I will get to ask each other one question we must answer honestly. It'll help us build trust."

Ruth stared at him blankly and shook her head. "Nope. You're going to have to work for every piece of information you learn about me, mister."

"Isn't answering a question about my own work enough?" She shook her head again. He shook his head. "Women, who can understand them?" he asked, earning another wildflower chain on the nose.

Later that evening, Michal was waiting for Cheryle in the garden. He'd sent a note saying he needed to speak with her, choosing this specific location in case there was any doubt in his heart as to her guilt. He'd heard it with his own ears and had seen it with his own eyes. Now she knew she couldn't have her way she was trying to manipulate the situation by any means necessary, which couldn't and wouldn't be tolerated.

The sun was setting, painting the sky with a multitude of brilliant colors. Birds chirped all around and the soft scent of roses was carried on the soft wind that cooled his face. He stood staring at the swan fountain when he heard a woman's light footfalls behind him.

Turning, he saw Cheryle was once again dressed in midnight blue, once his favorite color. She'd always worn it when they had quarreled and she wanted to apologize. Little did she know that, because of this fact, he now hated the color.

The moment he saw her she exclaimed "Oh, my love! I was so worried you believed the horrid lies that Ruth girl was spreading about me! I..."

Michal stopped her with an upraised hand and the shake of his head. "I did not ask you here because I wanted to reconcile. There is absolutely no hope for a future between us. If you believed otherwise, you've never known me at all. If you had, you would know that, once someone breaks my trust, they lose it forever. Unfortunately, you have made it abundantly clear the past couple of days you didn't understand this fact, so I've asked you here to clear up the confusion.

"We have no future together and not one aspect of my life includes you. My relationships, my time, my hopes, and my dreams will never include you again. As a matter of fact, after tonight I have no intentions of ever even speaking to you again. You sealed your fate on Valentine's Day, but you put the nails in the coffin of our love when you decided to try to attack my friends and family. If you ever try to interfere with any of my personal relationships again, I will personally banish you from this great country. Stay away from my sister, from Ruth, and from me forever. You may have my forgiveness, but you will never have my heart again."

Cheryle was silent for a moment, considering him. A gleam entered her eyes and Michal wondered if he was seeing what Ruth already had to face in the corridor of the castle. Cheryle had only ever put her best face forward around him, so, even though he knew the stories, he'd never actually seen this side of her.

"You're in love with her, aren't you?" she asked with a strange tone.

Michal only blinked. How dare she! Did he not just literally stand here and tell her his life was none of her business. Swallowing all the hateful words he wanted to yell at her, he simply made a small bow. "Goodbye, Cheryle. I hope you have a nice life." With that, he turned and started walking back toward the castle.

"I hate you, Michal! You never loved me! You are going to rue this night for the rest of your life!" Cheryle screamed at his back with a pitiful wail.

CHAPTER 5

THE GUEST

Withdraw thy foot from thy neighbor's house;
lest he be weary of thee, and so hate thee.

Proverbs 25:17 KJV

Océan, A.D. 907

Aamber took a swig of her water and wiped the sweat off her brow. She'd just finished her most recent lesson with the army. Michal nodded to her and they began walking toward the castle. She'd already taught the army how to hunt, make a fire, find water, and build shelter in the forest. She'd also talked the king into setting up evacuation sites for the people in the case of an invasion, even creating signals for entry. The army's training was going well, and Aamber was getting to know the men.

Ever since Cheryle's abrupt departure, the castle had been fairly peaceful. Her threatening Michal in the garden had been the last straw and she was promptly asked to leave, although she wasn't banished.

119

Each day, Michal became more himself; at least that's what Chrystal claimed and Aamber couldn't help thinking she liked Michal more and more every day. Aamber's evenings at the castle had become the highlights of her week. They'd eat dinner and then have self-defense/dancing lessons. The three young people would then stay up late discussing anything and everything. But Aamber kept having to remind her heart not to fall in love with Michal, knowing that doing so would be a big mistake.

When they entered the castle doors, a servant met them. "Excuse me, Miss Ruth. There's a young man here looking for you."

Aamber raised her eyebrows in surprise. "Thank you, Polly, who is he?"

"Well, that's nice! You not recognizing your best friend," a booming voice echoed off the foyer walls.

Aamber turned at the voice, a bright smile appearing on her face. "George!" she yelled, throwing her arms around his neck. Michal folded his arms and watched the man hug her. To him, it seemed that their greeting was a little too friendly. The man "George" had brown hair with unruly curls and bright green eyes.

"George, what are you doing here?" she said pulling back. Michal felt like breaking his fingers when he held on to her sides.

"What do you mean, what am I doing here? I'm visiting my best friend," the pompous man feigned indignation.

Aamber folded her arms and stepped back after George finally released her. It wasn't until then Michal realized he'd been holding his breath. "Really, George. Why are you here?" she asked again.

He feigned hurt. "Oh, I see how it is! I can't just pop by to visit you?"

Aamber eyed him skeptically. He raised one hand and put the other over his heart making his big greens eyes sincere. "On my honor, I'm only here to visit."

Michal cleared his throat and Ruth looked at him for the first time since George had entered. "Oh, goodness, Michal I'm sorry! I was just so surprised!" Turning back to George she said. "George, this is my coworker and friend Prince Michal Moore. Michal, this is George Honeycut. We went to school together."

The other man made a bow. "Excuse me, your highness. I didn't realize I was in the presence of royalty."

Michal eyed the man up and down, not missing the veiled insult. Michal nodded. "Any friend of Ruth's is a friend of ours. We were just headed to supper. Would you be kind enough to join us?" he gritted out, feeling as if the words scarred his throat.

Aamber turned hopeful eyes on the insufferable man. "Of course, I would never refuse such a kind offer!" George exclaimed. Michal wanted to grit his teeth but led the way to the dining room, wishing the man would shut up. He talked non-stop to Ruth, telling of his adventures, always making himself out to be a hero. Michal stopped and washed at his stand when they entered the dining room.

Aamber finally was able to get a word in with the man and clasped her hands in front of her waist. "You can wash with my water first, George."

"Why thank you, my lady," he said and splashed the water on his hands and face. How dare he? Ladies were always thought of first.

"Polly, could you bring another washbowl, please? We have another guest for supper tonight," Michal called.

"Right away, sir!" Polly hollered from the kitchen.

Aamber frowned. "That's not necessary, Michal."

"Oh, it's not a problem, Ruthie," Polly said, as she bustled into the room with a fresh bowl of water. She quickly switched the bowls and handed Aamber a fresh rag.

Aamber gave her a sweet smile. "Thank you both."

Michal noticed George was frowning at him. As far as Michal was concerned, if he felt bad it was his own fault. His father walked into the dining room, focused on some papers. He signed one and handed the stack back to his personal assistant. "Thank you, Jessie. That'll be all for today."

It wasn't until then he noticed their unexpected guest, his bushy white eyebrows rising in surprise. "Well, hello. Who do we have here?"

Michal motioned to George. "Father, this is George Honeycut. He and Ruth were school chums." Michal introduced him as simply as possible, earning him a surprised look from his father.

George bowed low. "It is the greatest honor of my life to meet you, my king."

The king laughed. "Oh, no need to be so formal. Any friend of Ruth is a friend of ours. Please have a seat. Have we already informed Polly?" Michal nodded. "Good, good. Tell us about yourself, Mr. Honeycut."

To Michal's chagrin, the man took the place on the other side of Ruth. He'd hoped he would sit by Chrystal. The man talked, and talked, and talked. When his mother and sister joined them, he charmed them with his dimples and made them laugh. Polly's wonderful cooking tasted like sawdust to Michal that night and he only picked at his food. He was relieved when the dinner was over.

"All right, Ruth! I'm ready for my defense lesson. But I'm warning you, I've been practicing!" his mother teased, pointing at Aamber. Aamber only laughed in response, and his father groaned, nodding in agreement with his mother's statement. Michal couldn't help smiling because his mother had been using his father to practice with.

George looked at Ruth, surprised. "You're training the queen? I heard you were training the army."

Aamber nodded. "Yes, I'm training the queen and the princess in self-defense, as well as training the army."

"Not the Prince? What's the matter, Michal? You scared you're going to get your butt kicked by a girl?" George challenged and narrowed his eyes.

Michal had to keep himself from punching the man in the mouth. Aamber quickly spoke up, knowing George had irritated him. "Michal trains with the army. Having worked with the army for a long time, he already knows the basics. Michal even surprised me the first day we met with his skills. He often acts as my assistant during his mother and sister's lessons." Michal looked at Ruth, surprised. *She'd noticed his fighting skills while facing down robbers? And then even after he'd tried to arrest her?* He thought to himself.

George gave the women a charming smile. "I would be happy to be your assistant tonight! At least, if that is all right with everyone else."

His mother and Chrystal just shrugged, unsure how to answer. "Well, how about you both be my assistant tonight," Aamber tried to smooth Michal's ire.

Michal shook his head. "By all means. He can be your assistant tonight."

"No, Michal, please. You've already practiced what I want to teach them," Aamber pleaded.

His wounded pride was soothed somewhat. "If you wish."

Aamber rewarded him with a bright smile. "Thank you!"

The group made their way to the ballroom, George talking the entire way. Aamber grabbed Michal's hand, holding him back before he entered. "I'm sorry if George offended you. I don't think he meant any harm," she whispered.

Michal tried to give her a reassuring smile. "Not a problem, my lady."

George was frowning as they entered. He noticed that they'd hung back for a moment. Michal wondered why he felt as if he'd won a victory. Aamber began the lesson, alternating between the two men with requests to help her. Michal kept an eye on George when he was working with his sister but Chrystal didn't seem affected by George's charms. Michal couldn't help thinking it strange how Chrystal didn't react to any of the gentlemen who paid her attention. Most girls her age ate such things up.

When they'd finished the self-defense lesson, his mother stretched. "All right, young ones. I'm tired. I'm afraid I won't be joining you for the dance lesson tonight. I've had a long day. George, might I ask where you are staying?"

The pompous man nodded feigning humility. "Oh, my queen. I'm a nomad and sleep wherever my head lands under the stars."

Michal rolled his eyes at the man's poetic response. His mother shook her head. "That won't do. You must stay at the castle tonight. Follow me and I'll show you to your room."

"I humbly thank you, my lady," George replied with a deep bow. "Until tomorrow, my dear Ruth," he said and kissed Aamber's hand.

Aamber rolled her eyes. "Stop being silly and do as the queen says." George winked at her, bowed to Chrystal and Michal, and followed the queen out of the room. Michal breathed a sigh of relief and could almost swear his sister did as well.

"Let's skip the dance lesson tonight, and just sit and talk," Chrystal suggested. Aamber and he nodded, both tired from the long day. They made their way down the corridor and settled into the large library with its overstuffed chairs. It had become their unofficial meeting place. Often after their lessons, they'd all sit and talk, enjoying each other's company. Chrystal and Ruth sat on the couch and Michal took the chair. Polly entered and offered them tea and cookies, which they gladly accepted. Once they'd settled into their seats again, they all stared into the fireplace.

"So, tell us about George, Ruth. He kind of appeared out of nowhere. I don't remember you ever mentioning him before," Chrystal said and took a sip of her tea.

Aamber nodded and swallowed a bite of cookie. "I was as surprised as you were. We went to school together. I haven't seen him since graduation. He left right after graduating to see the world. I honestly believed I would never see him again. We were close in school. I didn't really get along with the other girls and he was kind to me." She laughed and then continued. "He spent all his time getting us into trouble and I got us out. That's why I thought he'd needed help when he showed up out of the blue today. I'm sorry you ended up taking him in. That was never my intention."

Chrystal shook her head. "Don't worry about it. It wouldn't be appropriate for him to stay at your place."

Aamber blushed. "Oh, I know. But I could have found a place he could stay."

Chrystal patted her hand. "We know. There's no need."

Michal shook his head. "No offense, Ruth, but I can't help thinking it's not much of a friend who gets you into trouble and only shows up when they need something."

Aamber shrugged. "It's complicated. He was kind to me when I needed it. I couldn't turn him away now."

This made Michal dislike the guy even more. He was using Ruth's kind spirit against her. They talked for about another half-hour. Chrystal stretched like her mother had and said. "I'm headed up to bed. Goodnight."

"Goodnight," Ruth and Michal replied in unison.

When she was gone, Michal joined Ruth on the couch. "There's something I wanted to discuss with you. I've noticed Chrystal doesn't respond to any of the suitors who come by the palace for her and she didn't respond to George's flirting. At this age shouldn't she be noticing men and thinking about marriage?"

Aamber shrugged, surprised at his concern. "Yeah. Girls this age usually have started dreaming about such things but maybe she just hasn't found someone who interests her yet."

Michal shook his head. "It's more than that. She doesn't respond at all. Usually, comments from suitors would at least make a young girl like her blush, but she almost acts like she's receiving the compliment from my parents or me."

Aamber laughed. "And how would you know so much about how young women respond to compliments?"

Michal rolled his eyes. "Please! I had to learn the art of complimenting young women at ten! Women seem to refuse to leave our balls until I've complimented them." Aamber laughed. "Seriously, though, what do you think's going on? She's obviously not slow in maturing, so what could it possibly be?"

A slow smile spread across her face. "Maybe she's already in love with someone you don't know about."

Michal's jaw dropped and he knew he looked like a fish trying to say something and then closing his mouth again. Finally, he got out. "You think?"

Ruth shrugged. "It makes sense. It would explain why she's not interested in anyone else."

Michal rubbed his jaw. "Who could it be? One of the servants? A stable boy?" Aamber shrugged again and Michal rubbed the back of his neck.

Aamber nudged him. "Relax. Your sister has good judgment. If someone is courting her, I'm sure you'll know who it is soon enough.

But I can honestly say she's never mentioned anyone to me. I doubt she would, though. Your sister's a very private person, which means I wouldn't be able to tell you anyway."

Michal's eyes were serious, almost brooding. "But you'd warn me if there was something I needed to worry about?"

Aamber shook her head. "Your sister's almost fully grown, Michal. She can take care of herself. But if I ever think she's heading into trouble and she won't listen to me I'll warn you and your parents."

Michal leaned back on the cushion, seemingly relieved. He could feel Aamber looking at him. "You're a good big brother. I wish mine had been half as attentive as you are."

Michal looked at her, surprised. The fire created shadows dancing over her face and she looked away but he could see the pain in her eyes. "So, you and your brother weren't close?"

Aamber continued to stare at the fire and Michal wondered if she was going to answer. This was the first time she'd brought up anything personal since he'd taught her to swim. "I suppose we were as close as could be expected," she finally answered. Michal placed his hand over hers and she glanced at him surprised but didn't remove it. He rubbed his thumb in circles over the spot George had kissed as if he could wipe the memory away. He wondered at the feelings he'd been experiencing all evening. Why should he be jealous of Ruth's friend? It wasn't as if she'd indicated they were ever romantic. Why would he care if they were romantic? It wasn't as if Ruth and he were courting. But, as Michal looked at her amber-colored eyes reflecting the soft firelight, he couldn't help wondering what it would be like to kiss her soft, pink lips.

Two days later, when Aamber returned to the castle, George was still there. Michal remembered a Bible passage about false prophets who stayed longer than two days. Maybe he could use it as an excuse to make him leave. George had charmed and swindled his family long enough, including Ruth.

The previous afternoon George had joined Ruth on her daily adventures and Michal chaffed that he'd be alone with her for an entire afternoon. What self-respecting man didn't rise until noon? And didn't offer to do anything to pay for his free room and board? Michal was honestly starting to suspect he'd sought out Ruth because he'd heard she had connections to the royal family and wanted a free stay in the palace.

The day was hot and they all struggled to stay cool. Aamber even convinced Michal to end exercises two hours early, afraid the men would stroke in the heat. "I know, let's go swimming!" he suggested.

Aamber smiled, remembering the last time, when he'd taught her how. "Sounds good to me. Let's invite your sister, pack a lunch, and make a day of it."

Michal wouldn't admit even to himself that he hoped his sister was busy so he could be alone with Ruth but, of course, she wasn't. "That sounds heavenly! It's been too long since I've been swimming!" Chrystal clapped her hands together. They invited the king and queen, who declined, preferring to spend the afternoon resting in the hammocks under their big oak trees.

George came up behind them and said. "Swimming sounds like fun! I'm in!" Michal inwardly groaned. While the girls changed into their lightest dresses, Michal told the kitchen to pack them a lunch and the stable to saddle four horses. The lunch was ready by the time he returned to the castle and so were the girls.

Outside, they each went to their respective horses; Aamber on Cinnamon, Michal on Buck, Chrystal on her palomino named Cream, and George on a sorrel mare named Poinsettia. It wasn't long before they arrived at the stream with the rope. They dismounted and the men tethered the horses, Cinnamon being the exception, while the girls removed their shoes. Aamber immediately went for the rope.

"Whoa, Ruth. I didn't think you'd actually get in with us. You don't know how to swim," George called.

To Michal's surprise, since the first time George had entered their lives, Ruth seemed irritated with him. "Michal taught me," she called over her shoulder.

George side-eyed him. "Well, wasn't that gentlemanly of you."

Michal refused to be intimidated by this buffoon. "Why didn't you ever offer to teach her? Obviously, you knew," he challenged and narrowed his eyes.

George's light green eyes snapped. "I never felt the need."

Michal rolled his eyes. "It was obvious to me she wanted to learn the first day we came here."

The other man's eyebrows furrowed. "And how often have you two come here?"

"What's it to you," Michal shot back. He'd only taken Ruth swimming the one time but didn't think George needed to know that. They heard a splash and Ruth popped out of the water, swimming away so Chrystal could join her.

"Are you two going to talk all day or swim?" Ruth baited them as Chrystal made her flying leap. Michal headed toward the rope, not caring whether George followed or not, and immediately joined the girls. George joined soon afterward.

They got into a splashing war, boys against girls. Michal snuck up behind Ruth and tickled her again, then did the same to Chrystal. Michal could tell that George wanted to try the same thing but he somehow always managed to block him. The one time he did try Ruth almost gave him a bloody nose. Michal figured it was wishful thinking but thought it almost looked intentional.

They swung off the rope repeatedly, played every water game they would think of, teased, and enjoyed one another's company for the rest of the afternoon. When the sun began to set, they climbed up onto the stream bank to dry before the ride back to the castle. Chrystal persuaded Ruth to let her braid her hair and Michal watched them wondering how they got their fingers to twist the hair in such intricate ways. He honestly preferred Ruth's hair down, flowing in red waves that shimmered gold in the sun on her back. Chrystal put in several complicated braids, twisting them into a bun in the back.

George leaned up, examining Aamber when Chrystal was through. "Man, that looks weird. I don't think I've ever seen you without your two braids, Ruth."

Leaning toward Chrystal, he stage-whispered "She's always been very set in her ways. I've tried over the years to get her to loosen up a little, to no avail. I'd often call her a stick in the mud when we were young."

"Really," Michal spoke up. "She's never seemed that way to me. Maybe it's just you."

George glared at him. Aamber looked to Chrystal for help. "How about we eat. I think you boys are getting cranky," Chrystal said, standing to get the basket. Aamber went to help her retrieve the food from Buck's saddlebags.

"Thank you. I don't know what those two's problem is. I swear they seemed to dislike each other the moment they met," Aamber said when they were out of earshot.

Chrystal laughed. "I can't believe you can't see why."

Aamber looked at her confused. "You know why?"

Chrystal laughed again. "My brother is jealous of George."

Aamber raised her eyebrows. "Jealous of what? We're just friends. Besides, Michal and I are just friends, too. Shouldn't that make them more likely to get along, having a friend in common?"

Chrystal just shook her head and then rolled her eyes at the two men glaring at each other when they returned. After they prayed, the girls passed out the food. "Why is it food always tastes better after exercise?" Chrystal asked.

"I guess because your body needs it more," Aamber suggested. They ate the rest of their meal in relative silence. When they'd finished, they gathered the leftovers and repacked. Michal held Chrystal's horse while she mounted and Aamber and George mounted their own. After everyone was mounted, they set out at a leisurely pace back to the castle, which gleamed from sunlight on a hill in the distance. It was a picture-perfect scene and Chrystal tried to memorize it so she could draw it tomorrow. A soft breeze cooled their faces and the smell of pine trees surrounded them.

Chrystal broke the silence. "How'd you train your horse, Ruth? She's so gentle and well behaved."

Aamber's eyes glowed from the compliment. "I've had Cinnamon since she was born. There've been times in my life when I felt like she was my only friend. I guess you could say we are kindred spirits."

George snorted. "Kindred spirits with a horse. Ruth, you've got a lot more fanciful since I left."

Aamber's eyes snapped and Michal could swear he saw sparks fly out of them. "Maybe I've always been this way and you just never noticed."

George waved his hand. "Oh, please. I know you like the back of my hand."

"Really?" Michal jumped in. "Who's her mother? Her father? Where was she born? What's her favorite color? Does she have any siblings? What's her favorite pastime?"

George seemed shocked. "I'm just asking because if you know her so well you would know all these things," Michal said trying to seem nonchalant.

He glared at Michal. "And I suppose you know."

Michal shook his head. "She won't tell me much about her past. All I know is she has an older brother," he replied honestly. "Her favorite pastime I would guess to be three things: horseback riding, reading, and practicing her weaponry. I think her favorite color is red. I'm just saying, if you're going to claim to know her so well you should be able to back it up."

Chrystal laughed "You two would fight over anything you could think of," she said, once again trying to lighten the mood. The tension between the two men was palpable as they rode into the castle courtyard.

The next day, Chrystal was sitting on one of the castle balconies, enjoying the beautiful day. She worked on drawing the castle scene from yesterday, including Ruth and Michal riding their horses, side by side. Chrystal couldn't help wishing it had been her and a very special someone in that scene. She would draw that later. This picture was for Ruth.

Chrystal felt a presence behind her and glanced over her shoulder, almost jumping out of her skin. George stood behind her chair looking over her shoulder, watching her draw. A furrow appeared between his brows when he saw who was on the horses. Something felt off to Chrystal and a trickle of fear ran down her spine. She wasn't sure what it was about his presence but George made her uncomfortable. He had from their first dancing lesson with him but Chrystal didn't say anything afraid of hurting Ruth's feelings.

"You're very talented," he complimented her.

"Thank you," she said, hoping he'd take the hint to leave, and continued working. Instead, he walked around in front of her and leaned against the balcony railing, blocking her view of the countryside. She looked up. "Is there something I can help you with?" she asked, not trying to hide the annoyance in her voice.

"Oh, come on, Chrissy. Don't be like that. I know how you feel about me." Chrystal was baffled and she bristled at the hated nickname. She glanced behind her to see if there was a guard anywhere close by.

"What are you talking about?" she asked incredulously while still scanning for a guard.

George came and kneeled by her chair, putting one hand on its back and trying to take hers in his own. She immediately pulled away and he put his on the table. "I'm talking about our love for each other. We shouldn't have to hide it. We could sneak to the church tonight and marry. Then no one would be able to stand in our way!" he exclaimed and placed his hand over his heart.

Chrystal knew her eyes had to be as large as teacups. "George, I'm sorry if I've somehow misled you, but I have no romantic interest in you," she was finally able to squeak out.

A hurt expression immediately crossed his face, but to Chrystal it seemed rehearsed. "Please don't do this, Chrissy! You're the love of my life. Say you'll marry me," he begged, grabbing her hand again.

"George, I'm sorry but I do not love you," Chrystal insisted, the bad feeling in the pit of her stomach growing. She didn't miss the desperate look in the man's eyes.

Suddenly, George grabbed her by the upper arms and tried to kiss her. She turned her face just in time and he only kissed her cheek. "Release me at once!" she screamed, struggling to escape his grasp. Her arms ached and her stomach revolted at the feel of his slobbery lips on her cheek.

"No! Chrissy please!" he cried and tried to kiss her again.

Trying not to panic, Chrystal used one of the self-defense moves Ruth had taught her and shoved the base of her palm into his nose. His nose crunched and blood squirted out of it. He released her, grabbing his face with a roar. Chrystal dropped her sketch pad, ran into the palace to her chambers, closed the door behind her, and locked it. Her breath came in gasps and tears ran down her cheeks. Blood now stained her favorite dress, and her palm hurt. Sliding her back down her door, she buried her face in her knees. George's desperate eyes kept flashing through her mind, and she couldn't help wondering how far he would be willing to go. "Thank you, God. Thank you for protecting me," she whispered in prayer.

When her heart had stopped racing, Chrystal walked over to her looking glass and pulled up the quarter-length sleeves where he'd grabbed her. Sure enough, dark bruises had already started to form against her pale skin in perfect fingerprints. Blood stained her blouse and dried on her hand. While cleaning herself in a washbasin and changing her dress, Chrystal knew she would have to consider her next moves very carefully.

George hadn't actually done her much harm, other than scaring her out of her wits. Chrystal had even done more harm to him than he'd done to her. If she told her brother about the incident, he'd have George hung in a heartbeat and she was sure her father would react just as badly. Chrystal didn't think the offense was worth a hanging, but she definitely wanted the man to leave. She could tell her mother, but her mother didn't have much interaction with George, not like Ruth did.

Chrystal hated the thought of telling Ruth about what had just happened but, since George was her friend, she figured Ruth would have the most insight as to what Chrystal should do. Chrystal didn't think she could wait until tomorrow when Ruth would arrive for her lesson with the army. Chrystal wouldn't be able to sleep as long as that man was in the castle.

Chrystal unlocked her door and opened it a crack. No one was in the corridor. She took a deep breath and stepped out, trying to hurry but not make it seem like she was running. Chrystal reached the foyer just as a messenger came through the entrance. "Excuse me, I have a message I need you to take."

The man nodded. "Forgive me, your highness, but I have a message for the king. As soon as I deliver it, I'll return promptly."

Chrystal nodded and he disappeared down one of the long corridors. She heard footsteps and stepped into another doorway just out of sight. Michal emerged from one of the halls, so Chrystal breathed a sigh of relief and stepped out. "Whoa, Chris. You scared me. What are you doing, hiding there?" her brother asked, surprised.

Chrystal shook her head and shrugged. Michal laughed and headed toward another doorway. It was then that Chrystal saw George approaching her from the opposite direction, his nose black and blue. His eyes told her he intended to finish their previous conversation. "Michal, wait!" Her brother turned surprised. "Where are you headed?" she asked, trying to stall him.

He walked back toward her, so they weren't shouting at each other. She could tell he knew something was up but he answered her question anyway. "To my office. I've been working in my chambers and have some questions for father. You all right?"

George emerged from the doorway, eyeing Michal and Chrystal. Chrystal had to keep herself from shaking and sending him furtive glances. "I'm fine, but if you'll wait here with me for a moment, I'll walk with you."

Her brother continued to eye her suspiciously but shrugged. "Sure, if you want to." Michal glanced curiously at George's black nose but didn't ask. George waited for Michal to leave and leaned against the doorframe, not having heard their previous conversation.

The messenger returned and she sent him for Ruth. "Why are you sending for Ruth on her day off?" Michal asked her curious.

They'd begun walking down the hall and she was relieved that George didn't follow, but she could feel his eyes boring into the back of her head. "There's something I need to discuss with her," Chrystal said to ward off her brother's suspicions.

Chrystal followed her brother to his and her father's joint offices, almost jumping out of her skin when a servant down the hall accidentally dropped a vase that crashed to the floor. She grabbed Michal's arm and he laughed at her jumpiness. Michal preferred working in his chambers because of the privacy it afforded him. His father, on the other hand, had grown accustomed to the constant interruptions. Once Michal had his answers to his questions from their father, the two siblings headed back to their chambers. When they reached Chrystal's door, Michal crossed his arms.

"You want to tell me what this is all about?" he asked, raising his eyebrows, but his older brother interrogation techniques weren't going to work on her this time.

"Do I need a reason to walk with you?" she shot at him, becoming irritated. He shook his head but gave her a look that said he wasn't buying her story. She opened her door and began to enter when he grabbed her arm. Chrystal was relieved it was her forearm. She didn't think she'd be able to keep from wincing if he'd grabbed her upper arm.

"Hey, you know you can always come to me, right?"

Tears sprung into her eyes, and she had to look away from his penetrating blue eyes. "Of course I do." Her response seemed to satisfy him and he finally let her go.

Chrystal refused to leave her chambers until Ruth arrived. When the servant knocked on her door, she wasted no time in pulling Ruth into the room, thanking the servant and closing the door behind her. "Chrystal, what's wrong?" Chrystal pulled up her sleeve and showed her the bruises in response. Then she picked up her soiled dress and showed it to Ruth. A dark look came over Ruth's face. "Who did this to you?"

Chrystal sat on the edge of her bed, trying to keep the tears at bay. "George. I don't think he meant to hurt me. When I was drawing on the balcony this morning, he joined me and I had this funny feeling. Next thing I knew, he knelt before me and tried to grab my hand. He claimed he loved me and insisted we run away together tonight and get married so no one could stop us. When I refused, he tried to kiss me, grabbing me by my upper arms. I used the palm move you taught us and I think I broke his nose. I ran into my chambers and stayed until I calmed down. Then I immediately sent for you. Oh, Ruth, I didn't know what else to do! He scared me so bad! But I was worried if I went to my father or brother, they'd have him hung. Like I said, I don't think he meant to hurt me. I thought about my mother, but since she doesn't know George and he's your friend I thought it would be wiser to ask your advice first."

Aamber felt like someone had taken a branding iron to her skin. She'd never imagined George was capable of such a thing! Aamber didn't believe he would ever take it farther than trying to steal a kiss, though, and agreed with Chrystal that he shouldn't be hung. Aamber chewed on her bottom lip, trying to rein in her anger. She'd trusted George and once again she'd been betrayed. The thought that she had furnished the door that this man had walked through so he could dare to touch Chrystal broke her heart.

Aamber sat on the bed beside Chrystal. "Oh, Chrystal. I'm so sorry! I never imagined him capable of such a thing."

Chrystal seemed surprised. "Ruth, this isn't your fault. None of us suspected him of being capable of such a thing. I mean he's been staying at the castle for two weeks now. And remember, we're the ones who invited him to stay here. You tried to get him to go somewhere else."

Her words were like a healing balm to Aamber's soul. "I think it would be wise to go to your mother first. Having both of us discuss it will help convince her he didn't mean to hurt you, which will go a long way in convincing the king and prince. I can only imagine what their reaction will be." Chrystal nodded. Both girls dreaded the hours ahead of them.

By the time the day was done, George was facing a year in prison and then banishment from the castle forever. Chrystal and Aamber had hoped to convince the king to just banish him but a year in jail was the lightest sentence he was willing to allow. If George had just declared his love, they wouldn't have punished him at all, except for maybe asking him to leave. But the fact that he'd laid hands on Chrystal and had left bruises couldn't be excused.

That evening Michal stood on the balcony, watching the sun set. Aamber slowly approached him from behind. He'd been hurt when Chrystal hadn't gone straight to him about George and neither had her parents, but they understood when she'd explained her reasoning. Michal was a different story altogether. He stood now holding one elbow, with the other hand covering his mouth.

Aamber stopped next to him, placing her hands on the railing. The view was beautiful. It went from the stream and field surrounding the castle on the hill, to a stretch of forest, to the city, and to the ocean beyond. The sun turned the sky and clouds red, orange, and pink and the ocean reflected the splendor. Herds of cows and flocks of sheep grazed in the distance, sometimes bellowing at each other or other members of their group.

Aamber watched him out of the corner of her eye but he didn't move. "I'm so sorry, Michal. I understand if you blame me for bringing George into your sister's life. I never would have if I'd known this would happen," she whispered.

He looked up to the sky and rubbed his hand down his face. Then, to Aamber's utter shock, he turned and pulled her into his embrace. "This is not your fault, Ruth. I'm not angry with you or my sister. I'm just devastated I wasn't there for her," he whispered into her ear, holding her tight.

"You couldn't have known," she whispered back.

He shook his head. "I should have. I was so distracted by my jealousy I missed his true intentions. All he ever wanted was to try to catch either you or Chrystal to get into my family and swindle them."

Aamber gently shook her head. "You put too much responsibility on yourself."

He pulled back and looked into her eyes. "And you don't?" Then he buried his face in her neck, breathing deep as if holding her was the only thing that brought him comfort.

CHAPTER 6

THE BALL

*But thou, O Lord, art a shield for me; my
glory, and the lifter up of mine head.*

Psalm 3:3 K JV

Ocean, A.D. 907

Aamber helped Chrystal into her dress for her birthday ball. It was a gorgeous light blue that brought out the blue of her eyes. It flowed in waves around her and she had a mask outlined in pearls to accompany it, along with a pearl necklace. The ball was a costume masquerade. Chrystal was going as the ocean. Aamber was going as an orange rose and the irony was not lost on her. "It just fits your personality perfectly and brings out the color of your eyes," the queen had insisted when Aamber tried to convince them it was too elaborate.

Aamber had now been training the army, Chrystal, and her mother for over a year. No more incidents of disrespect had occurred since the first day and she'd taught the army almost everything she believed they needed to learn. Now all that was required was for them to practice and perfect their skills, which they didn't need her for. Soon she would only be training Chrystal and her mother.

Over the past year, Aamber and Chrystal had become as inseparable as sisters. Chrystal was very mature for her age, negating any potential problems that could arise from their age difference. The king and queen had become almost another pair of surrogate parents to Aamber, but the relationship that surprised her most of all was Michal's and hers. Aamber had figured their relationship would be only professional, and barely that, but since the first day of training, they'd truly become friends. The queen even referred to Michal, Chrystal, and Ruth as the three musketeers.

Aamber had noticed Chrystal being strangely quiet the past few days. Chrystal had been planning her sixteenth birthday ball for weeks and had never faltered in enthusiasm before. Once her dress was cinched, Aamber said, "Turn around and let me look at you." Chrystal slowly pivoted, insecurity brimming in her beautiful blue eyes. "Oh, Chrystal. You look absolutely stunning!" she exclaimed, trying to lift the younger woman's spirits. Chrystal quickly averted her gaze. Leading her over to their special sitting area in Chrystal's room, Aamber said, "All right, it's time we talked about what's been bothering you the past few days."

They took their seats, and Chrystal fiddled with a fold in her skirt. Aamber waited patiently, knowing her well enough to realize she was considering whether she wanted to confide in her or not. Chrystal knew she could fully trust Aamber but was still a private person. Finally, Chrystal looked her in the eye, her own eyes filled with worry. Aamber reached for her hand. "Hey, come on. What's going on? You've been acting funny the past few days and this is the night you've dreamed of for years."

Once again Chrystal stared into her lap, but she finally cleared her throat and said. "Promise you won't laugh."

"Of course, Chrystal. I will never laugh at you," Aamber tried to reassure her.

Chrystal sighed again and finally began her story. "I've never told anyone this before. You see when Michal was younger, his best friend was Gideon Promesse, prince of Montagne. They are still best friends, but since they've grown older and assumed more responsibilities, they naturally have much less time to spend together. His last visit was over two years ago."

Aamber nodded. She wasn't sure where this story was going. Michal had told her about Gideon before and she'd noticed Chrystal was always strangely quiet when he was discussed. She had even wondered if he'd done something to Chrystal in the past. She'd been meaning to ask her about it but hadn't found the right time. Now that she thought about it, Chrystal had been acting strangely ever since it was mentioned that Gideon would be attending her birthday ball. Was she afraid of him? Aamber's hackles immediately began to raise.

"Well, Ruth, you see. I've kept this secret from everyone since I met Gideon, even though I was only five at the time. I didn't think anyone would ever believe me. Oh, goodness, this is so embarrassing," Chrystal said and covered her hands with her face.

Aamber pulled her hands away and held them between her own. As gently as she could, she asked "Chrystal, did he hurt you?"

Her sky-blue eyes became as large as saucers. "No! Oh, no, not at all. I'm so sorry, Ruth. I never meant to give that impression. I didn't consider you've never met him."

Aamber breathed a sigh of relief. She knew the shame of having her innocence taken by a man. The thought of Chrystal carrying such shame made her blood boil. "No, he's never hurt me. Quite the opposite, actually. Even though Michal and he are so much older than me, he always treated me with kindness and included me in their games. He was almost like a second older brother to me. If I ever had any trouble or needed to talk something out with anyone, I knew I could trust him as much as any member of my family. So, you see, I started growing feelings for him from a very young age. By the time I was seven, I knew I was in love with him. But he's never seen me as anything but a little sister. He's 20 now, same as Michal. A four-year difference between our ages, which of course is not large in the grand scheme of life but, at this age, I'm sure it seems like a hundred years to Gideon. And I know how crazy it sounds! A five-year-old falling in love and keeping the love tucked away in her heart all these years! It sounds ridiculous.

"But Ruth, I have tried to convince myself it wasn't true. I've even forced myself over the past year to consider the early suitors who have called on me. But Gideon is the only man I'm ever able to picture the rest of my life with. And since I'm 16 now, tonight I was hoping his viewpoint would change and he would see me as an adult, not a kid sister. Ruth, his coming has made me so nervous I can barely breathe."

Aamber smiled. "Chrystal, I don't doubt your sincerity for a moment. I know you're not a girl who would take saying she was in love with someone lightly. It actually answers a lot of questions," she chuckled. "Michal mentioned he was surprised you never seem interested in the suitors who visited like a normal fifteen-year-old would be. I even had a feeling it meant you already had feelings for someone.

"Chrystal, I don't see how this Gideon could not see you as the mature young woman you are. Since the first day we've met, you have impressed me with your maturity, so I don't think you need to worry about trying to convince Gideon of it. I almost believe you should be reserved toward him. Tonight, he'll see the men buzzing around you like magpies and will realize he would be stupid not to try to win you for himself. Even if he doesn't, don't you ever try to change yourself for a man. You're perfect the way you are.

"If Gideon is the one God made for you, but he doesn't match you now, he is the one who will have to grow and mature to deserve you. If he never does, then you know he's not the one God meant for you and you move on, no matter how hard it is. Because I promise you, Chrystal, there is a special young man out there waiting to meet you who will treat you like the precious jewel you are. Promise me you'll wait for him, no matter what."

Chrystal ducked her head again and nodded. "But, Ruth, what if he meets someone else before he notices me?"

Aamber put her finger under Chrystal's chin until she met her eyes again. "Chrystal, if he's the man for you, you must trust God to bring you together in his own time. If you try to force it on your own, you'll just mess everything up. All your faith must be firmly placed in Him."

Aamber saw the strength grow in Chrystal's heart and the fear melt away from her eyes. Chrystal suddenly threw her arms around Aamber's neck, pulling her in for a tight hug. "Thank you, Ruth," she whispered into her ear.

It wasn't long after they'd finished their talk that they had Aamber ready for the ball as well. When Chrystal had fastened the last button on Aamber's dress, Chrystal's mother walked in, wearing a soft gray dress. Chrystal had told Aamber her mother wore the same dress to every ball because she believed it wasteful to keep making new ones. "Oh, my dears, you both look stunning!" Aamber didn't miss the tears in the queen's voice.

After giving Chrystal a quick embrace, she said, "Chrystal, your father wants to have a talk with you before the ball begins."

"Did I do something wrong, Mother?" Chrystal asked, concerned.

"Of course not, my dear! Now run along. I'll help Ruth finish getting ready and we'll meet you in the foyer." When Chrystal left, the queen picked up Aamber's silver cross from the dressing table. She'd removed it to keep the chain from tangling in the complicated braids Chrystal had put into her hair. "Turn around, dear, and I'll snap this for you." Aamber did as she was told. Something felt wrong but she wasn't sure what. "This necklace is beautiful."

"Thank you, ma'am. My mother gave it to me," Aamber replied as she watched the queen snap her necklace behind her in the mirror.

After she'd finished, the queen kissed her on the cheek and whispered into her ear. "An amber rose for an Aamber Rose."

Aamber felt all the blood drain from her face and watched herself grow pale in the mirror. Slowly, she turned and faced the queen. "What did you say," she replied barely above a whisper.

The queen smiled. "I said an amber rose for an Aamber Rose." All Aamber could do was stare at the queen, dumbfounded. The only two people she'd ever told her background had drowned in the Atlantic over two years ago. How could the queen possibly know who she really was? Had she sent Chrystal out so her father could tell her in secret and the queen could have Aamber arrested?

"We've always known your true identity, Aamber. At least the king and I have. It wasn't long after your escape from the *Calder* we heard rumors that the only daughter of Viking Captain Einar Egil had died before she could marry and unite the Uffe clan with her own. Many believed you'd escaped the ship and considered you a hero, even though your family insisted they'd found your blood-soaked shawl. If the Uffe clan had united with yours, there would have been rivers of bloodshed.

"The king alerted his spies to be on the lookout for anyone matching your description because we'd heard our land was the closest to where you'd escaped. It wasn't long after you arrived that one of them came back and informed us the Cullards had taken you in and you'd begun to live with Ellen under the name Ruth. Our spies watched you for a while, making sure you were here only because you'd wanted to escape your former life.

"It was then we invited Captain Cullard to the castle and asked him what your intentions were. He assured us you were simply a young girl who'd come from a bad situation. That you had escaped and begun a new life, so the king and I decided to let you live in peace. You'd begun to create a good Christian life for yourself and we respected that. But we kept tabs on you, mostly out of curiosity. We wanted to know what you would make of yourself. A couple of years later, rumors started circulating about a young woman who was making a profound difference in the lives of our people. It didn't take us long to make the connection. I knew who you were the day you saved my son and me from the robbers.

"We invited you to the palace not only because you saved our lives but also because we wanted to meet this amazing young woman we'd watched grow up. Not only that, but we'd also been hearing rumors that the Egil clan was becoming desperate, which is why we wanted so badly for you to train our army. The countries they used to loot have become too strong for them to overpower and we would have been an easy target. Little did we know how important to us you would eventually become. I love you like a daughter, Aamber, and I am truly sorry we haven't been straight with you from the beginning. I do so hope you understand, but we will understand if you're angry with us.

"We basically tricked you into teaching us how to defend ourselves from your family, even though we didn't think of that at the time. It wasn't until we took a step back and considered our actions did we realize how deceitful we'd been. We are truly sorry, Aamber, and would understand if you didn't want anything to do with us anymore."

A slow trickle of tears had begun falling down the queen's cheeks as she spoke and her lips trembled. Aamber was stunned. They'd known who she was the entire time she'd been in the country? Yet instead of arresting her and locking her away for her connection to her family, they'd allowed her to live in peace? They had told her they wanted to make sure their country wasn't an easy target, and Aamber had suspected there was more to the story, but it wasn't as if they'd lied to her or tricked her. She knew exactly what she was doing. The fact that she was training their country to defend themselves from people like her family had been the whole reason she'd agreed to train them in the first place! She loved the Moores! Not because they were royalty but because of who they were and how they treated her! They had never wronged her and, as far as she was concerned, she had wronged them by not admitting who she was from the beginning!

Aamber reached out and took the queen's hand in hers. "My queen, I have fallen in love with you and your family, too. You're like a mother to me. And you did not deceive me into doing anything. The only reason I agreed to train your army is because I knew it would help you defend yourselves from people like my family. I'm the one who should be apologizing for not telling you who I was from the beginning. So please, think nothing more of it and let us enjoy Chrystal's special night."

The two women embraced, holding each other as if it would be their last chance. When they'd pulled back, Aamber asked "Shouldn't we tell Michal and Chrystal who I really am?"

"The king and I actually decided to leave the decision up to you. We'll tell them if you want us to but we understand if you don't."

Aamber nodded. "I would rather you not. I trust them to know but I cannot stand the thoughts of them being hurt by someone trying to use that knowledge against them."

The queen shook her head. "You are one of the most selfless people I've ever met, Aamber. Anyone else would have immediately said yes, so they wouldn't have to carry the burden alone any longer by sharing the load with others. Instead, you think of what's best for the people you love and carry the burden yourself."

The two women embraced one last time and exited the room arm in arm.

Michal couldn't help wondering what was taking Ruth and his mother so long. Ruth was always the first one to finish getting ready. Michal turned and watched as father told Gideon a joke. Chrystal was on his father's arm and even Michal couldn't believe how beautiful and grown-up she looked. Gideon had barely been able to take his eyes off her since she entered the room, and Michal was starting to wonder if his best friend was falling for his little sister. Surely not, she was too young for him, but the way it seemed as if he almost had to force himself to watch Michal's father while he spoke gave Michal pause.

Michal heard footsteps on the staircase and looked up. Ruth and his mother were descending arm in arm. Ruth was wearing an orange, almost amber-colored dress whose folds were arranged to look like rose petals. The dress's blouse was green and her mask almost looked like a leaf framing her head like a halo. If it weren't for her amber-colored eyes Michal wouldn't even have recognized her! All the breath left his lungs and he felt as if he'd been sucker-punched. He'd never denied Ruth's beauty but tonight she took his breath away. And, with her abundant inner beauty, Michal wondered how she'd managed to stay single for so long.

When they'd made it to the landing, he could read the insecurity in Aamber's eyes. Even though she'd accompanied Chrystal to multiple events over the past year, it was nothing compared to a royal ball. Father spoke up first. "You two ladies look lovely," he said, which earned him a tentative smile from the pair.

Releasing Ruth, Mother clapped her hands together and said. "I had an idea while I was helping Ruth finish getting ready. Why not, instead of Michal escorting Chrystal to the ball, have Gideon escort her and Michal escort Ruth?" Chrystal's panicked look to Ruth wasn't lost on Michal. Ruth seemed to respond with an almost imperceptible rise of her shoulders. Almost as if Chrystal was worried that some secret she'd confided in Ruth had been passed on to their mother. And Ruth was reassuring her she hadn't.

The two young couples eyed the queen warily. What was she up to? "Fine with me," Michal replied with a shrug and Gideon nodded, but Michal found the nod a little too enthusiastic. When he looked back at Ruth, it almost seemed as if she was struggling to hold back a smile. What was going on here that she knew about and he did not? He would have to corner her tonight and find out. Which, being now that he was her escort shouldn't be too difficult. The six of them paired up and headed toward the ball.

They were announced by couple as they entered the ballroom; Chrystal and Gideon first because it was Chrystal's birthday, then mother and father, then Michal and Ruth. Michal had a strange feeling that this couples' arrangement might be permanent but couldn't fathom where it came from. Everyone watched them enter and Michal felt Ruth's hand on his arm tighten. He gave her a reassuring smile. He could only imagine how scary this was for her and he'd be lying if he said he wasn't nervous as well. This was the first ball he'd attended since Valentine's Day and it was starting to stir up bad memories.

It wasn't until they'd begun to make their way among the people that it seemed as if everyone returned to their previous conversations. All the different costumes were overwhelming, and the elaborateness made Michal chuckle. "Care to share the joke with the rest of us?" Aamber asked, taking a sip of the wine he'd brought her.

"I'm just amazed at the different costumes. I'm really struggling, trying to recognize who is who." Aamber nodded. Michal had noticed several young gentlemen eyeing him with envy and Michal decided he wasn't going to leave her side through the night. His blood boiled at the thought of Ruth with another man. He didn't understand the overwhelming feeling of protectiveness that surged through his chest. He, of all people, should know that Ruth was very capable of taking care of herself.

Instead of a formal meal, Chrystal had opted to have tables set up with finger foods around the ballroom. That way people could dance longer. Suddenly the musicians began playing the song he'd danced to with Ruth during their first dance lesson. After that night, every time his mother and sister had a self-defense class, they'd been teaching Ruth to dance and she was a fast study. Michal wasn't surprised. If Ruth was anything, she was smart and agile. "May I have this dance?" he asked with a flourish.

Aamber looked up at him, a teasing glint in her eyes. "Why sir, aren't you afraid you'll fall in love with me?" It was almost the exact same barb he'd thrown at her that night.

Leading her out onto the floor with the other couples, he said, "I'm afraid, my lady, you've already got the rest of my family snowed. Why should I be any different?" To his utter shock, it wasn't the response he'd wanted to give. He'd almost had to catch himself saying. "I already have, madam."

He didn't understand! After all that Cheryle had put him through, he'd sworn to never fall in love again! Michal thought he had built strong stone walls like a castle around his heart. And besides, he'd only known the woman before him for a year! But it had happened so subtly. Like the weakening of a dam from a trickle of water that was able to make it through. It was almost as if his heart had slipped through his fingers like sand right into Ruth's hands!

How could it happen so fast? He'd tried everything to prevent it! Did he feel this way only because she was the first kind woman he'd met after Cheryle? He knew in his gut that wasn't the case. And, as he found himself getting lost in her amber-colored eyes, he knew he was completely and utterly lost forever. He was going to have to do a lot of praying to decide if this was God's will or if he'd once again decided to try to force his will onto God.

After a few dances, they made their way over to where Gideon and Chrystal were standing and talking. Michal was surprised that Gideon hadn't made any effort to dance with the other young ladies, even when other young men stole Chrystal away. But now that he thought about it, he had done the same thing when other men stole Ruth away from him. The only time the two couples weren't each other's partners was when they'd traded with each other or with the king and queen, except naturally when the other men tried to steal the girls away. When they made it to Chrystal and Gideon, Gideon clapped Michal on the shoulder and said, "Why don't you and I go find the ladies a drink? Ladies, we'll be right back."

Once they were out of earshot, Aamber was quick to lean in and whisper to Chrystal. "I didn't tell your mother anything. I had no idea she was going to suggest that Gideon should be your escort and Michal mine. You believe me, don't you?" The fear that her friend was mad at her had gnawed at Aamber's stomach since the queen made the suggestion.

Chrystal nodded. "Of course, I believe you. I know you would never lie to me! After my initial shock wore off, I was able to see yours." Chrystal looked around her to ensure that no one was listening and leaned even closer to Aamber, whose conscience was smarting from Chrystal's comment about never lying to her when she didn't even truly know who Aamber was. "I'm so very glad she did, Ruth. It has given Gideon and me the excuse to spend the entire evening together! He hasn't said anything but I definitely believe he's starting to see me as something more than a little sister!"

The look of joy in Chrystal's eyes brought tears to Aamber's. "Oh, Chrystal, that's wonderful! But can I tell you a secret? The moment we walked down the stairs and I saw how Gideon was looking at you. I had no doubts."

A sly look came into Chrystal's eyes, and she gave Aamber a small, secretive smile. "Really? Because I had the exact same thought when I saw my brother look at you."

Aamber's jaw fell open but, before she could respond, the men returned with their drinks. "Can we get you ladies anything to eat?" Michal asked. Both women shook their heads. Neither of their stomachs would be able to hold food after the events of the evening and the conversation they had just had. Michal hadn't forgotten that he wanted to corner Ruth and grill her about what was going on with his little sister and, while Gideon and he had gotten the drinks, he'd had a brilliant idea as to how, but he would have to let his father know what he was doing before he proceeded. "Excuse me, ladies and gent, I'll be right back."

Michal weaved his way through the crowd, over to where his mother and father were standing and talking to each other. Michal was surprised to find them standing alone. Usually, he had to fight off a crowd to talk to them during a ball. "Hello, Michal! Are you having a good time?" his mother greeted him. He could tell she was worried about him, this being his first ball since he and Cheryle had broken up. He tried to give her a reassuring smile.

"Actually, I'm having a wonderful time, mother. And are you enjoying yourself?"

This reply earned him a brilliant smile from his mom. "Of course, dear. Now, what was it you wanted to speak with us about?"

Michal was taken aback but didn't know why. His mother had always been able to read him like a book. "I just remembered that I'd never had the chance to show Ruth the view from the central tower. But I wanted to let you know what I'd planned so no untoward rumors could be spread about us."

His father nodded approvingly. "Wise decision, son. Don't tarry too long. I trust you but I wouldn't want Ruth's reputation to be tarnished in any way."

Michal nodded. "Yes sir."

He made his way back to his group. Gideon was regaling the girls with a story of their misadventures as boys, even though Chrystal had probably heard the story a hundred times. He'd just finished when Michal reached them. "Hey, Ruth. I just realized we've never shown you the view from the central tower and it's even more beautiful at night. Would you like to accompany me? I promise we won't tarry long."

Aamber shrugged, setting her empty wine glass on the tray of a servant who passed by and thanked them. "Now, behave yourself, young man. After meeting this delightful young lady, I would have no qualms about running you through if you tried something untoward. But from the stories Chrystal has told me, neither would she," Gideon teased and laughed at Michal's red face.

"I could give you the same warning," Michal threw over his shoulder. He didn't miss the delicate blush that appeared on the cheeks of both young ladies or the look of chagrin that entered his best friend's eyes. Michal inwardly groaned, no longer able to deny that his friend was falling for his little sister.

As they were climbing the tower steps, Aamber asked. "What is it so important you had to get me alone to speak with me about?"

Michal shook his head. "Am I that transparent?"

Aamber smiled in response. "Only to your mother and I."

Michal chuckled. "I think you already know what I'm going to ask you about."

Aamber shook her head. "I assure you, sir, I couldn't possibly have any idea," she teased.

Michal rolled his eyes. "Well, either way, I've been meaning to show you this view for a while. I think you'll like it."

They'd reached the top and Michal helped her through the trap door. When they were both safely on solid ground, she looked around, her face transforming into a look of appreciation. "Oh, my goodness! It's absolutely lovely up here. I can't believe you waited so long to show me! It's almost as if you could reach up and take a star in your hand!" She walked around the small, circular space and placed her hands on the stone rail. "Oh, it's so beautiful," she said, her voice airy.

"Yeah, beautiful," Michal said while watching Ruth's face. His eyes were solely for her.

Aamber risked a glance over her shoulder, sensing the true meaning behind his words. Michal could read the uncertainty in her eyes. Nervous, Aamber turned around again and looked out over the open country to the ocean. Michal walked up behind her and placed his hand on her side. He followed her gaze, wondering what she was looking at. He was surprised she'd allowed him to place his hand on her side. There was nothing inappropriate in the gesture but she'd never been a touchy-feely friend, except maybe with Chrystal.

"Do you have a telescope, by any chance?" she asked. Michal looked at her face. Her voice had a strange ring to it. There was a small, wooden box on the top of the tower where his guards left a telescope for others to use. He reached down and took it out, handing it to her.

Aamber took it and stared once again at the horizon. Michal looked to where she pointed the telescope and he could barely make out a ship in the distance. After slowly lowering the telescope, she handed it to him. Her hands were trembling, and her face had turned as white as snow. "Please tell me that's not who I think it is."

Michal took the telescope and examined the ocean. A ship was headed toward their shore but it was a long way out. A mermaid with her hands stretched out to the sea was on its stern. The Egil Viking Clan flag flew proudly above it. Michal slowly lowered the telescope in the same fashion Aamber had, feeling his heart drop with it. "Come, we must warn the others."

CHAPTER 7

THE ATTACK

For the mountains shall depart, and the hills be removed; but my kindness shall not depart from thee, neither shall the covenant of my peace be removed, saith the LORD that hath mercy on thee.

Isaiah 54:10 KJV

Océan, A.D. 907

Aamber and Michal raced down the tower steps, trying not to trip over Aamber's dress. Every moment was precious. Once the Vikings made land, they would kill and mutilate anyone and anything they could find. Aamber was not going to let that happen to her home and family. Upon reaching the doorway to the ballroom, Michal grabbed her arm. She stared at him, surprised he would hesitate, trying to catch her breath.

"If we go in there in a panic, it will cause all the people in that room to panic, which could cause someone to get hurt." Aamber nodded and took his arm and they entered as if nothing was amiss.

They made a beeline for the king and queen, ignoring the calls from friends as they passed. When the king saw their faces, he froze, knowing something was wrong. "What happened?" he whispered when they finally made it to him.

"The Egil clan. They're coming. We must sound the alarm," Michal responded in a winded whisper.

Michal didn't understand why his father suddenly looked at Ruth and asked. "Are you all right?"

She nodded resolutely. "I'm fine, sir. My loyalty lies solely with you and your people. You are my family, and I will lay down my life to protect you."

Where did that come from? Why did Ruth think his father would ever question her loyalty? Especially at a time like this? But Michal didn't have time to ponder these questions. "Get Gideon and Chrystal. Head to our sitting room and tell them what's going on. Tell the kitchen staff to prepare four sacks of food and I want all of you to change into hardy clothes. Grab your Bibles and your weapons. Prepare for war," the king commanded them.

They immediately turned to do his bidding but Michal had no intentions to tell the staff to prepare four sacks of food. They would only need three. The pair hurried and pulled Chrystal and Gideon off the dance floor. Michal whispered. "Follow us," and they headed toward the sitting room.

"Ruth, you tell them what's going on and what to do while I go talk to the kitchen staff. We'll meet back here after we're all changed and ready," Michal barked when they'd reached the sitting room and he ran out.

"Ruth, what's going on?" Chrystal exclaimed.

"When Michal and I were in the central watch tower, we spotted the Egil Viking ship headed our way. We must prepare for war immediately. Gideon, go change into hardy clothes. Grab your Bible and your weapons. Leave everything else. Chrystal, follow me."

Gideon nodded but, before leaving the room, he gave Chrystal a concerned look and her hand a gentle squeeze. The girls immediately headed for Chrystal's chambers. Aamber was surprised at how calm Chrystal was. Most young women her age would be utterly hysterical, especially since it was her special night, but Chrystal had never been a normal young woman. Aamber wondered how long Chrystal's calm would last when she found out what she was going to have to do next.

The girls changed quickly, hiding as many weapons on themselves as possible. Aamber didn't have to tell Chrystal what to do. She was smart and grabbed only what Aamber did. They were done within ten minutes, each wearing a sturdy dress, sturdy shoes, a cloak, and a single light bag containing their Bibles and even more weapons. Aamber clasped the strap of her tarp bag, looked Chrystal in the eye, and nodded her approval before they left, hoping to assuage some of her friend's uncertainty.

They reached the sitting room just as everyone else did. "We announced to the people what was going on. The soldiers are preparing for battle and a few hundred of them are heading to the villages and cities to help the people get to the prearranged hiding spots," the king immediately informed them. "Ruth, do you know someone who could get you kids out of the country and go to Promesse to ask for reinforcements? They're the closest of our allies."

Aamber nodded. "Yes sir, but I have no intentions of leaving. I'll get your children and Gideon to the ship safely but I'm staying here to help fight." Her voice left no room for argument.

"I'm not abandoning our country in its time of need, father," Chrystal said.

"And there's no way you could blast me out of here," Michal added.

Aamber's heart broke for the king and queen. She could tell they were proud of their children but wanted to protect them. "I agree Michal should stay. He's one of the main leaders of the army and they would lose hope if he left. But I think Gideon and Chrystal should go. If both plead our case, it would help tremendously, and knowing at least one member of the royal family is still out there would give Océan hope if worse comes to worst."

The group fell silent for a moment, knowing this was the wisest plan. The king turned toward the queen. "You should go too, my love." Aamber's heart broke at the gentle look of love and sadness in the king's eyes and she wondered if someone would ever look at her the same way.

Immediately the queen shook her head. "Our fates will be the same, my love, and they will be the same as our people."

They all looked to Gideon. He was the only member of the group who hadn't said anything. "I'll do whatever is required of me. I am at your service. I would prefer to stay here, though, and help with the fighting. Ruth can protect Chrystal on her own."

The king shook his head. "She'll only be with her until the ship. And you requesting assistance from your father will only strengthen our case. I have no doubt he'd believe Chrystal, but another voice couldn't hurt."

Chrystal bit her lip and growled. "I don't need protection, father. Ruth has taught me how to take care of myself."

The king approached Chrystal, put his hands on her shoulders, and pressed his forehead to hers. "I have no doubt, my daughter, but I still think it wise for Gideon to accompany you. I know Ruth would only send you with someone she trusted but, if the men on his ship were to stage a coup, you would be at their mercy. At least with Gideon along, you would have one more protector besides yourself and God." Tears started pouring down Chrystal's porcelain cheeks. The king kissed her forehead and pulled the other two members of their family into a large embrace, who then pulled Aamber and Gideon in. "Oh, Father God, we ask you to be with us in this most trying hour. Put your hand of protection over our land and family, and may your will be done in all things," the king prayed.

Shouts of soldiers began to ring through the palace. "Follow me," Aamber said, "I know of a tunnel that leads from the palace directly to the shore."

"Ruth, wait," Michal said. He turned her toward him and drew her in for a desperate hug. After kissing her cheek, he said, "I'll see you soon." Aamber couldn't look at him as the trio left. She already knew what their fates would most likely be.

In the kitchen, they grabbed the bags of food the staff had prepared and left on the table for them before leaving to help their families. Large amounts of food that was supposed to be for the ball lined the counters and dishes were strewn everywhere. Aamber led Chrystal and Gideon to the trap door behind the produce in the pantry. During her time working at the castle, Aamber had been given free rein and had taken advantage of it, exploring every nook and cranny of the large structure.

After they'd climbed down the rickety, wooden ladder, Gideon moved the produce back in front of the door before closing it behind them. As he was doing that, Aamber lit one of the torches from the wall of the tunnel. Soon they were off, almost running through the dark structure. They had about a fifteen-mile trek ahead of them. For the first few miles, they were as silent as mice, wondering what was happening at the castle behind them.

Michal fought back-to-back with Joseph Burges and his father and mother fought back-to-back. Michal jabbed his sword through the Viking he'd been fighting, then quickly turned to block another Viking's blow. He didn't understand! From the rumors he'd heard, the Egil clan didn't have more than 200 members. His country had about 10,000 soldiers. At least half of them had been at the castle that night! How did so many Vikings make it past their lines of defense?

When he threw up his sword to block another blow, Michal saw the Uffe clan colors tied on the arm of his attacker; so the Egil and the Uffe clan had united after all. That meant that they had at least double the number of Océan's soldiers and, with half of Océan's soldiers already spread out over the countryside, it hadn't taken long for the Vikings to siege the castle.

As Burges was dragged away to the dungeon with the other soldiers who had survived the vicious attack, Michal and his parents were bound and forced down on their knees in a line. Michal knew what came next. The Viking clan leader would get the honor of killing each of them as he saw fit. "Please God, let Your will be done in all things," was all Michal could think to pray.

Michal looked at his parents. They'd both fought valiantly. Michal had been thoroughly impressed by his mother's swordsmanship. Ruth had taught her well. His parents stared back at him, their eyes brimming with love and fear. "We love you, son. And we know you love us. Remember what we taught you to do in this situation," his father cautioned him. Michal nodded, his throat too full of tears to say anything back.

"No talking!" their captor said, giving his father a slap. Michal jumped up to defend him but just got another blow to the chin for his efforts.

"Got some feisty ones, do we?" a deep, sinister voice said from behind them, making them freeze. Two men who were mirror images of each other stepped around into their view. One was older and a single scar ran from his forehead to his chin on the right side of his face and the other had lighter hair. They both had eyes of such a dark brown that were virtually black. They had to be Einar and Elof Egil, the leaders of the Egil clan. A small woman with blond hair followed them. She settled on the couch behind the men as if she were tired. When she looked at Michal and his parents, her eyes seemed dead, but there was something familiar about those eyes, something in the shape and color.

Einar crossed his arms over his chest and raised his eyebrows as he said. "The only reason we haven't killed you yet is because, to our surprise, your soldiers used our own fighting techniques against us, leading to many of our men's deaths. Even though your forces were not able to fight us off, you were somehow prepared to minimize the damage we could cause even before you knew we were coming.

"You evacuated the city and surrounding settlements, so there is almost nothing for us to plunder. Obviously, you couldn't have taught yourselves to do these things on your own, so now you're going to tell us exactly who it was who taught you and where they are. Until tonight, I'd thought not a single person had ever escaped my ship. Apparently, I was wrong. And now that this person has decided to teach you to use our own techniques against us and therefore committed the greatest sin possible against their clan, they will pay!"

After giving his speech, the older gentleman squatted down before Michal's father to look him in the eye. His father stared straight back without even blinking. Then, without any warning, the Viking ran his sword through his father's heart. "Noooooo!" his mother screamed, trying to get to him, but another Viking held her down by her shoulders.

Michal fought as hard as his mother but was also unable to break free. When his father lay dead between them and they realized resistance was futile, they calmed for a minute to catch their breath. The Viking squatted down in front of Michal. Michal stared him straight in the eye, just as his father had done. "Well. Do you have anything to say?"

To the Viking's utter shock, Michal slammed his head against his, knocking him backward. The Viking behind him held the point of a knife to Michal's throat while Einar arose, blood running down the side of his face. He had the audacity to chuckle. "I like this kid." Then turning toward the queen, he gave her a sickening smile. His poor mother looked to the blonde woman behind Einar for help but received nothing in response. "What about it, mother? Are you willing to let your only son perish for this person you're protecting? Whoever they are, they cannot be a good person, having come from my clan," Einar sneered. Michal's mother looked him in the eye and Michal could tell she was struggling between the love for her daughters and the love for her son. But she knew, just as well as Michal did, that the moment she told them what they wanted to know they'd kill them.

Giving his mother another sickening smile, Einar turned toward Michal and asked. "What about you, son?" The man squatted before his mother. Taking his vile finger, he caressed his mother's soft cheek. "What are you willing to let your mother endure for the sake of this person?"

Before Einar could say another word, Michal's mother turned and spat in the man's face. The blond looked at her, surprised and seemingly impressed. Einar roared in anger, backhanded the queen so hard she fell backward, and then ran his sword through her heart. Her husband's blood mingled with her own. Michal fought with all his might. "Nooo, nooo, nooooo! Mother, noooo!" Tears streamed down his face as he fought. He couldn't see anything but white. "Oh, God, please help us!" Michal wailed.

"Take him to the dungeon. Later we'll see how many of his men's lives are worth this person he's protecting," Einar spat.

Once they were a safe distance from the castle, Gideon finally broke the silence. "So, who's this contact that's going to take us to Montagne?" he asked while reaching back to make sure Chrystal didn't trip over a root. The tunnels were solid packed dirt with wood beams for bracing. Several tree roots had grown through the walls and the trio had to maneuver through them, increasing the time their journey took tenfold.

"He's an old friend of mine that owes me a favor," Aamber replied, hoping Gideon would take the hint to leave it alone.

"That all you're going to tell us? Don't you think we should know a little more about who we're going to be stuck with for a month on a ship?" he replied incredulously.

Aamber inwardly groaned. No wonder Gideon and Michal were friends, since they were both so stubborn. "I don't think you want to know more about him. He's not exactly the type who'll give you fuzzy feelings. But I know he'll do as I ask and ensure your protection."

"And how exactly do you know that?" Gideon stopped and crossed his arms, challenging Aamber.

Aamber turned to face him, not trying to mask the irritation in her voice. "If you must know, he's a smuggler. He couldn't make a living as a fisherman, so he turned to a life of crime. I've been working with him for months, trying to teach him how to fish in our waters so he could turn away from that life. And, through this process, I've tried to lead him to Christ. Many fear him and he has a scary demeanor. But he's never been a violent person unless you challenge him, so I suggest you keep your attitude in check." She turned to leave, thinking the conversation was over.

"Seriously? You're trusting our lives to a criminal?" Gideon threw at Aamber's back. Chrystal gasped. He turned to look at her, and she held her hands over her mouth, eyes wide. "It's all right, Chrystal. I have no intention of trusting your safety to any smuggler," Gideon tried to reassure her.

Aamber dug her fingernails into her palms, turned, and met Gideon toe-to-toe. "She didn't gasp because she's scared of my contact," she snapped. "Chrystal knows I would never put her life in danger. She gasped because she knows I can't stand people who look down on others. Is turning to a life of crime ever all right? No. But when you have four starving kids and a wife to worry about, you get desperate. So yes, I'm trusting your lives to a criminal. A criminal who spends his days trying to help people escape lives of persecution and misery. A criminal who is one of the best fathers to his children I have ever met. A criminal who has spent his life working his fingers to the bone, fighting pneumonia in the freezing rain just to feed his family.

"Is he scary-looking? Yes. Is he the best conversationalist? No. But he would never hurt anyone who wasn't hurting him. Especially not a young woman, since he has four young daughters of his own. Now, if you want to live to see another day, Prince Promesse, I suggest you follow my lead. And if you don't want to trust me, you can trust King Richard, because he's the one who trusted me enough to task me with finding someone who will give you safe passage." Aamber turned, knowing she'd flung her braids hitting him in the face, but didn't care. Gideon looked back at Chrystal, who was hiding a small smile.

They traveled a few more miles in silence. Aamber wasn't sure how Gideon and Chrystal couldn't hear the blood pounding in her head, considering how angry and scared she was. Gideon sighed. "I'm sorry Ruth. I shouldn't have snapped at you like that. I'm just worried." Aamber was surprised. Men were rarely ever humble enough to apologize to her, at least when there were witnesses around.

Aamber heaved a sigh of her own. "Me too. I understand. But if we're going to make it through this, we must trust each other. I know that you and I only met tonight but your friends trust me and I know they trust you. That's just going to have to be enough for now. No more talking for now, we're reaching the tunnel exit. We don't want to alert anyone to our presence. I'll go first and, if the coast is clear, I'll chirp like a cardinal." They could see the mouth of the tunnel ahead. The stars winked at them as if their whole world hadn't just been turned upside down. Aamber worried her lower lip. They probably only had a couple more hours before the sun rose and they'd lose their most powerful ally, the cloak of darkness.

After extinguishing their torch, Aamber inched her way to the mouth of the opening. It was small and she would have to army-crawl to get out. Before pulling herself up, she rustled the long grass overhead. When she didn't hear any cries from the Vikings who were sure to be trolling the woods, she slowly inched her way out. The tunnel opened onto the edge of a clearing on the side of a hill. They'd be exposed for a few hundred yards and would have to make a run for it, but the shore was just beyond the tree line in the distance and they could hide in the long grass covering the field if they had to.

When Aamber had pulled herself fully up, she strung her bow and scanned her surroundings. Nothing stirred. She gave the signal and Gideon's head popped out of the hole. Once he was free, he turned and helped Chrystal out. Dirt covered them all from head to toe, which was a good thing, Aamber thought. The more they could blend into the forest, the better.

"Come on, we must hurry," Aamber whispered. They ran toward the trees, staying as silent as they could. Suddenly, an arrow flew past Aamber's ear. "Get down!" she yelled, causing Gideon and Chrystal to drop in the long grass.

Aamber and Gideon moved in a zig-zag motion toward the trees, alternating popping up and shooting arrows at their attackers. Because Chrystal didn't have a bow, she stayed low behind her friends. Three Vikings hunted them. Aamber's first arrow hit one in the shoulder, and Gideon's arrow hit the same one in the knee. The Viking collapsed with a scream of pain and a slew of curses. Gideon dodged an arrow and Aamber shot the next Viking through the eye. Only one chased them now. Suddenly an arrow pieced Aamber's bicep, causing her to gasp in pain. Gideon shot one last arrow and hit the last Viking in the heart.

When they at last made the trees, Aamber let out one long whistle. Before anyone else said a word, she yanked the arrow out of her arm and tied off the bleeding with a strip of cloth. The pain was excruciating but there was nothing they could do about it, so Aamber just gritted her teeth against it. Cinnamon came crashing through the trees. "Come quick!" she called to her companions.

Aamber leaped onto Cinnamon's back. Gideon interlocked his fingers to give Chrystal a boost and then swung up behind her. They could hear yelling in the distance. Cinnamon didn't like the extra weight but obeyed Aamber's commands. All three fugitives prayed they wouldn't have to dodge more arrows. Soon they were racing through the forest and the yells grew so faint they could no longer hear them.

When she was sure no one was following them, Aamber slowed Cinnamon down to a trot. She hated pushing the little horse so hard with triple the weight she was accustomed to but knew she was sturdy enough to handle it. It took them about half an hour to reach the far south shore, where Aamber knew Sea Dog would be docked. Because of his chosen profession, Sea Dog avoided the main docks and had built a small one for himself on the opposite side of the island. Now it had become a hidden haven for smugglers and someone had even built a tavern where the men could wet their whistles and enjoy some female company. Aamber got them as close as they could on Cinnamon. The dock was surrounded by cliffs, which was how it stayed so well-hidden. The average citizen didn't know about the well-traversed paths down to the little field the tavern and docs were built upon.

"All right, we have to dismount here. The path is too dangerous for a horse from this point on," Aamber whispered. Gideon slid off first and helped Chrystal dismount. Aamber swung down before he could do the same for her. "I know the paths to the harbor well, but there are some narrow parts. Follow close behind me and only step where I do. When we reach the bottom, pull your cloaks up around your faces. Follow me into the tavern but don't say anything or look at anyone. Understand?"

Both of Aamber's companions nodded and they began their descent. Aamber could only imagine how surprised they must have been as she showed them the well-hidden paths. Each turn in the paths had another camouflage. At one point on the path, they barely had enough rock to fit their feet on and had to walk sideways. Chrystal tripped over a stone and almost fell, her gasp echoed off the surrounding cliffs. They were all relieved when they made it to the bottom. Gideon and Chrystal followed close behind Aamber, holding their cloaks close about their faces. Gideon was surprised Ruth didn't do the same.

When they walked through the swinging doors they were greeted loudly by the man behind the bar. "Hey, Ruthie! How you been? You come to preach at us some more? Don't worry, girlie, we always enjoy hearing you talk. Who's your friends?"

"Hey Jo, they're no one of consequence. Have you seen Sea Dog here tonight?" Aamber replied, hoping he would take the hint.

The bartender nodded over toward a man nursing a large beer in the corner. "You all right, Ruthie? Need help with anything? I heard Vikings have attacked the city. They bothering you? You're lookin' nervous and your arm's bleeding," he said with a concerned look while wiping a glass clean.

"Don't worry, Jo. They know better than to mess with me. You have a good one," Aamber replied, hoping she sounded convincing. Blood had soaked through her makeshift bandage and she knew she had to be pale from the loss of blood. These men might be willing to lay down their lives for her but, for the princess, not so much, so involving them would only make things worse.

Aamber slid into the booth across from Sea Dog. Nobody knew his real name. Aamber often wondered if he even remembered what his real name was. His long white hair was always pulled into a messy ponytail and his long white beard was mostly stained yellow from the tobacco he chewed. He was large and muscled for his 60 years and Aamber knew he could outwork men half his age.

Gideon and Chrystal stood to the side, just behind Aamber's shoulder. A simple candle sat in the rough, wooden table's center, casting an eerie glow over their filthy surroundings, reminding Aamber of her one and only family meal aboard the *Calder*. The entire tavern smelled like cheap perfume, sweat, and stale beer. The floor was dirt and Jo had never even heard of wiping off a table before. Aamber counted them lucky; he at least cleaned the glasses between customers.

"Hey, Red. What brings you here tonight? You usually save your visits for Thursdays," Sea Dog said in his raspy voice. Before Aamber could answer, one of the women sitting on a man's lap in the corner let out a loud squeal, causing Gideon and Chrystal to jump. Sea Dog cast them a glance, obviously suspicious about who they were.

"I need your help, Sea Dog. I need safe passage for my two friends here to Montagne," Aamber replied, hoping to distract him from recognizing Chrystal.

"What's the catch? You wouldn't have come to me just for passage," he said, taking a large swig of his beer.

"As you know, the city docks have been seized by the Egil Viking Clan. I need you to smuggle them past the Egils without detection. I also need you to make sure they make it to the Montagne castle safely," Aamber replied, holding her breath. It wouldn't be an easy job for anyone, but she was confident that, if anyone could manage it, Sea Dog could.

Sea Dog considered her. "That's a tall order, Red. I've come toe-to-toe with Einar Egil before and I ain't looking for a rematch. What would be in it for me?"

Aamber reached into her pocket and tossed a sack of gold coins onto the counter. She'd always kept some emergency money tucked away with her weapons for a situation like this. "Will that cover it?"

Sea Dog examined the coins. "I'm surprised Red. I ain't ever seen you with a penny on ya or does it belong to your friends here? Where'd you get this, if you don't mind me asking? I just don't want someone coming after me accusing me of stealing their money."

"I assure you, Sea Dog, it's not stolen. I've always kept some money away for emergencies," Aamber reassured her friend.

He tapped his fingers, considering her offer. "It's going to be hard, Red. I'm not going to lie to you. Now that the Egil clan had united with the Uffe clan, they've practically taken over the entire ocean."

Aamber held her hands out to the man. "If you need more money, I can get it for you. I'll just need some more time."

Sea Dog leaned forward and replied in a low voice. "That's not what I'm saying, Red. I'd be willing to do the job for half this. I'm just saying I won't be able to guarantee anything. I'll do my best, and you know I'm a slippery old fish, but I can't make any promises."

Aamber nodded. "I know that, Sea Dog. But you're the best in your line of work."

Once again, Sea Dog leaned back, considering her, almost seeming confused. "I thought you wanted me to get out of a life of crime. And now you're paying me?"

Aamber shook her head. "This isn't a crime, Sea Dog. They're not criminals running from justice. I've never condemned you for helping those escaping dangerous situations or lives of persecution. This is the exact same thing."

He continued to stare at her. "They must really mean a lot to you for you to be willing to do this."

Aamber met his gaze, hoping he read the sincerity in her eyes. "They're like family to me, Sea Dog. Just like you."

He nodded solemnly. "All right kid. You've hired yourself a smuggler. We'll leave immediately."

Sea Dog tossed Jo one of the gold coins and headed out the back door. The trio followed close behind. When they'd reached his ship, Sea Dog walked the plank and started barking orders to his crew. The ship wasn't large but it seemed sturdy. *The Ghost* was painted on the side. Aamber stood on the shore with Gideon and Chrystal. "All right, it's time we part ways. Don't worry. Sea Dog will protect you. He might have expressed some reservations but I have no doubt he will be able to get you there safely. I've seen his work firsthand and, like he said, he's a slippery old fish," she said with a wink, trying to lighten the mood.

Chrystal looked at her, her blue eyes brimming with tears. "Ruth, the trip takes a month in good weather. Who knows how long it will take having to sneak around? And then it's another month back. How will the people ever survive that long?" she asked, her voice trembling.

"Hey, hey, hey. You're forgetting we have God fighting on our side. And no Viking clan could ever be a match for Him. Don't worry. We'll make it through this with His help." The two girls embraced each other with tears streaming down their cheeks, wondering if they would ever see each other again.

"Come on up, blue-bonnet, we'll hide you first," Sea Dog hollered down to them. Chrystal looked at Aamber, confused, and Aamber just laughed and shrugged in response. Sea Dog had the habit of giving his acquaintances nicknames.

Chrystal walked up the plank slowly and Gideon and Aamber were left alone. Aamber turned to him and begged him, "Gideon, I don't know what's going to happen during the time we're waiting for reinforcements. It is possible not one person will be left for her to return to. Please tell me you'll always take care of her."

For the first time since their argument, he looked her straight in the eye. Aamber could read the sincerity in his green ones as he spoke. "I love her like family, Ruth. I always have. I won't ever abandon her."

Aamber nodded, knowing she'd left Chrystal in good hands, and couldn't help smiling. "Are you sure you love her like family? Or do you love her like a wife?" she teased. A look of shock came over his face and Aamber laughed before saying seriously. "May God go with you."

Aamber watched until *The Ghost* set sail. She'd already scaled the cliff and was sitting upon Cinnamon. The ship pulled out of the harbor just as the sun began to rise. Aamber wondered how it could be so cheery when their lives had fallen apart during the night. "Oh God, please protect them. Get them there safely. And please let some of us survive until their return. But in all things, let Your will be done and not our own," she prayed, taking in a deep breath of the morning air.

Aamber turned Cinnamon around and headed straight into the forest. Last night, King Richard had dispatched soldiers to the surrounding cities to get citizens to their prearranged evacuation sites. There were five sites, each in a valley with a well-hidden entrance and a clear stream through the middle. Some citizens were sure to have got lost or injured and Aamber planned on spending the day searching the forest for them. She was also sure to find injured and lost soldiers or some who'd been separated from their troops during the night. Vikings were also sure to be trolling the woods, looking for victims. The more she could pick off the better. Right now, her focus had to be on regrouping and forming a plan of attack.

Aamber had been surprised last night at hearing that the Egil clan had joined with the Uffe clan, after all. For Viking clans to unite, a marriage between the clans' family leaders was required. Aamber's brother Elof had probably been forced to marry one of Rafiq Tacitus's daughters. It wouldn't have been as satisfying as Einar Egil's daughter marrying the Uffe clan's leader, but it would do.

Birds chirped and the leaves of the trees rustled in the wind as Aamber let Cinnamon set a leisurely pace because of how tired the little horse was. Aamber took a deep breath. The forest was one of the only places where Aamber had ever felt at home. A scream split the peaceful silence of the woods, causing Cinnamon to jump, and Aamber rode toward the sound, hopping off Cinnamon and taking cover behind a tree when she drew near the whimpering sounds of a young woman.

An Uffe clan Viking had a young woman pinned against a tree with a knife at her throat and the other hand covering her mouth. "Now, now don't be like that," he crooned sinisterly into the girl's ear. "We wouldn't want anyone to interrupt our fun, now would we?" He laughed and began kissing the girl's neck. The girl clawed at his arms and kicked, but he outweighed her by at least 200 pounds.

Aamber strung her bow. Taking aim, she fired while her injured arm protested profusely. The arrow hit the Viking squarely between the shoulder blades. He slowly turned around, a shocked expression across his face, and fell facedown, dead. Aamber was finally able to get a good look at the girl. She couldn't be more than 14 with blond hair and large brown eyes. Her mouth was red where he'd covered it with his hand and bruises were already forming on her wrists. Tears streamed down her cheeks as she stared at Aamber in shock.

Before the girl could say a word, Aamber held her finger to her lips. Where there was one Viking, there was always another. Aamber motioned the girl toward her but, before the girl could take a step, an arrow flew past her head. Instead of running, the girl crouched on the ground, covered her ears, and screamed. Aamber ran to her and dragged her to cover. Arrows flew past them and one hit the girl in the shoulder, causing her to scream more. When they had cover, Aamber covered the girl's mouth with her hand. "Calm down! You're going to get us killed." The girl whimpered and Aamber released her, praying the child would be silent.

When she peeked around the tree, another arrow flew past Aamber's head, causing her to duck. Aiming at the place the shot came from, she fired. A Viking fell forward holding his thigh, a stream of curses flowing from his mouth. Aamber was stunned for a second, realizing she knew him from *the Calder*. He was one of the watchmen. The Viking looked up at Aamber, and a shocked expression came into his eyes as he said, "You!" But, before he could say anything else, she shot again and he was dead.

Turning to the girl, Aamber stretched out her hand. The girl hesitated. "I'll get you to the evacuation spot, you have no reason to fear me," Aamber tried to reassure her.

The girl stared up at her and, to Aamber's surprise, anger flashed in the girl's eyes. "You're one of them, aren't you?"

Aamber considered her. Maybe this girl wasn't such a nitwit after all. "No. I am not a Viking. My name is Ruth. I'm a servant of King Richard. He hired me to be his daughter's bodyguard about a year ago. Now please, let me help you," she pleaded and held her hand out to the girl again.

Surprise flashed in the girl's eyes and she finally took Aamber's hand. Aamber turned her to see where the arrow had struck the girl in the back of her shoulder. It wasn't deep or life-threatening. She picked up a stick and handed it to the girl. "Bite down on this. I'm going to have to pull out this arrow before we go anywhere. You'll be fine, it'll just hurt like blazes."

Nodding, the girl put the stick in her mouth. Aamber didn't give her any warning, knowing it would make it worse, and ripped the arrow out. Blood gushed out of the wound and Aamber quickly pressed her handkerchief to it. She untied the rope from around her waist and made a sling for the girl so her arm wouldn't pull on the injury. The girl reached up with her other arm to remove the stick from her mouth. She'd bitten straight through it.

"Wait here a minute. I'll be right back," Aamber told her, hoping the girl would take a minute to recompose herself.

Aamber peeked around their tree and, when she didn't see any movement, she ran to the dead men. She pilfered their arrows and weapons, knowing that, if she left them for other Vikings to find, they would be used against her and her soldiers in the future. After returning to the girl, she took her hand and led her to where she'd left Cinnamon. She boosted the girl onto Cinnamon's back, swung up herself, and headed in the direction of the nearest evacuation site. Aamber held onto the girl's waist to keep her from falling sideways.

Aamber didn't ask the girl her name or how she'd got separated from her group. Talking would only put them in more danger. To Aamber's surprise, the girl didn't try to make conversation either, but she was probably in too much pain to try. They hadn't even traveled a mile when they came upon a lost soldier. He'd been separated from his troop in the chaos of the night and he'd also lost his weapons. Aamber supplied him with the ones from the Vikings she killed, gave him directions for the nearest evacuation site, and told him to be on the lookout for any injured or lost people on his way. Aamber wouldn't have minded taking him to the evacuation site herself but, since he wasn't injured, she decided he would be of more help walking the distance. He would have a greater chance of coming upon someone she might have missed.

Near the end of their trek, they came across three more lost soldiers and supplied them with the rest of the Vikings' weapons, and then Aamber spotted a little boy. She swung off Cinnamon and squatted down before him. "Hey, little guy. What's your name?"

He was hiding in the underbrush, clutching a blanket for dear life. He didn't say anything but, when Aamber held out her arms to him, he ran to her, grubby arms clutching her neck with all their might. Aamber carried him back to Cinnamon. She noticed the girl was pale and knew she had to hurry because the girl was losing too much blood.

They were soon on their way again and, when they reached the entrance to the evacuation valley, Aamber called out the signal that they were friends and not foes. This entrance was a thin pass through the rock of a mountain, barely large enough for a horse to fit through. If Aamber stretched her arms out, she could touch both walls.

Riding into the valley at a trot, she descended the gradual slope and called out, "Quick! She's bleeding and needs a doctor." People of all ages ran toward them, both men and women. Many ragtag soldiers led the charge.

A man pulled the girl from Cinnamon and carried her over to the group of tents. People surrounded Cinnamon, who almost balked at the attention. "Commander Ruth! Do you have word of the royal family? When will the Vikings leave? What news do you have? Have you seen Johnny? What are the army's next moves?"

Aamber held up her hand to quiet them. She pulled her cloak aside to reveal the boy, whose arms were wrapped around her chest. "Johnny!" A young woman screamed and pushed her way through to the front. Upon hearing his mother's voice, the boy cried and reached for her. Aamber gently handed the boy down, happy that the mother's grief was over." "Oh, thank you! Thank you, Commander Ruth!"

Aamber was uncertain how she'd got the title "Commander" but now wasn't the time to be worried about formalities. She looked out over the crowd, who were all looking to her to find what they were to do. It was frightening to know she was their leader. Aamber swallowed hard. "Are there any other army commanders here?" All heads shook. "All right, I want every able-bodied soldier to grab their weapons and form a group by the stream. The highest-ranking soldier among them is responsible for the count. Any men between 18 and 50 who are not soldiers are responsible for hunting and fishing, along with any younger ones who have the ability. Who among you can be responsible for the hunting parties and keep the men from getting themselves killed?"

An older man with gray hair raised his hand. "I can, Commander. I've been a trapper my whole life. My name is Kyle Manning."

Aamber scanned the crowd's faces. "Any objections to Mr. Manning leading the hunting party?" No one said a word.

"I need a woman or a doctor who can oversee nursing. They'll need to be able to organize the workers into alternating shifts and alert me about what they need. I know how to make cloth from a common plant in this valley and many different medicines. But my time would be better spent fighting. Is there anyone here who knows these things?"

An elderly woman raised her hand. She had gray hair and weathered cheeks. "I can. I was a nurse for 20 years. My doctor showed me how to create the cloth you're talking about, as well as many herbs. My name is Carla May."

Aamber scanned the crowd. "Any objections?" Once again, no one moved.

"Mrs. May, can you also be responsible for the production of the cloth?" The older woman nodded.

"Is there a teacher among us who could watch and teach the young ones during the day?"

This time two women raised their hands. "All right, you will work together. This will free up parents to help in other areas. Now, is there anyone who could oversee cooking for the camp? I know many are capable of cooking individually but our food will stretch farther if we all eat together."

This time several women raised their hands. "All who raised their hands, step forward."

They complied. "Which of you have experience cooking for large groups?"

Only two raised their hands. "Then you'll oversee cooking together. Teach the others who want to learn." Both women nodded.

"I also need a man who can oversee the burial of the dead and the marking of graves. As you know, we've already lost many and they deserve to be buried like heroes."

This time, a middle-aged gentleman raised his hand. "I'm a carpenter, ma'am. I've made many coffins and helped bury many dead. I will treat the remains with the honor they deserve." Aamber nodded. She didn't even need to ask if the others approved.

"Is there a preacher among us who can pray with us and lift our spirits during these trying times? Who can also hold church services and funerals?"

A young man raised his hand. "I am Pastor Farid. I'm young but I'm willing to answer God's call."

Aamber nodded. "That's all that's required, Pastor." Turning back toward the people, she said, "You now have your leaders. Every person is expected to help during these trying times. Each leader is to determine who their workers are and to let me know if there's something they need I can obtain for them or if they need help carrying out their duties. As for the royal family, the only one I have any news of is the princess. She's safe and is fighting the war on a different front. Saying any more would put her in danger. Our priority right now is to find the citizens who are lost and soldiers who are injured. Once we've made a thorough search of the forest, we'll regroup.

"Until reinforcements come, we don't have the numbers to take the Vikings on directly but the Vikings are going to be searching for us. So, while we heal and wait for help, we're going to pick them off one by one when they are alone by alternating sending out platoons. While your soldiers search today, I'm going to make my way between the other evacuation sites and try to find word about the rest of the royal family, how other citizens are faring, and what they need as well. I know you're scared, tired, and hurt. But let me assure you, God is fighting on our side, and we will defeat this foe if we depend on Him. Now, Pastor Farid, please lead us in prayer."

They all bowed their heads as Pastor Farid began. "Dear Heavenly Father, we come to you in our hour of need. Please, stretch out your hand of protection over our army and our people. Please, give us strength for the days ahead and healing from the days past. Please touch the Vikings' hearts and give them compassion and show us how we may be the example to bring them to You. In all things let Your will be done. Through Jesus's most precious and holy name I pray, Amen." Murmurs of "Amen" traveled through the crowd, and they started to disperse.

Aamber turned Cinnamon to cross the stream. The soldiers stood at attention on the other side. They were a ragged-looking group but Aamber knew their strength. There was something different about them from the day they'd first met. They now had the pain of battle in their eyes; it reflected the pain in her own. What could she possibly say to them to give them the hope they needed?

A middle-aged soldier stepped forward as she approached. "How many, soldier?"

"Seven-hundred and 52, Commander." Aamber nodded, thinking about how it would be best to split up their resources.

"Does anybody have news I should know?" she asked.

One young soldier, with long brown hair hanging in his eyes, pushed his way to the front of the crowd. He stood at attention and saluted her after he made it to the front. She saluted back and asked. "What do you need to tell me, soldier?"

Shy, he avoided her eyes. "They're looking for someone, Commander. I heard a Viking talking to his comrade near the castle last night. They couldn't figure out how we knew their methods. They're searching for you, ma'am. It's why they're not looking harder for the people. They want you." Aamber felt her heart sink to her feet, as the young soldier continued. "But we'll defend you to our dying breath, Commander. You've helped our people and families in our time of need. You could have left us to our own devices. But you didn't. We stand behind you."

Tears sprang into Aamber's eyes. They wouldn't, if they knew who she really was. "Thank you, soldier." Her voice was guttural, and she had to clear her throat before she could continue.

173

Turning back to the original soldier, she said, "Split the men up. Leave about half to defend the camp. Once again, split the remainder in half. One half will rest while the rest go out scouting. Alternate as you see fit. You'll scout at night. Start at sunset and have one group go out and come back about every three hours. Stay within a ten-mile radius of the camp. And always remember, watch out for Vikings. Take the weapons off any that you kill so they can't be used against us later. I would also throw their bodies off the cliffs into the sea if you can. It'll keep the Vikings from narrowing down the search for our hiding places. We'll make them disappear into thin air. I'll come back as soon as I can to give you updates and see if you need anything. Any questions?"

The soldier nodded. "How do we determine who's in charge among the troops, ma'am?"

"Go by the highest-ranking soldiers who are here. If they're all the same rank put it to a vote. If it's a stalemate, flip a coin," Aamber replied.

"Yes, ma'am," the soldier said solemnly.

"Any other questions?" The soldier shook his head. "May God be with you."

She began to turn her horse around. "Wait, ma'am! What about you? When will you rest?" the soldier called after her.

She threw him a smile over her shoulder. "Not until I'm dead."

CHAPTER 8

THE RESCUE

Behold, God is my salvation; I will trust, and not be afraid: for the Lord Jehovah is my strength and my song; he also is become my salvation.

Isaiah 12:2 KJV

Océan, A.D. 907

Michal's eyes popped open when he heard his cell door swing open. He was lying on the floor on his side, chained to the wall by one leg. He'd lost weight and had suffered innumerable interrogations. They'd taken his shirt and his pants were in rags. His feet were torn to pieces from the rough cell floor and they hadn't given him any food or water in days. His eyes were almost swollen shut and he didn't know how much longer he could hold out. But he would never give up Ruth or his people. They'd just have to kill him.

Einar picked him up by his hair, his signature move. Michal was too weak to stand and didn't want to help the Viking, anyway.

His black eyes stared into Michal's as if trying to read his thoughts. Michal was surprised he'd come down himself. All the previous interrogations had been done by his henchmen. Before Michal could catch himself, the Viking dropped him hard, bruising his shoulder. "You know, kid, I've sailed from one side of the world to the other. I've tortured and killed men twice your size and twice as mean, making them cry like babies. They begged me for their lives. Some of them were my own brothers. I've never even spared my kids." *Kids?* Michal had only ever met Elof. Did Einar have more on the ship?

He walked back and forth in the small cell's expanse as he talked. "The only type of people who've ever been able to resist my techniques are either in love or have religion. And, unfortunately for you, you're both. You love your people, and have a strong faith but did you know that, by protecting the person that trained you, you're subjecting the people you love to a criminal?"

Squatting down to look Michal in the eye, he said, "You know whoever you're protecting is a Viking. Not only a Viking but a member of my clan. Which means they've robbed, lied, and even killed innocent people. They've taught you techniques only a member of my clan could know." Suddenly, the old Viking froze, causing Michal to look up at him in surprise. "Actually, they've taught you techniques I've only ever taught my kids."

Grabbing Michal by the hair again, he slammed his head against the wall, holding him off his feet. Michal saw stars and struggled not to black out. "Where is she!" Einar screamed through gritted teeth.

Michal squawked out through his dry throat, "Who?"

Michal had thought he'd seen evil in the eyes of this man, but it wasn't until this moment that he saw the devil incarnate. "My daughter. Aamber Rose Egil. She disappeared off my ship six or seven years ago. We thought she was dead. But your soldiers knew a technique I'd only ever taught her. At first, I just figured another Viking saw me teach her but now I realize, you're in love with my daughter. That's why you've never cracked. And she is the reason you've been a step ahead of us the entire time. No king has ever been smart enough to prepare for our arrival and Aamber's the smartest woman, maybe person you'll ever meet. She not only abandoned her responsibilities toward her clan but she's also taught others how to defeat them."

Michal's head was spinning. *Her cross with the rose, her weaponry abilities, her dress the night of the ball. His father knew, his mother knew! That was why his father asked her if she was all right when she told them about the Vikings. This was Ruth's, no, Aamber's father! The woman's eyes! Those were Aamber's eyes! Her mother! This was her family, why she hid so much of herself from everyone. His father was right. She'd been taking an enormous risk by teaching his soldiers! She'd risked everything in the new life she'd built! And now she was exposed, and the life she had fought for was gone. Her family knew she was alive and she would never be safe until they were gone.*

Matching Einar's glare, he said. "You'll never find her." Einar roared, slammed him against the wall, and everything went black.

Aamber rode Cinnamon between the camps. From the tallies she'd done, about half of their army had survived the battle. They were killing more Vikings every day but there were still so many more. Aamber knew they couldn't do this forever. She just prayed they'd still be alive by the time Gideon and his army returned, if they returned at all.

For the past two days, she'd been riding back and forth between the camps, taking them supplies and helping the commanders she'd appointed. At this point, she knew the king and queen were dead but there was no word on Michal. That would change tonight. She'd gathered five soldiers she trusted to help rescue Michal. Little did the Vikings know, a tunnel ran under the castle, straight into the jail.

Aamber hadn't slept in four days and needed to rest to be at her best for the long night ahead of her. Releasing Cinnamon, she climbed the tallest tree she could find, sat on one of the branches, tied her legs to it, and leaned back. It had been about a week since the invasion. Aamber had been hearing rumors in the camp. Apparently, Molly, the girl she'd rescued that first day, had been telling everyone who would listen that Aamber was a Viking though no one had been brave enough to confront Aamber to see if the rumors were true.

Aamber's heart squeezed. The life she'd built for herself was over. It wouldn't be long before everyone knew her true identity if they survived that long. Worse, though, was that Michal would know. The thoughts of Michal learning she'd lied to him broke Aamber's heart. She'd always known there was no hope of a romantic relationship between them but her stupid heart hadn't listened to her and got involved anyway. These worries consumed her until she fell asleep.

Aamber awoke with a start. The sun was starting to set and she would need to head out soon to meet the rescue team but she could hear male laughter below her. Slowly looking down, Aamber saw six Vikings. They'd stopped to rest and hadn't seen her sleeping above them. They were all members of the Egil clan, and Aamber tried to remember their names; Crook, Basse, Jaw, Scar, Lucifer, and Elof, her brother.

"Did you hear your dad thinks it's your sister who trained the army to fight against us?" Jaw asked Elof. Aamber's heart leaped to her throat.

"Yeah, I heard, but I don't think he's right. The night she died, there was a raging storm and we weren't anywhere near land. Even if she had made it off the ship she would have drowned, her not knowing how to swim. Besides, we found the shawl she wore all the time soaked in blood, and no lifeboats were missing from the deck. Not to mention Odin was found dead that same night. Maybe he'd tried to get her again, and she killed him, and then someone saw her and killed her. At least that's been my theory the past seven years."

The six debated back and forth about whether she was alive or not, so her plan had worked. They'd thought she was dead. Aamber held her breath, hoping they would say something about Michal. Scar spoke up. "I heard the prince confirmed it. Apparently, he had the guts to tell the boss he'd never find her when he'd figured out who it was. Boss says he's in love with her, which is why he hasn't given her or anyone else up yet. Plus, he says he's a Christian and you know how difficult they are."

"Well, then why is he keeping the squirt alive?" Jaw broke in.

"Boss apparently won't leave until he's killed Aamber and all the people. They know too much, having lived with her for so long. He plans on using the prince as bait." Aamber's stomach dropped. Her father wasn't going away and it was her fault. She groaned inwardly.

The sun was almost set and Aamber began to worry that they were planning on camping there for the night. Michal was alive but she knew he wouldn't be much longer. At least they knew their mission tonight wasn't all for naught. But, if they did stay, Aamber would have to kill them. Could she kill her own brother? She didn't think so.

Elof leaned against her tree trunk and closed his eyes. Aamber held her breath; he was sure to see her if he opened them again. Before she could decide what to do, arrows started flying past the Vikings' ears. Their attackers had killed three of them before they were able to take cover. Elof was injured and continued to lie at the tree below her. She knew he wasn't dead and was pretending to bring his attackers in closer to kill them.

Aamber strung her bow and shot the other two Vikings who were crouching behind some bushes before they could kill her men. Climbing down the tree, she landed on her feet with a thud. Elof didn't move. The five soldiers who were to help her later tonight came up behind her, arrows ready to fly. "All right, Elof, enough. I know you're faking," she challenged, but he still didn't move.

"Ruth, who is this guy?" Gregory asked her.

"He's the son of Einar Egil. The next leader of the Egil clan and a valuable hostage. He's Einar's last chance to pass on his family line," she replied, without looking at him.

"What about you?" Elof shot at her. The five soldiers behind her jumped, brandishing their weapons.

Aamber stared at Elof blankly. He rose and yanked the arrow out of his shoulder. Looking at the blood on the tip, he said, "You could give Father a grandchild. Maybe even one with royal blood, considering how close you and the prince are."

Aamber could feel her men's eyes, questioning her, and her face turning red. "Shut up Viking. Jackson, tie him up."

Elof chuckled. "Oh, Aamber. You know you're the only one who knows how to tie me up so I can't escape."

"Ruth. What's he talking about?" Jackson asked.

Elof gave her a sinister grin. "So, you haven't told your buddies here who you really are."

This time it was Jasper who told Elof to shut up. "Look, Viking. We're not going to believe anything you say. You're just trying to turn us against each other. We all know Ruth has a past and we don't care. She's stood by our side during our battle. Nothing you say can negate that!"

Elof looked at him lazily. "Not even if she's the daughter of the man who's caused all your pain? Gentlemen, let me introduce you to Aamber Rose Egil. She's been dead for almost seven years. You are traveling with a ghost."

Aamber had never heard the forest so silent. Jackson went toward him to tie him up. "Wait," Aamber called, after seeing the look in Elof's eyes. Jackson froze. "Give me the rope."

"No, Ruth. He's egging you on," Jackson replied, never taking his eyes off Elof.

Aamber shook her head. "Give me the rope. He's going to try to kill whoever comes near him. I know him. I might have a chance."

Jackson turned and stared at her. "So, it's true. You are who he says?"

Aamber looked up, trying to keep the tears from falling. "Does it matter?" she asked but the men just gave her a look. Finally, she took a deep breath and said. "Yes, I was Einar Egil's daughter. But haven't I proven my loyalty? Blood doesn't matter. Family are the people who love you. Not who you share blood with."

The men looked at each other, then Jason laughed. "I don't know how we didn't figure it out sooner. I mean you showing up out of nowhere. Aamber disappearing at the same time from the *Calder*. All your fighting techniques. Even the color of your eyes."

By the time he'd finished, all five men were laughing. "Aamber, actions speak louder than words. I guarantee you not one man in the army doesn't have a story about how you've saved their life. You being an Egil just helps us because now we know we have an inside man.

You've been our sister in battle but, more importantly, you're our sister in Christ. Our loyalty is with you," Jasper said. Aamber almost shook her head. Jasper had come a long way from the cocky, young soldier she had to pin on their first day of training.

The tears flowed freely now, even though Aamber tried to wipe them. "Thank you."

Turning toward Elof, she headed toward him with the rope. He smiled at her again. "So, you went and got religion. Who'd have known it was possible of an Egil? But you've always been the black sheep of the family. I mean you being stupid enough to let yourself get raped by Odin is proof enough."

Aamber felt the men behind her tense. They started circling her brother to block off any paths of escape. Elof crossed his arms. "We going to do this or not, Sis?"

Aamber stopped, considering the man her brother had become. "Elof, why don't you join us? You could leave the life of the Vikings like I did. You've seen how good of a life I've built for myself. I could help you. God could help you."

Elof stared at her, hatred in his eyes. "You left me, Aamber."

Aamber was shocked. "I didn't ever think you'd want to come with me. You've always loved the life of a Viking," she ventured hesitantly.

Elof shook his head. "No. I just pretended to so I wouldn't face father's wrath the way you did."

"Then you're a coward. If your little sister got out, you could have. You only have yourself to blame," Joseph snapped. Aamber turned toward Joseph, shocked; he never talked. Elof was angry now.

Aamber went at Elof again, knowing the fight she was facing; she could see it in the twitch of his foot and the set of his jaw. But, before Elof could strike a blow, Jackson came up from behind and hit him in the head, making him crumple at Aamber's feet in a heap. Aamber chewed her lip. Turning to her comrades, she asked. "What are we going to do?"

Aamber could see the pity in the men's eyes and knew what they were going to say. They couldn't take him to the camp because he would most likely break free and then lead his comrades back. If they had men guard him offsite, he'd overpower and kill them. They had only two options: let him go or kill him. Aamber looked to the sky. Remembering where her help came from. "I...I c-can't. You do it but I can't watch," she stuttered. She walked away, praying for forgiveness.

About a stone's throw away, Aamber fell on her knees and sobbed. "Oh, God. I can't take much more. Why?! Why did you let this happen? I escaped and tried to live my life for you. Is this punishment for all the things I'd done before? But I was only a kid! Please, HELP!" A peace that transcended all understanding entered her heart and it was almost as if the Lord was reaching down and giving her a comforting hug.

Aamber heard a scuffle behind her; she jumped up and ran back to the men. Two of her men were lying on the ground, and the others were pulling them up. Elof was nowhere to be found. "What happened?"

The men looked at each other. "He woke up and overpowered us." Aamber stared at them. She couldn't believe they'd be willing to let him go because of her. She avoided their eyes and said, "Thank you."

They smiled. "My lady. Whatever for?"

A while later, they were making their way through another dirt tunnel, with Aamber leading and the men following like a row of ducklings. Aamber wondered who had built these tunnels. Whoever they were, she wanted to thank them. She'd been exploring these tunnels for a long time, ever since she'd learned of their existence. One day she'd been out riding and stumbled across the entrance to one. Ever since she'd been obsessed with finding the rest of them.

Gregory let out a long whistle. "I never knew this was here. Are there any more, Aamber?"

Aamber still couldn't get over them using her actual name. "Yes. There's a whole network of tunnels leading to and from the palace. I've found a total of five, but there could be more."

"Where does this one lead to?" Jackson asked.

"The jail. At the end, there's a trap door that leads right up into one of the cells. From there, I can pick the cell's lock. We'll get all the soldiers we find and the prince. One of you needs to stay in the tunnel to help them down. They're bound to be wounded and weak, so expect a long trek ahead," she cautioned.

"What about the guard? Would you be able to pick the lock before he sounds the alarm?" Joseph asked, concerned.

Aamber laughed. "He'll be sound asleep. It's a well-known secret among the Vikings that guard duty is nap duty." She sobered. "The prisoners are in such bad shape that even if they tried to escape, they'd be too slow to ever get away." What Aamber didn't tell them was, if they succeeded, these would be the first prisoners to ever escape the Egil clan. She didn't want to discourage them.

They came to the end of the tunnel and Aamber handed her torch back to Jasper. Aamber climbed the ladder and pushed the trap door up a crack. Dirt rained down around her. As she'd expected, she could hear the guard snoring and men moaning. The pungent smell of human urine, feces, sweat, and blood hit her strong, and she heard one of the men below gag.

She pushed the door the rest of the way open slowly. It creaked the entire way. At one point the guard snorted and smacked his lips but soon returned to sucking in the walls. Once up. Aamber looked to see who occupied the cell with her. Why they had the tunnel leading into a cell instead of the walkway, Aamber would never know.

To her surprise, Michal was chained to the wall. Aamber ran to him, scared he was dead. He was breathing. The weight fell off her shoulders like a waterfall. He was alive. She wasn't expecting how much her heart hurt at seeing him in so much pain and refused to contemplate it. He was her friend and would only ever be her friend. She couldn't believe she had to remind herself of this right now.

Blood was dried on his head. She picked the lock on his shackles, being careful that they didn't make a noise when they fell off. Aamber turned him onto his back and his eyes flickered open. "Aamber?" he whispered.

"I'm here. I'm here. You're safe now," she reassured him while pushing a lock of his blond hair out of his eyes.

"Aamber, go pick the lock. We'll get him," Jasper whispered. Aamber almost jumped. She hadn't realized he'd already climbed up behind her. Joseph picked Michal up and handed him down to Jackson, who'd stayed below. Her heart broke at his whispered, "Wait, wait. Aamber, don't go."

After making quick work of the lock, she slowly swung the door open. The snoring Viking woke up but Joseph ran him through before he could sound the alarm. Aamber went down the row, picking the locks to each cell door and each soldier's shackles. The men took one man to the tunnel after the other. Jackson was giving them water and broth to drink, hoping to give them some strength for the journey.

When they'd finished, they had released ten men, including Michal. Five soldiers were already dead in their cell. "Jasper," Aamber said, "let's lower the dead into the tunnel. We can send men back for them later. I can't leave them here like this." He nodded.

They were in and out of the jail in 20 minutes. Aamber heard a yell as she closed the trap door. She felt no pity for the Viking they'd killed. It was more merciful than what her father would do to him. They'd stacked the dead in a little curve in the tunnel, covered with Aamber's cloak. Five of the soldiers could at least walk by leaning against the tunnel wall, which left five who needed support. Michal was in the worst shape, having been tortured significantly more than the rest and Gregory had to carry him.

Aamber led the way with her torch, letting each of the walking soldiers take turns leaning on her. They were all covered in blood, sweat, vomit, dirt, and tears. The soldiers had various injuries but Aamber was happy that it seemed as if malnutrition was the worst of it. No bones were broken, and they all had various scrapes but they didn't seem life-threatening…except for Michal, and she couldn't tell the extent of his injuries.

"Let's stop here and take a break," Aamber called behind her after an hour. Gregory sat Michal against the wall and Aamber kneeled beside Michal to give him a drink. She reached up and pushed his blond hair out of his eyes. He'd been unconscious during most of the walk but now his eyes flickered open. "Aamber. You're all right. You came for me." His voice was soft, but it was the most beautiful sound in the world to Aamber.

"Of course, we came for you. We would never leave you behind," she replied.

He almost smiled, his dry lips cracking and beginning to bleed. "My love came for me," he whispered and fell asleep. Aamber stared at him, sleeping peacefully. His love? He loved her? He had to be delusional.

"What'd he say?" Jasper asked her.

Aamber shook her head. "He wasn't making any sense. Mostly that we'd come for him. I think he has a bad concussion."

Aamber leaned back against the wall, pulling Michal's head onto her lap so he'd be more comfortable. She wiped the salt from his cheeks where tears had left their trails. Laying her head against the wall, she sighed. Michal's finally being safe had lifted the weight off her chest and she could finally breathe again. She hadn't realized she'd been holding her breath since they'd parted.

Aamber realized several of the men were staring at her. "What?"

Three of them leaned back and smiled. The rest looked away. Of course, only Jasper was brave enough to say what they were all thinking. "You're in love with him."

Aamber scrunched her eyebrows. "Says who?"

This earned her several laughs. "Says you. He's the only one you've ever looked at that way. Anyone with eyes can see you love each other. It's nothing to be ashamed of, so why not just admit it?"

Aamber stared at the ceiling trying to hold her tears at bay. "You know who I am. There could never be a future for us."

Jasper raised his eyebrows. "Why not? What's wrong with who you are?" Aamber didn't respond and continued staring at the ceiling. *Everything is wrong with who I am,* she wanted to say. Except she was a child of God. It was her only strength. Little did they know that

Michal was listening to this entire exchange and couldn't help smiling. She did love him, otherwise she would have flat out denied it.

It was a long journey, about seven miles, and it took them the rest of the night. The sun was peeking its smiling face over the horizon when they finished and they breathed a collective sigh of relief. But they still had to make it to camp. They hobbled over to the tree line, hoping no Vikings saw them.

Suddenly, Aamber heard a grunt behind her and turned to see what it was. Jasper stood, wide-eyed, and fell facedown, with an arrow sticking between his shoulder blades. "Run!" she screamed. Arrows flew past them as they went. One of the injured soldiers got shot in the same spot as Jasper and fell dead. Aamber let out a whistle and Cinnamon came crashing through the bushes. They boosted Michal onto her back, along with two of the remaining injured soldiers. "Get them to camp and send reinforcements," she said as she handed Cinnamon's mane to the least injured one. He spurred the little pony and they took off.

Turning toward the others, she called, "All right men. We don't run. We fight." They raised their weapons in response and turned toward the battle. Aamber strung her bow and took cover behind a tree. A group of about ten Vikings was hunting them. When one stood to take a shot at Joseph, her arrow hit its mark. Men were dodging in and out of bushes and from behind trees everywhere and it was almost hard to tell who was a Viking and who was a soldier.

Suddenly, Aamber felt a presence behind her. She ducked and rolled just in time to avoid the sword. She unsheathed her dagger and brought it up in time to block the attempted thrust that would have gone through her. "Elof?" she asked, shocked.

"Thought I'd spare you since your men spared me, did you? I thought father taught you mercy was weakness," he snarled.

Aamber blocked more of his blows and twisted her path, trying to get the high ground. "My Heavenly Father taught me mercy takes strength. He came to earth and died for my sins when he had never made a mistake in his life."

"Good gosh. You're farther gone than I thought. How the once mighty have fallen. You've already shown you're too weak to kill me, so why are you even fighting back?"

He blocked Aamber's blow, their weapons making a cross. She looked her brother straight in the eye. "You've already shown you don't have the heart to kill me, too. When my men let you go, you could have easily come and snapped my neck. Why didn't you? Have you realized your soul is searching for Jesus too?"

Elof shoved her away and they stood staring at each other. Aamber began pleading with him. "It doesn't have to be like this, Elof. Join me. Help me defeat the Viking clan and end the misery and suffering for good. I now know I was wrong to leave you. I thought you were happy in this life. Now I realize no one could be. I'm sorry. Please, let's start over. We could fight this battle as brother and sister and build new good lives for ourselves. I could tell you about how God has saved my soul. I know your heart and I know you've always felt a deep hole in it that's been begging you to be filled for years. I know because I felt the same way. I felt dead inside until I found Jesus. And when I let Him into my heart the most beautiful things this life has to offer followed. Joy, peace, friendship, family, hope, and most important of all love. Love filled my heart, Elof. John 3:16 says, 'For God so loved the world that he gave his one and only Son, that whoever believes in him shall not perish but have eternal life.' Please, Elof, let us show you the love of God."

Elof couldn't believe the glow that had come over his sister when she talked about her God. Anger and hatred welled up in his heart until all he saw was red. He hated these people for their happiness and wanted nothing more than to destroy them. No one deserved to be so happy. The love that emanated from his sister and her comrades was more than anyone deserved. They loved her and that was their weakness. Elof suddenly knew how they would defeat this army.

Then Elof realized his men had been defeated and Aamber's were beginning to surround him. "This isn't over," he growled and disappeared into the forest like a mist.

Elof made his way back to the palace, trying to forget what his sister had said. He refused to believe there was some mystical God out there controlling his destiny and anyone who believed that there was had to be crazy. But then, why did it seem as if, no matter how hard they tried, they couldn't defeat these people? They were farmers! The weakest prey of all in his mind.

Einar and Elof had sent out their best soldiers and trackers left and right. They either were finally brave enough to come back empty-handed or not at all. It was almost like their men vanished into thin air because, when other scouts went out, they found no trace of their comrades or even the horses they had ridden. Many of the Vikings were beginning to believe the island was cursed or that these people really had a God whom they had offended. Elof suspected this was why Aamber had chosen the techniques she was using. She knew Vikings were superstitious and would read more into the disappearances than if they thought her army was picking them off one by one.

Since his run-in with his sister, he'd gone straight to the palace to get reinforcements so he could hunt her down. Little did he know that the party with her had been the very soldiers they'd had locked up in their dungeon. He had no intention of telling his parents that he had now seen and spoken with Aamber twice. They would ask him why he'd not brought her in. "Sir! Sir!" a Viking cried out, hailing him.

"What!" he barked.

"The prisoners have escaped!" the man said and braced for Elof's reaction. Elof's gut twisted. He should have known Aamber would try something like this. They knew the prince was in love with her. Why shouldn't they have assumed she was in love with the prince? Otherwise, she wouldn't have been so stupid as to break him out of prison and humiliate their father. Of course, their father had done a great job of humiliating himself. Ever since he'd learned that Aamber was alive, all he'd done was drink and eat himself into a stupor.

The Vikings wouldn't last much longer with their leader in his cups and the rest left to their own devices. Elof was not going to let his clan be defeated. His sister had abandoned him, his clan never had. They were his family. And he was tired of them having to serve a leader who didn't lead and humiliated them regularly. Well, tonight Elof was going to fix that. A plan formed in his mind.

That evening Elof put together a dinner for his parents. It reminded him of the dinner they'd put together the night they told Aamber they were selling her to the Uffe clan, with its abundant food and flickering candles giving the room an eerie glow. Elof couldn't believe he'd actually pitied his sister at that meal. Now he realized she would have deserved any abuse she received at the Uffe clan's leader's hand and more. He'd been forced to marry the Uffe clan's leader's daughter, who was only two months old at the time because of Aamber. He supposed his wife would be nice to have in his old age.

His father ate like a pig, and his mother picked at her food. Elof had never been close to his mother. She'd always preferred Aamber over him. Since Aamber had supposedly died, she'd become gray and sullen. She never talked or ate, and just drank her life away in her bed of satin. Elof picked up his wine glass and held it up. "Let's have a toast. To the Egil clan and Aamber's ultimate death."

"Hear, hear!" his father shouted, taking a deep gulp of his wine. His mother weakly raised her glass and took a sip. They immediately began eating again. His parents had never been much for small talk.

Elof eyed his parents over the rim of his cup. "Mom, Dad, I just wanted to tell you that you were the worst parents a kid could ever have, and I am forever grateful for the horrible, wretched man you have made me. Now we shall toast to your ultimate death."

His parents froze; his dad's fork was halfway to his mouth. Elof raised his glass and took a long drink. His dad started to choke, bringing his hand to his throat. His mother wasn't far behind. Elof watched them slowly choke to death, unable to breathe because of the poison he'd slipped into their wine. His father grabbed for a knife on the table but couldn't even make it out of his seat and ended up sprawled out over the tabletop. His mother just laid her head down, her misery finally at its end. Elof smiled darkly and continued eating, satisfied that now he was the leader of the Egil clan. Now he'd proven to himself he was strong enough to kill his family. Next, Aamber.

The men returned with horses, including Cinnamon. Aamber rode Cinnamon, who plodded along. The small horse was as tired as Aamber was. Cinnamon was not accustomed to carrying more than Aamber's weight and, in the past week, she'd been carrying multiple passengers. Jasper lay across Cinnamon's back behind Aamber, covered in a cloak. The rest of their trek to the camp was uneventful and, when they appeared through the large stone pass, the people cheered.

Aamber swung down. The people took the last of the injured soldiers away and also took the dead to be prepared for burial. "Hey, guys, wait," Aamber called to the rest of the original rescue team.

The last four of her comrades turned to face her, tired and sad for their lost friends, but happy they'd completed their mission. "I'd appreciate it if you'd keep what you learned about me to yourselves. Not everyone in the camp would see things as you do."

All four nodded and headed toward their tents without ceremony. Aamber found Carla May. "Where's the prince?"

She motioned to a small tent with four soldiers guarding each corner. "How's he doing?"

A bright smile wreathed her face but Aamber could read the sadness in her eyes. "I'm hopeful, dear. He's young and was in good shape. He's got that much going for him. But they beat him bad, dear, and he lost a lot of blood. I'm getting as much broth and fluids down him as possible, but he's starting to develop a fever. I'm worried infection is setting in his wounds. I'm honestly not sure whether he'll make it or not. It's up to him and God now. He's going to always need someone by his side until he's better but I don't have a nurse to spare.

"He'll need his bandages changed every few hours, broth spooned into his mouth, and a cool cloth kept to his head. Someone to sponge-bathe him and keep his bedding clean. The army is doing well with their scouts now and I believe they should be able to spare you. But, oh, commander. You have no idea how much it raised their spirits when you rode in with the prince alive. I'm afraid if he dies the army will lose hope." Carla May paused, shaking her head. "Are you up for the job of nursing him?"

Aamber nodded. The whole Egil clan couldn't stop her. "Great! Go ahead and go see to him. I'll make sure to send you fresh broth and supplies every few hours. What you need for now should already be there." She waved Aamber off with her dark hand.

Aamber walked to the tent. The soldier standing guard opened the flap for her as she entered. She gave him a thank-you smile and ducked in. Michal was lying in the middle of the small tent on a pallet of animal skins. His skin was pale and a pained expression graced his face but his chest rose and fell in a smooth rhythm.

Aamber took off her weapons and tarp bag and put them in the corner. A bucket of drinking water was next to his head and there were a few clean rags beside it. Aamber dipped one in the water, wrung it out, and placed it on his forehead. Carla May was right. His skin was on fire. Bandages covered the cuts all around his arms and a cloth had been wrapped tightly around the wound on his head. They'd bathed him and removed his clothes to allow for easier nursing care. He was under a light blanket to keep him warm but to allow the heat of the fever to escape. They'd even cut his long blond hair and trimmed what was left of his broken nails.

Aamber knew the Vikings had pulled many of his toenails and fingernails off. Only a few bits of nail remained on each. They'd cut him slowly on the most sensitive parts of his skin and Aamber knew many would leave scars. He'd be forever branded by what he survived on the inside and the outside, and her heart hurt that he would forever have the reminders on his very skin. But, to her, he was the most beautiful, bravest man she'd ever met. It was then the realization hit her full force like a sucker punch. She was completely and irrevocably in love with Michal.

Aamber pushed the thoughts out of her mind and continued to bathe his face, then noticed the small bowl of broth beside the water bucket. Michal had yet to open his eyes once but Aamber knew nutrients would be desperately needed if he was ever to get better. After propping him into a sitting position on some pillows, his eyes finally flickered open, but not for long.

Aamber picked up the broth and spoon. Blowing on the steam, she whispered, "Michal, you need to drink some of this broth to help you get better. Your citizens need you. Your country needs you. I need you to get better." She spooned the broth into his mouth; a little leaked out the side of his lips but he swallowed. She took another of the clean cloths and caught what was spilled.

"Good, good, Michal. That's it! At this rate, you're going to get better in no time!" She continued this process until she ran out of broth and then helped him lie back down. He started shivering and his teeth chattered. She tucked the blanket around him but it didn't help.

Carla May stuck her head in the tent. "You might have to hold him, girl. There's nothing better than body heat. Here, I'll stay in here a while until you get him warm to preserve your reputation." Aamber knew her cheeks flushed bright red but she pulled Michal up, got behind him, and pulled him into her lap. She wrapped her arms around his chest and before long he clung to her arms, shivering.

Aamber put her chin on his head. Despite all he'd been through, he still had his distinct smell of fresh air and fresh spring grass. He was heavy on her lap and Aamber reached down and pulled his blanket up around his shoulders. Seeing his chest made her cheeks burn and she had a hard time averting her eyes.

"He had fluid buildup on the top of his head where they'd held him up by the hair so much," Carla May informed her solemnly. Aamber's eyes stung. It was one of her father's classic moves. That was why she always kept her hair in two braids. He had to work twice as hard to grab all her hair. Aamber wondered if she'd ever spent more than the time it took to wash her hair with it down in her life except for the time Michal and she had gone swimming. Women often strolled through the town, their hair flowing in waves down their backs. Aamber envied their freedom but could never bring herself to do likewise.

Aamber brought her face down and pressed her cheek to his, salty tears running down her face. "Oh, Michal. I'm so sorry. This is all my fault. If I'd only stayed on the *Calder* and never left, my father would have never come here and tortured you so. I'm so sorry," she whispered in his ear.

Aamber continued to cry, holding him in her arms. To her surprise, he reached up his hand and clasped hers. He slowly turned his head and looked into her red eyes. Reaching his shaking hand up he pushed a stray lock of hair that'd escaped one of her braids out of her eyes and whispered back, "It's not your fault." Then he fell right back to sleep.

Carla May watched the young girl hold the prince and saw them whisper something to each other. She'd heard rumors they were in love but didn't believe it until she saw it for herself. Both kids had experienced so much pain in their young lives. They looked at each other the same way her husband and she looked at each other all those years ago. She hoped they were smart enough to hang on to each other but that young woman was in so much pain she wondered if she'd continue to push him away.

When he'd stopped shivering, Aamber got out from behind him and settled beside him, making sure she tucked the blankets comfortably around him. Carla May decided to risk asking the girl a question. "Why don't you two just have the preacher marry you? That way I wouldn't have to sit in here too."

Aamber tossed her a surprised look over her shoulder but wouldn't look away from the prince for long. "We're only friends. Besides, I'm not royalty. He needs a queen who can help him lead his people."

The older woman chuckled. "Oh, please. You're the only reason the people have been able to keep it together! Without you, we'd be dead! And besides, you are royalty. You are a Viking princess, aren't you?"

The older woman saw the girl's shoulder tense. Without looking at Carla May, Aamber replied. "There's no such thing as a Viking princess."

Carla May decided to press. She had no interest in causing the girl harm and wanted Ruth to realize that, no matter what her past was, people could still love her. It wasn't as if she had any control over what family she was born into. "Well, they may not call it that, but it's the same concept. I mean, your father is basically the king of the *Calder*. It's just a ship instead of land. Which would make you the princess."

The girl finally faced her, her face unreadable. "Who told you Einar Egil was my father?"

The older woman smiled. "Well, Michal did, indirectly anyway. When they brought him in, he kept saying something about Einar and Aamber Rose and Ruth." She shrugged. "I put two and two together when I remembered the story of Einar's daughter dying a few years back. But don't worry, dear. I'm the only one who heard. Your secret's safe with me."

Aamber evaluated the older woman, considering whether she could trust her or not. She was plump with chocolate brown skin. Her eyes were like dark coffee and her hair was pulled back into a tight braid. She sat on a chair knitting, never taking her eyes off her work. She seemed sincere, and Aamber honestly wondered how many secrets the older woman did know. Obviously, the woman was sharp and didn't miss much.

Aamber hated the fact that many were figuring out her secret and she knew it wouldn't be long before everyone knew. Captain Cullard had told her she wouldn't be able to run from her past forever; that it would catch up with her someday. Maybe all this was happening because of her lying for five years about who she was, but why would God punish her for that! She'd truly tried to become Ruth. How could she deflect suspicion without lying?

"I never said it was true," she shot at Carla May, hoping to create reasonable doubt.

"You never denied it, either. Just as you've never denied being in love which Michal." Aamber was getting irritated. Why did everyone think it was their responsibility to tell her and Michal how they felt?

She turned back to Michal and wiped his forehead again. "Even if I was in love with him, it would never work. I'm not royalty and he needs someone who can help him lead his people. Someone who they will always trust, who doesn't have a past like mine. Someone good enough for him." Aamber honestly wondered if she was trying to convince Carla May or herself.

"Child, if anyone's proven their loyalty to this country, it's you. And you're one of the best leaders I've ever seen. The only others I've seen that could compete with you are the royal family themselves. You're everything Michal could ask for in a queen!"

Aamber just shook her head and the older woman sighed. "You're an amazing Christian and that's what's most important."

Aamber looked up at the tent ceiling. "I agree being a Christian is what's most important. But I'll only ever be Michal's friend. He's too smart to try to make me his queen."

The two women sat in silence for a few moments. Carla knew the girl's low self-esteem was the product of her childhood. She'd tried. Now it was up to Michal to convince her she was the one for him. Aamber didn't realize how much of an open book she was. Many said they could never tell what she was thinking but Carla believed they weren't looking closely enough. Everything the girl did was for God, Michal, and the people. She never thought of herself or her own safety. What more did they need to know?

"By the way, everyone's been wondering where the princess is. Rumors have been flying and no one is sure what to believe."

Aamber leaned against one of the tent's posts and closed her eyes. "I can't tell you where the princess is."

"You mean you don't know? Everyone says you're the only one who knows," Carla replied surprised.

"No, I know where she is and what she's doing. But, like I said in the beginning, she's fighting the war on a different front and, if I say any more, I could potentially put her and others in danger. All they need to know is that she is safe and is fighting for them. It's up to Michal whether he wants to tell them or not when he gets well."

Carla nodded. Then she decided to press Aamber on their earlier conversation just a little bit more. "What if Michal feels differently than you do about you becoming his queen?"

Aamber looked at the older woman, who'd finally stopped her knitting to watch her reaction. "I guess we'll cross that bridge if we get to it." The older woman smiled, then continued her work, seemingly happy with Aamber's answer.

A week later, Aamber was asleep with her head on the edge of Michal's pallet. She'd been catching a few hours at times when he didn't need her. His fever had left but he was still very weak and hadn't stayed awake more than a few seconds at a time. Aamber was exhausted from the constant praying, nursing, and worrying. Carla May hadn't been able to peel her away from Michal's side for a moment.

Michal opened his eyes and wondered where he was. Everything was blurry and his stomach felt as if it was on the sea in a storm. The last thing he remembered was being in jail. Then he had flashes of an angel with red hair setting him free and caring for his wounds, even holding him when he couldn't get warm. How long had he been out? He turned his head to the side and squeezed his eyes shut, hoping the world would stop spinning.

When he opened his eyes again, he noticed Aamber's head resting on the edge of his pallet. It dawned on him that she'd been the angel and, even though they'd only known each other for a little over a year, she'd been protecting his people and nursing him back to health. She slept with one hand under her head, her face pointing toward his head, her long red eyelashes contrasted against her bright porcelain skin. Freckles dotted her nose and her fingernails were long and caked with dirt. Her slender hand lay next to her face and her hair was in its usual braids, but several locks had come loose. She hadn't redone them in days. A sliver of sunlight came through a crack in the tent, making her face glow.

It took all his strength, but he reached over and stroked her soft, silky hair. Her amber-colored eyes fluttered open and looked up at him. To his surprise, she didn't move and allowed him to continue stroking her hair for a few seconds. "You're awake. How are you feeling?" she almost whispered, her voice groggy from sleep.

He smiled, feeling how cracked his lips were. "Weak, but I'm powerful hungry and could drink the whole ocean."

A beautiful smile bloomed on her face like a rose in the spring. "Thank goodness! That's a good sign. Here, let me give you a drink and then I'll go get you some food."

She helped him into a sitting position; To his horror, he realized he was naked. He pulled the blanket to his chin when she reached over to get his water. When she turned back toward him, she seemed confused, and then it dawned on her, making her cheeks blush a beautiful pink. It was obvious to Michal that she'd been there a while and had ceased to be uncomfortable with his state of undress. She brought the ladle to his lips, not meeting his eyes.

He drank deep, wanting all she was willing to give him. After he'd finished, he leaned back, the cool water making him feel refreshed. "I'll go get you your soup now." She practically ran out of the tent and Michal had to laugh at her childish excitement.

An older woman entered the room not long after Aamber had left, carrying a bowl of soup and a shirt. "Well, well! Looks who's finally decided to wake. Goodness, boy, you had us scared to death. I'm Carla May. Miss Aamber put me in charge of nursing in this camp. But when she returned after rescuing you a week ago, she wouldn't leave your side. No siree! You're awful lucky to have a friend like her. She wanted to bring your soup back but I told her I could manage to feed you while she washed up and got some sleep. I told her she wasn't allowed back in this tent until tomorrow, I did! But don't worry boy, your girl will be back in the morning. It's evening now," she said with a wink.

Michal continued to hold the sheet around his chest. The woman set down her load and turned to him with a shirt, then rolled her eyes. "Boy, I've raised four sons. You ain't got nothing I've not seen before. Now put on this shirt and I'll get your soup. It's mostly broth at the moment but it has more in it than the broth Aamber's been spooning into your mouth the past week. I imagine it'll be a while before you're up for solid food."

Michal quickly dressed. "Would you happen to have any pants, ma'am?"

She crossed her arms and considered him. "Can you get them on and off as needed, son? You're still pretty weak." He was quick to nod. He didn't like being so exposed. Carla shrugged. "All right, I'll go get you your pants while your soup cools. That way, you'll also be more comfortable while I feed ya." The woman left in a bustle and Michal felt as if a tornado had left his tent. He couldn't help contrasting Carla and Aamber's presence. Aamber felt like a gentle summer breeze.

When he woke up the next morning, Aamber sat by his side again. She looked refreshed and was darning some clothing. He tried to push himself up and she reached down to help him. "Good morning," he breathed. Michal couldn't believe just sitting up winded him. He had a lot of work ahead of him.

"Morning," she replied. Michal could feel the awkwardness between them. He didn't like it and decided to get right to the point.

"So, what should I call you, Ruth or Aamber?"

Her sewing froze, and she refused to look at him. Finally, she sighed and began to explain. "I'm sorry I didn't tell you. I was hoping if you didn't know who I was, you would be safer. Someone can't torture you for information you don't have. I was wrong. I hated lying to you and Chrystal, but I didn't feel like I had any other choice. And, if word reached my father that I was alive, he was sure to try and hunt me down, which ended up happening, anyway. I'll understand if you want me to leave and never see me again," she said, with a single tear running down her beautiful cheek.

They sat in silence for a moment. "Aamber, look at me." She shook her head. Michal pulled her chin to meet his eyes as he'd done the first time they danced together. Her amber eyes finally met his, the fear and pain emanating from them. "If you ever try to leave me,

I will hunt you down, tie you up, and never let you out of my sight again. I'm considering doing that, anyway. You are the best friend I've ever had. I understand you were trying to protect us. But from now on, no more secrets. We fight our battles together with God as our leader. Agreed?"

Aamber turned her face into Michal's hand. "Michal, I've been hiding so many secrets for so long. Letting that go scares me more than anything but I want to. I'm going to make mistakes and you're probably going to have to forgive a lot but I want to try and be completely open with you. I just don't know how right now."

Michal's heart broke. He could only imagine all she had had to suffer at Einar's hands and the thoughts made his blood boil. "Aamber, it's scary for me too. I've never been completely open with anyone outside of my family, and I'm going to mess up just as much as you. But we'll figure it out together. All I'm asking is we try." Aamber just nodded, holding his hand to her cheek with her own.

For the next month, Aamber nursed Michal back to health and he slowly regained his strength. They'd heard about Elof murdering his parents and the Vikings had started looking hard for their camps but, by the grace of God, hadn't found one. The Vikings had dramatically decreased sending out scouting parties because they doubted that any more lost citizens or soldiers would ever be found. Also, the Vikings had taken to traveling in large numbers. Picking them off little by little had become more and more difficult.

Michal told Aamber to tell the people reinforcements were coming. They'd hoped to keep the news from the Vikings but the people so desperately needed hope and the knowledge that they weren't just sitting ducks. They'd also started working with the soldiers again, continuing their training and making weapons. They had a big battle ahead of them and, with God's help, they would be ready.

On one sunny afternoon, Aamber and Michal were working together, making arrows and watching the soldiers practice their weaponry while sitting on the bank of the stream that flowed through the middle of the valley. It reminded Michal of the days they'd gone swimming and he wished desperately they could go back to that day if only for a minute. Michal had decided only to call her Aamber in private. They would tell the people who she really was after the war was over, at least those who'd not already figured it out.

Michal knew Aamber well enough to know she was considering asking him something. When she was deciding something. she always chewed on her bottom lip and scrunched her eyebrows, an expression he found quite adorable. "Penny for your thoughts?"

He chuckled at the shocked look on her face. After looking back down at her work, she asked, "What would you say to us sinking the *Calder* and the other Viking ships?"

"What?" he asked, dropping his work into his lap.

This time it was Aamber's turn to be amused at his shocked expression. "The Egil clan is weaker now than it has ever been before. If we were to destroy their ships, we would destroy the clan's weapon resources and home. They wouldn't be able to escape and we could finish them. That way they'd never be able to hurt anyone like this again."

Michal chewed on the inside of his cheek, which Aamber had noticed was his habit when deciding something. It was a long time before he said anything again and, by the end of his reverie, he'd given up working on the arrow and stared out over the soldiers. She was right but that would mean the Vikings wouldn't be able to leave if they decided to—but then they could always come back with reinforcements and destroy his country all over again. He couldn't let that happen and he couldn't let them do this to anyone else. "Let's do it."

Aamber nodded. "All right, now we have to figure out how we are going to get close to the ship without being seen and, once we get there, how are we going to sink it?"

Michal leaned forward and picked a hallow reed off the bank. Aamber would often use them to make flutes as presents for the children stuck in camp and bored. Michal cut the ends even and then headed into the water. He put the reed in his mouth and went under with the top of the reed sticking up. He even swam around a little.

After settling back on the bank, Aamber said, "Showoff. You could have just showed me." She avoided staring at how his white shirt clung to his well-formed abs.

He shook the water off his head at her. "Where's the fun in that? And, as far as sinking the ships, I figured we could saw holes in the side. Think of it. We'll send four swimmers toward each ship from different directions, so the watchmen don't see the reeds coming. Then they'll each saw a hole in the bottom of the ship. Multiple holes will ensure the Vikings can't stop them all before enough water has leaked through."

He began chewing the inside of his cheek again. "What about prisoners kept in the hulls?"

Aamber hadn't considered that. A slow smile crept over her face. "I have an idea."

CHAPTER 9

SINKING THE SHIPS

For the eyes of the Lord are over the righteous,
and his ears are open unto their prayers: but the
face of the Lord is against them that do evil.

1 Peter 3:12 KJV

Océan, A.D. 907

Later that night, Aamber rode Cinnamon through the dark forest and Michal followed her on Buck. She'd insisted on going alone but Michal had refused. They were headed back to the secret tavern. Aamber had another contact she believed could get them the information they sought. After giving Michal the same instructions she'd given Chrystal and Gideon that night, they descended the cliff and headed into the tavern.

Jo called out his usual greeting. "Hey, Ruthie! Where've you been? We've been missing you."

Aamber walked up to the bar and placed her hand on it. Tonight, musicians were playing loud music and the place was packed. Apparently, many would rather escape here than deal with the war in the cities. "Hey, Jo! Sorry I haven't been here in so long. I've been busy."

The old man nodded. "We figured you were off fighting the war."

Aamber nodded. "I probably won't be able to visit regularly again until it's over. Have you seen Oct around?"

Jo pointed at a table in the middle of the room. Men were surrounding a smaller gentleman, getting ready the beat him. "Hey, hey, hey what's going on?" Aamber asked as she stepped in the middle. Michal couldn't believe she'd just stepped in the middle of a brewing brawl and grabbed the hilt of his sword.

"He cheated us at cards and stole our money," Rusty growled.

Aamber rolled her eyes. "Oct, just give them the money and come with me. There's something I need to discuss with you."

With reluctance, Oct gave up the coins and followed Aamber and Michal out of the smoky tavern. They led the little man over where their horses were waiting for them. "Gosh, Ruth. Can't you ever give me a break?" Oct whined when they were alone.

Aamber stared at the little man blankly. He was short with black hair and shifty brown eyes. "I did, Oct, I just saved your hide in there."

Oct crossed his arms. "What do you want? I haven't swindled any of your friends in a long time. I thought we were square."

Aamber made a tsk-tsk sound. "You shouldn't be swindling anyone, Oct, and besides, I told you the day we met you'd never be rid of me."

This time it was Oct who rolled his eyes. "Who's your friend?"

"That's not what you need to know." Turning to Michal, she said. "This is Octopus. We all call him that because he's the best actor slash conman you can find. He can blend with any crowd." An idea of what she was planning started forming in Michal's mind. Turning back to Oct, she continued. "I have a job for you. One that, if you

203

complete it, will get all your crimes forgiven and even land you a steady job if you want it."

Aamber could tell she'd piqued Oct's interest, and he said. "I'm listening."

"You're not going to like it," she warned.

Oct shrugged. "You think I like being a conman?" Michal wondered what job she was offering this man.

"We need you to sneak onto the Viking ships and release any prisoners on board."

The little men tried to bolt, but Aamber was too quick and grabbed his arm. "Are you crazy?! That would be suicide! And why would you want me to do that anyway?" Oct practically yelled at her.

Aamber didn't flinch. "It's none of your business to know the why. All I need to know is if you could do it."

Oct looked to the sky. "Of course I could do it! I'll need your help though. What makes you think there's prisoners on the ships anyway?"

Aamber just narrowed her eyes and stared the little man down. "All right, all right, all right. I'll do it. But what is the job you're promising me?"

"Court jester."

"Are you serious?" the little man's eyes bulged.

"Yes. You would be perfect for the job. Instead of using your talents to cheat people, you'd be using them to bring people joy."

The little man sighed. "So, you're trying to reform me?"

Aamber shook her head. "Only you could do that. I'm just trying to give you the opportunity to; that is, if you want it. Otherwise, I can find someone else to do the job." Michal was surprised. They hadn't had a court jester for years, but if that's what it took, he was more than willing to do it.

Michal watched the little man consider Aamber's offer. "Are you sure there's going to be a royal court by the time this is all over?"

"I have faith," Aamber replied with a shrug.

He considered her some more. "Fine, but that doesn't mean I'm going to be converting to your religion."

Aamber nodded. "I know that."

He sighed. "All right, when do you need the job done?"

"Tomorrow night."

"That isn't much time!" Once again, Aamber just stared at him. Oct started pacing back and forth formulating a plan. "How many men would I have at my disposal?"

Aamber shrugged. "However many you need, but the fewer the better."

"I want at least two guards and someone who knows how Vikings talk to coach me in their nuances and protocols. Not to mention I'm going to need Viking clothes and help with the whole armband thing. And you'll make sure your men won't try and attack me, won't you?"

Aamber nodded. "I can help you with all that."

He sighed. "Fine. For us to be ready we must start preparing now. Let's go to your camp."

Shaking her head, Aamber said, "You will not be going to our camp. I have some men who are going to meet us in the forest with supplies. If you're captured by the Vikings, I don't trust you not to flip on us."

"Whatever," the little man growled. "Let's just get this over with."

Aamber swung up on Cinnamon. Oct tried to pull up behind her but Michal put his horse between them. "You're riding with me."

Oct furrowed his brows and looked to Aamber. "This your boyfriend or something? He's a little possessive, don't you think?"

"Just shut up and do what he says, Oct."

Michal reached down his hand and pulled Oct up behind him. "Good luck with her, buddy," the little man said. "I can't tell you how many men I've seen her put in their place over the years. I actually pity the poor sap she allows to catch her someday if she ever does."

Aamber tossed him a glare and spurred Cinnamon on. Michal couldn't help smiling. "I've seen her put a couple in their places but the man who's smart enough to be patient and wait for her to be ready will be a lucky man indeed."

Oct chuckled. "Oh, man. You're that far gone are you." Michal didn't answer and they continued the rest of their journey in silence.

Joseph and Jackson were waiting for them at the prearranged spot with Viking clothes and bands. Jackson raised his eyebrows when they swung down off the horses. "This is your contact?" he asked incredulously. "He isn't any bigger than a kid!"

Oct crossed his arms, angry at the insult. "You're more than welcome to attempt this job yourself."

"Better than putting our lives on the line to trust a kid!" Jackson shot back.

"All right! Enough! Both of you!" Michal spat. "I don't care if you hate each other. You must work together on this job. After that, you'll never have to speak to each other again, God willing. Now, let's get your costumes fitted."

They spent the next hour fitting the men in the pilfered Viking clothes, with Aamber using the needle and thread she kept in the pocket of her dress to make alterations. When Oct noticed her fitting the clothes to Jackson and Joseph, he paused. "I thought you and your boyfriend would be my guards!"

Aamber used her teeth to snap the thread she'd been sewing with. "Nope, meet your guards, Jackson and Joseph," she said. motioning to the two men respectively.

"But why can't you do it!" he whined.

"None of your business," Michal snapped. There was too large a risk of one of the Vikings recognizing Aamber or Michal. They hoped to get the prisoners off the ship with the least amount of bloodshed possible.

"Man, why are you sending me in without any information as to why we are doing this! Don't you think that's important for me to know?" Oct grumbled.

"No, we don't. Now, let's go over the plan again. You'll sneak onto the first ship. The prisoners will be kept in the hull. Avoid eye contact as you go but walk like you belong there. You'll probably have to kill the guard before he can sound the alarm. Afterward, Joseph and Jackson will ensure no one sneaks up on Oct while he's picking the locks. Then you will rush the stairs, jumping off the side of the ship, or reclaiming your boat. There'll be swimmers in the water to help the prisoners get to shore. You three will swim to the next ship, claiming you'd been tossed off the previous ship in the chaos. At this point, the alarm will be sounded and the Vikings will be distracted. Use that to your advantage. Work as quickly and quietly as possible," Aamber recited.

They finished the fittings and Oct piped up. "Now I need someone to coach me on how they walk and talk."

Jackson and Joseph looked to Aamber, who continued adjusting the clothes as she spoke. "Vikings always walk with a purpose. They're some of the laziest people you'll ever meet and therefore never walk without one. You almost never see a Viking smile. They're always either bored or irritated, so be careful about facial expressions. Body language is important. Vikings are smart, otherwise they wouldn't still be alive. As far as the way they talk, do any of you men know ship lingo?"

All three shook their heads. Aamber spent the next few hours coaching them on ship terms and, by the time they'd finished, she believed they'd created some very good Viking look-alikes. She tied the Uffe clan colors stripes on each man's bicep. Because of their large numbers, it wouldn't be uncommon for a Viking not to recognize an Uffe clan member.

"All right men, I think you're ready. Spend the rest of today sleeping. You'll need to be well rested for your adventure tonight."

Jackson yawned and stretched. "You don't have to tell me twice. Good luck with the rest of the men," he saluted and began to climb a tree.

Joseph began to climb up behind him. Oct looked at Aamber. "You're sure about this?"

Aamber nodded, and then she and Michal mounted their horses. Oct climbed up behind the other men and they headed back to the camp. When they were out of earshot, Michal pulled Buck up beside Cinnamon.

"You sure about that guy? I mean, I trust your judgment, but he seems kind of unreliable."

Aamber sighed. "He is, but he's the best of the best. I think Jackson and Joseph will be able to handle him easily enough. He's slick but Joseph is sharp and sees everything. Jackson's more brute force," she chuckled.

Michal nodded. "So, let me make sure I understand the plan. We're designating two hundred swimmers to saw holes in each ship as those three release the prisoners. Another 50 will be in small lifeboats around the ships, but out of sight. The swimmers who've finished their part of the sawing will help the prisoners get to the boats. Once a boat is full, they'll meet more men on the shore, who will take care of them as needed." Aamber nodded. "A lot could go wrong with this plan because of the sheer number of people involved but, if it works, not only will we cripple the Vikings but we'll also most likely gain some more soldiers in the form of escaped prisoners."

"We'll probably need to station soldiers around the rescue crew on shore," Aamber replied.

Michal nodded. "It's going to be a long night."

Joseph woke up around sunset and nudged Jackson, who was sleeping on the branch next to him. It was time to head towards the shore. He reached into his bag and pulled out their bread and cheese, handing some to Jackson, whom he had to nudge again to wake. He then handed some up to the little guy Aamber had hired to help them. He hoped this little guy wouldn't let them down.

"So, do you think they're a couple?" Jackson asked around a mouthful of bread.

Joseph rolled his eyes. Jackson's favorite subject was to speculate whether Aamber and Michal were a couple when they weren't around. It was the most popular subject among all the soldiers but Joseph didn't care. He wished them well, but he refused to speculate on their personal lives. They deserved more respect than that.

"I do," Oct piped up enthusiastically.

Joseph couldn't help himself. "And what makes you think you would know? You just met them!" he said, leaning to the side so he could look up at the strange little man.

"I still don't know who the boyfriend even is but I've known Ruth a long time. Last night, when they came to hire me, the guy refused to let me ride behind Ruth on her horse. Little does he know, if any other guy had tried to dictate who could ride with her or not, she'd have taken his head off. She didn't even flinch when I made the remark about him being possessive of her."

Jackson shook his head. "That doesn't mean anything. They've been through a lot together now. Any one of us would try to protect Ruth. She's like a sister to us."

"You didn't let me finish. When I teased the guy about her torturing the poor sap who was actually able to catch her he told me the guy would be lucky."

Jackson shook his head again. "We all would have told you likewise."

"All right, then how do you explain me seeing them making out through the window of the tavern before they came to get me?" he shot at the men below.

"You did not," Joseph shot back. "I know that's a lie because even if they did make out, which they wouldn't, they'd never be careless enough to be caught by anyone. And I won't have you tarnishing their reputation that way."

"Well, maybe I didn't see that. Either way, I think they're a couple," Oct conceded.

Soon they were headed off toward the sea. The sun had just set when they arrived. The small boat was sitting where Aamber had said it would be. This was also the signal that the rest were ready and waiting. They climbed in and headed toward the first ship, which was anchored in the deep waters just offshore. It was going to be a long night with 51 ships to sink, each with the carrying capacity of about four hundred people.

When they reached the ship, they tied their boat to one of the waiting hooks and climbed up the ropes that hung down the side. The man on the moon watched them with his concerned face, while the stars twinkled. They reached the top and jumped over the side. Looking around, there weren't many Vikings on the ship and hope filled the small group's hearts. Without reaching back to help his comrades as Aamber had instructed, Joseph headed toward where Aamber had said the door to the prison would be. No one noticed them. Joseph felt their footsteps pound in their ears.

They reached the door and headed down. Oct couldn't help wondering how Ruth knew exactly where the door would be. When she'd described its location, he figured she'd been guessing but she had given too much detail for that to be true. The guard was leaned back in a chair against a wall, with its front two legs off the ground. His snores echoed off the ship's walls. Oct began picking the two prisoners' chains, while Jackson watched the door and Joseph watched the guard. He wouldn't kill a man who was asleep and, if he stayed asleep, he wouldn't have to kill him at all. They were surprised there weren't more prisoners on the ship but figured they'd probably be keeping most of their prisoners on land. The men on the ships were close to death anyway.

Now for the most dangerous part. To his surprise, Oct helped a man up without having to be asked and Jackson helped the other. They headed up the stairs, Joseph walking backward to prevent the guard from waking and attacking them from behind. When they'd made it to the deck, someone yelled "Hey!" but they were over the side of the ship before another word could be spoken.

They swam back toward their small boat after handing off their prisoners to the underwater swimmers, who stuck hollow reeds in the prisoners' mouths and went back under the surface. The Vikings still onboard were yelling as the men began rowing toward the next ship. Oct looked back and noticed the large ship was beginning to sink, its hull deeper in the water than its stern. "Oh, my gosh. You're crazy! You're sinking the Vikings' ships! That's what this was all about?!"

"Shut up," both men called back to him.

They repeated the same process on the next four ships, springing a total of 12 prisoners. The Vikings never noticed them. The guards had even left their posts trying to help the Vikings on the other ships stay afloat but the Vikings had begun swimming toward their other ships, making their anonymity harder to keep. One even pulled himself up onto their lifeboat.

"Can you believe this! How are our boats sinking? They're the thing we take the most care of," the Viking exclaimed when he was safe in their boat. He tapped his chin. "Actually, they're the only thing we take care of. I haven't seen any citizens that could have done it!" His long greasy hair dripped seawater. He wore no shirt, no shoes, and his pants were in rags. The men shook their heads, trying to look incredulous as they kept rowing.

The Viking studied them. "I don't think I've ever seen you three before."

"Excuse me! How dare you question us! We're the ones kind enough to give you a ride in our boat. As a matter of fact, get out!" Oct said and pushed the large man overboard.

Jackson and Joseph inwardly panicked, but when the Viking resurfaced, he no longer had any suspicion in his eyes. Joseph looked back at the strange small man. "I'm finally beginning to understand why Ruth insisted you come along. You really know how to read and interact with people." Oct laughed.

They continued their work through the night and finally began to climb the side of the last ship, the *Calder*, which was their biggest ship of all. When Joseph grabbed the railing of the ship, someone suddenly cut the rope. Luckily, Jackson grabbed Joseph's ankle and Oct grabbed his just before they fell. "Hey, what's the big idea!" he called up.

A Viking leaned over the side and looked down at them. "If we let everyone on this ship she'll be overwhelmed. Swim to the shore!"

"NO!" Joseph called up, pulling himself and his comrades up with all his strength. When they'd finally all made it on deck, the Viking who'd cut their rope rolled his eyes. "Whatever. At least no more can make it up here." The three stood catching their breath and then headed toward the prison.

"Hey, where ya goin'?" the Viking called to them.

Oct turned to face him. "What's it to ya?" he called back. Joseph felt his blood pressure rise. They were starting to attract the attention of others.

The Viking's eyes narrowed and that's when they knew they were in deep water. "I'm the first mate of this ship. When the captain's gone, everything goes through me. But if you three were really Vikings, you would have known that" he said, drawing his sword. The ten other Vikings on the ship followed suit. They surrounded the three men, backing them into a corner.

"What are we going to do?" Jackson whispered to Joseph.

Michal and Aamber had been two of the swimmers. The cold, salty water burned their eyes and they were chilled to the bone. They were responsible for any Vikings who discovered how the ships were sinking and attacked their people. The plan had gone off without a hitch until she didn't see any men jump off the *Calder*. Aamber poked her head above the surface and saw Michal fighting with a particularly large Viking.

Aamber quietly swam up behind him and ran him through with her dagger. He slowly released Michal and sank into his watery grave, blood staining the water. "Thanks," Michal breathed.

"I think the men are in trouble. I saw them head toward the *Calder* a long time ago but no one ever jumped off."

They began swimming toward the ship. They could just hear the men's voices on deck. "But if you three were really Vikings, you would have known that," Aamber heard a familiar voice saying. Kevin. He had been Einar's best friend when they were kids and was one of the only other children to survive the *Calder*.

When they arrived at the side of the ship, the climbing ropes had been cut. An idea popped into Aamber's head. "Follow me."

They swam to the front of the ship, and Aamber turned to Michal. "Can you help me reach the mermaid's tail?"

Michal picked her up so she could reach the tail of the mermaid. Aamber grabbed the slimy wood and she began using the grooves in the mermaid's scales to climb. Aamber's dress kept tripping her and getting in the way. Somehow Michal had pulled himself up and was climbing behind her. Aamber slipped and almost fell but Michal grabbed her until she could regain her grip.

When they reached the edge of the railing, Aamber looked over to assess the situation before hopping aboard. Eleven Vikings surrounded her men, swords drawn.

"Hey, hey. we're from the Uffe clan! We can't be expected to know every Egil clan leader!" Oct was saying.

Aamber inwardly groaned. Every Uffe clan member would have known who Kevin was since he was second in command on the *Calder*. She hopped over the side, making sure no one heard her, and turned to help Michal. Jackson pushed in front of Oct. "Listen guys, this is my kid brother. He's as stupid as a box of rocks. That's why we didn't recognize you. Please, we don't want any trouble. We were just headed to relieve the men downstairs."

The men weren't buying it. Aamber and Michal each ran one through with their swords before they even had a chance to turn around. The fight was on. Michal and Aamber fought back-to-back. To Aamber's surprise, it wasn't taking them long to defeat the remaining nine. After defeating another Viking, she turned to face Kevin.

"Well, well, well," he said, "the rumors are true. Little Miss Aamber is still alive. Too bad Odin isn't here to see this. I imagine he would be right pleased."

Aamber refused to let him make her angry because she knew anger could lead to mistakes. She slashed at him but he blocked her blow. They went back and forth a few times. "Kevin, why am I not surprised you're still my brother's lackey?"

Her words hit their mark and Kevin begun slashing crazily, his brown eyes snapping and his red hair falling in his face. They twisted so that she could see that Jackson was struggling with his man but Michal had defeated his adversary and went to help. Oct had snuck down to the dungeon during the fighting and was carrying the prisoners up one by one and tossing them over the sides.

Kevin and Aamber continued fighting. Aamber saw Oct go over the side of the ship after he'd finished freeing the prisoners and the floor began to tip. Their people must have done their job. Next thing she knew, Michal, Joseph, and Jackson were leaning against the rail of the ship, watching her and Kevin fight like they were watching a ball game.

"So, tell me, Aamber. Is it true women lose all their self-esteem after a man steals their innocence?" Aamber could see Michal's face over Kevin's shoulder and inwardly cringed. She'd never told Michal about what Odin had done to her and his shock and anger were instantaneous.

Aamber blocked another of Kevin's blows while she was on one knee and their swords made a cross. "My worth comes from my Heavenly Father, not from any bad experience," she gritted through her teeth.

Before Aamber knew what happened, Michal had run his sword through Kevin's side, and Kevin fell dead before her. "Is it true?" he asked, worry shining from his blue eyes.

Aamber refused to meet his eyes, instead staring down at Kevin's lifeless brown ones. It was hard enough for her to be standing on the deck of the *Calder* again, let alone having this conversation. He grabbed her by her shoulders. "Aamber!"

Aamber twisted out of his grasp. "Michal, don't! We'll talk about this later. Let's go! This ship is sinking."

They jumped over and swam as far from the *Calder* as possible so they wouldn't be sucked under the water with the ship. Their men were waiting for them when they made it to shore. They'd stayed well-hidden and no Vikings had discovered them. The prisoners they'd rescued were already being taken to the camp.

The sun was peeking over the horizon when they made it back to camp and collapsed after their long adventure. They were glad their mission had been successful and, by the grace of God, they hadn't lost a single man. The atmosphere in the camp overall had improved and people now had hope in their eyes. But Aamber knew things between Michal and her were bad. He refused to even meet her gaze. She knew him well enough to know he didn't blame her for her being raped. He was hurt she hadn't told him after they'd promised they wouldn't have any more secrets from each other. Aamber hadn't told him because it was humiliating and she was afraid he'd think less of her or see her as a victim. Unfortunately, though, neither of them was up to addressing the problem today and they immediately retreated to their tents until the next morning.

CHAPTER 10

THE ULTIMATUM

*And thou shalt love the Lord thy God with all
thy heart, and with all thy soul, and with all thy
mind, and with all thy strength: this is the first
commandment. And the second is like, namely this,
Thou shalt love thy neighbor as thyself. There is
none other commandment greater than these.*

Mark 12:30-31 KJV

Océan, A.D. 907

When they awoke the next morning, their men had news for them.
They'd put out feelers the previous day to determine how badly the
Vikings had been crippled from the sinking of their ships. Aamber
worried about how her brother would take the news. The *Calder* had
been the only home he'd ever known and, even after all the terrible
things he'd done, she didn't want him to be in pain. She'd yet to reconcile the fact that he had killed her parents and truly believed it was

216

simply a rumor. Still, the question kept her up at night. She'd replay their two previous meetings repeatedly in her head, wondering if she could have said anything differently to convince him to join them.

Her brother turned out to be a strong leader and had rallied his forces. He was determined to get revenge and had intensified the efforts to find their camps. Aamber went to find Michal, who was practicing his fencing with Joseph. If the men weren't out patrolling the forest, sleeping, or hunting, they were practicing their weaponry skills. "Michal," she said coming up behind him, seeing his back tense at the sound of her voice. "I've received news from the feelers we put out yesterday."

He turned to her, his face an emotionless mask. "The Vikings are naturally quite angry we've sunk their ships and have intensified their search for our camps," she told him "I believe they're getting desperate. Vikings might know how to fight but they don't know how to hunt or survive in the woods. Being able to escape on their ships has always been their greatest weakness, and food stores at the castle are running low. They can always fish but their men are becoming restless and their anxiety is greatly increased. I believe they'll be turning against each other by the time our reinforcements arrive." Michal nodded and returned to fencing with Joseph. If he wanted to be like that, it was fine with her. She went to the nursing camps to help out.

"Sir, may I speak frankly with you?" Joseph asked Michal after Aamber had left.

Michal was surprised. Joseph was one of their older soldiers, being in his mid-thirties, and mostly kept his opinions to himself. Which meant when he did have something to say, most people were smart enough to listen. Michal shrugged. "Fire away."

"You're being a huge jerk," he stated in a manner of fact tone. Michal stared at him open-mouthed as he continued. "That girl has been through horrendous things no one should even hear about and you're angry with her because she didn't tell you? The fact that someone as independent and brave as she is having been raped must cause her a lot of shame and make her feel as if it's her fault. When you learn something like that about someone you love, they need your support. People like her don't keep such things as this away from the people they love because they don't trust them. They keep them away because they're too ashamed to talk about it and fear their loved ones will either look down on them or pity because of it."

Michal was floored. This was the most he'd ever heard Joseph say at one time. Michal swallowed hard. "But we promised each other we weren't going to have any secrets from each other."

Joseph shook his head. "These things take time. Keeping secrets is what has kept Aamber alive all these years. Letting that go has to be hard. What you need to do is to be patient with her and trust in God to reveal all things in due time. The girl trusts you, Michal. More than she's ever trusted anyone in her life, but that doesn't mean it's easy for her."

Michal was very ashamed of his actions and nodded to the older man. "Sounds like you've had a personal experience with this," he ventured. The older man looked down at the sword between his hands, twisted the tip in the dirt, and then looked Michal in the eye. "My daughter went to a dance one night with a boy that we'd forbidden her to be around. On their way home, he raped her. She didn't tell anyone until she discovered she was pregnant. I was heartbroken she'd not told me. It took me years to understand why she hadn't, which put a huge strain on our relationship. I wish someone would have set me down and had a talk with me then and I refuse to stand by and let you make the same mistakes I did."

Michal nodded. "Thank you."

Later that day, Michal took the bowl of soup the serving girl offered him and watched Aamber from a distance. "Are you all right, sir?" the girl asked, seeming to read his mind.

"I'll be all right," he replied, not sparing the girl a glance.

"May I sit with you?" she asked, surprising him. He shrugged and she settled down on the ground next to him. "My name is Macy."

"Nice to meet you," he said, still focusing on Aamber. She was talking with Jackson and Joseph while eating her soup.

"Is it really?" Michal finally turned to his companion, confused by her strange question.

"Of course," he replied, studying her. She had brown hair pulled back in a French braid and large brown eyes. He wouldn't have guessed her to be over 13 until he noticed the small wedding band around her finger.

He nodded toward it. "Who's your husband?"

A gentle look of love appeared on her face. "Conrad Weathersby, he's out on scout right now."

Michal nodded. "How are you two doing after having to move to the camp so suddenly?"

The young woman shrugged. "As well as could be expected. We'd only been married for a day when it happened, so our marriage has got off to an interesting start," she chuckled.

"Oh, gosh," Michal laughed. "I couldn't imagine."

Macy sobered. "You seemed troubled. I was wondering if you needed a friend to talk to. And since my husband isn't here, I figured I could keep you company. Sometimes it helps to talk things out with a stranger."

For the third time in their short conversation, she had surprised Michal. He sighed "I've wronged my friend. I'm trying to think of the best way to apologize to her."

Macy nodded thoughtfully. "Even though my husband and I haven't been married for long, I've noticed after the few tiffs we've had the best results come from us sitting down and being honest with each other." She leaned toward him and whispered. "Ruth's very kind. I'm sure whatever you've done she'll forgive you for."

Michal laughed. "I'm that obvious!"

Macy shrugged. "It might go a long way if you were to tell her how you really feel about her while you're at it."

Out of the corner of her eye, Aamber watched the serving girl Macy sit with Michal and begin a conversation. She couldn't help thinking about how beautiful Macy was. Well, if she's who Michal wanted why should she care? It's not like Michal and she had been courting or anything. Another pang of jealousy went through Aamber when she saw Macy whisper something to him, causing him to laugh. Good riddance, she thought, trying to convince her heart it was how she felt.

Michal tried for the rest of the week to get Aamber alone to apologize but he never could. She was always helping with nursing or cooking or army training or even riding around the camps to see how others fared. He desperately missed their conversations. She'd been the only comfort he'd had during these trying times. One day, he knew he would have to slow down and mourn the death of his parents but for now he simply tried to push thoughts of them from his mind.

He wished he had word of Chrystal. She would be heartbroken when she learned of their parents' demise. Michal hoped he'd be the one to tell her, so he could be there for her in her grief. He shook his head of these thoughts and tried to focus on the task at hand. Aamber had called a meeting to discuss a new technique she'd come up with for picking off the Vikings a few at a time.

"I have an idea. The Vikings are traveling in large groups now and, unless we wage a full battle, we won't be able to kill them all at once. My idea is, instead of sending our soldiers out in groups trying to kill every member of the Viking groups they find, we send them out two by two. What they would do is ambush the Viking groups, killing off a few, and escape into the oblivion of the forest. Two men trying to hide is much easier than ten. And we could try and focus the attacks in areas far away from our camps. This will make the Vikings think our camps are in those areas and search for us there. The close call last night has made me nervous and I believe we need to get more proactive."

The men surrounding her nodded in agreement. The plan was solid and they soon had it arranged with their soldiers. Aamber whistled for Cinnamon so she could travel to the other camps to discuss the plan with them. Michal set about saddling Buck so he could join her.

When he rode up, her face was blank. "Mind if I accompany you?" Her reply was a nonchalant shrug. Before they could exit the valley, though, he motioned for them to stop by putting his closed fist in the air.

"What's wrong?" she asked immediately.

"Aamber, I need to speak with you," he said, desperate.

He could tell he'd only angered her further. "Can't it wait? We need to go," she snapped, spurring Cinnamon on. Riding between the camps took the rest of their day. Not only were the camps large distances from each other, but they also had to avoid Viking patrols and be as quiet as mice. When they were on their way back, they passed near the castle. Suddenly, a male voice rang out through the woods from the direction of the castle.

"This message is for Aamber Rose Egil! Our standoff has gone on long enough. You sunk our home, and now it's time for you to face your punishment. Instead, you and your people hide among the trees like animals, refusing to accept the inevitable. Now hear this!"

Michal and Aamber dismounted their horses and made their way to the edge of the tree line. Elof stood in the middle of the field before the castle drawbridge, calling out his message while holding a sword in the air.

"After tonight, each day you refuse to give yourself up, I will kill a child by cutting off their head at sunset!" Another Viking pushed a little girl forward. The girl was dirty, skinny, and could barely stand. Her hair was gold and, even from their distance, Aamber could tell her eyes were a bright blue. Aamber imagined she looked just as Chrystal would have when she was small.

"It's up to you, Aamber! How many children's lives are worth yours? I don't even care about your people. The only one I want is you!" Michal turned to look at Aamber. Fear unlike he'd ever seen shown in her eyes. He shook his head, having no intention of letting her turn herself over to him. It was a bluff. Michal turned and watched them shove the little girl back into the castle courtyard.

Elof continued. "Or if you'd like, I can stand here and tell your friends all your secrets! Are you listening, soldiers? Did you know the woman you've been following is my full-blooded sister? That she's one of us and has been feeding us your secrets this entire time? She killed your king! She killed your queen! She killed your princess! And she is using your prince! Aamber has stolen, lied, and killed for her own personal gain! She's been playing us all this entire time!

"I thought this was supposed to be a Christian country! How could that be if she's the kind of leader you follow? You will never meet anyone more two-faced. You might think you know her, but I promise you don't. Besides, what else can you expect when you make a woman your leader! Ha! Pain and suffering are what you can expect! She's the one who has caused all your misery. The suffering will never stop until she's dead. So, you decide! Will it be you or her?"

Finally, Elof had finished his tirade and Michal turned back to go to their horses. To his horror, Aamber was gone. Something glittered off the side of Buck's saddle. He walked over, and Aamber's silver cross with the amber rose hung off his saddle horn.

Michal spent the rest of the night searching for Aamber, almost getting caught by the Vikings on multiple occasions. He begged God to help him find her. If she turned herself over to the Vikings, they wouldn't just kill her. Killing her would be too merciful. They would slowly torture the life, spirit, and soul out of her. He knew. It's what they'd been doing to him before he was rescued.

Several of his men joined him on his search, never stopping until the next evening. Not even one believed Elof's lies, but now everyone knew she was Elof's sister, which could create distrust for her among the people. Michal prayed they were wise enough to look at all that she'd done for them instead of only looking at her bloodline.

Michal stationed men all around the forest edge to the clearing. He was not going to let her do this. She'd never be able to survive long enough for them to rescue her. At best, reinforcements were still two weeks out and that was only if they'd had no delays on the journey there and back and had turned to leave the same day they'd arrived to request reinforcements.

Elof brought out the child, a chopping block, and stood sharpening his sword. "Please, Aamber. Please don't do this," Michal whispered, but he knew she was looking at the girl's wide, frightened eyes too, and knew there was no hope of stopping her. Michal heard a rustle beside him and Aamber stood there, looking at him. She was at the very edge of the tree line, just out of his reach. He began running toward her. Not a single tear marred her face but Michal could only imagine the fear of what she was about to do. "I'm sorry," she mouthed, and stepped out into sight.

Michal watched as she placed both hands on the back of her head and walked toward her brother with her head held high. To his surprise, he noticed her dagger wasn't tied at her waist, and he looked around. It stuck out of a tree to his right, pinning a sheet of paper to the rough bark. Michal slowly removed the dagger and held the letter in his hands. It read,

"My dearest Michal,

First, I would like to begin by apologizing for not telling you about Odin. I kept it from you not because I didn't trust you, but because I was ashamed. I'm so sorry for hurting you. That was never my intention. I should have let you talk this morning, but I was still so angry. It wasn't until this afternoon I realized I wasn't angry at you, I was angry at myself for not telling you, and about how jealous I was when I saw Macy talking to you. It wasn't as if you'd made a commitment to me, and you have the right to talk to anyone you want. I hope someday you can forgive me for my pettiness.

I know you think Elof is bluffing, but I know him. The years have changed Elof and turned his heart to stone just as our father's heart had been. I'm sorry to do this to you, but I've prayed all day while watching you search. I know in my soul this is what the Holy Spirit is telling me to do. Please forgive me, my love. Don't try to rescue me. The Vikings have lost prisoners before, and they won't let that happen again.

I don't know if we'll meet again in this life, but I know we'll see each other in the next. I only pray someday you'll find it in your heart to forgive me. I have many regrets, but the largest regret is I never told you how much I love you. My heart has been yours from the moment we met. If I had to do it all over again, I wouldn't change anything.

Forever yours, Aamber Rose Egil."

Aamber walked through the clearing toward her brother, the blood pounding in her head. Even from this distance, she could see a smug, evil smile on Elof's face. At that moment, she knew the rumors were true. He'd killed their parents and now he was going to kill her too.

When Elof's lackey had her hands tied behind her back, she broke the silence. "I knew you were a coward, Elof, but I never imagined you would stoop so low as to threaten a child's life to get your way."

Her brother backhanded her, reminding her of the evening her father had backhanded her on the deck of the *Calder* for mouthing off. He was their father reincarnate. Elof motioned for the other Viking to set the little girl free, who then ran to the woods, throwing a look of gratitude and pity to Aamber over her shoulder.

Her brother turned to enter the castle. The Viking holding her tried to get her to follow, but she refused to move another step. She'd already done most of their work for them by turning herself in and had no intention of cooperating further. Aamber made herself dead weight. Unfortunately for her, though, the Viking lifted her as if she was a feather.

They entered the courtroom and her brother sat on King Richard's throne. Her captor dropped her onto the hard stone floor. She managed to turn just in time to land on her stomach, not her side. Landing on her side could have broken her shoulder. Either way, she ended up bloodying her nose. Elof clucked his tongue. "Soooooooo stubborn. You've already started making things harder on yourself. Search her for weapons."

The Viking picked her back up again while another searched her, finding nothing and taking too much time for Aamber's comfort. She kicked the man in the groin, causing her brother to laugh. "Oh, my dear sister. I'm disappointed in you. You've gone so far as to walk in here without any weapons."

Elof descended from the throne, reached down, and undid Aamber's braids, his disgusting hands feeling like slime on her head. Her red hair piled around her as he leaned down and whispered in her ear. "I remember how you hated it when father grabbed your hair." Elof then gathered her hair by a handful, pulling her head to face him.

Aamber smiled and for the first time looked her brother in the eye. Blood ran out of her nose, over her smile, and her cheek had begun to swell. Trying to avoid getting blood in her mouth, she said. "I have a weapon stronger than any other. It's one you could never defeat nor even control. My weapon is the Holy Spirit, who lives in my heart, which is something you could never take from me. It's only something that can be shared."

The look was back. The one that had scared Elof so badly in the forest that fateful night. Her eyes glowed, and all the love of her heart shone out. Elof leaned forward slowly, his anger growing by the second. His black teeth were only inches from her nose and foul breath assaulted her as he said, "We'll see about that."

A few days after Aamber had turned herself in, Michal rode Buck through the forest, stopping at the tree line that met the ocean. He was alone, save for Joseph who sat a few horse lengths back. Michal had had to get away from everything. He wanted to run away from all the pain, the crushing responsibility, and the regrets. He couldn't help wondering how much longer his people could hold out. The Vikings were getting closer and closer to discovering them, and Aamber being captured had deflated their spirits tremendously.

Aamber's note was in his breast pocket next to his heart, burning itself into his skin. Over the past few days, he'd read it so often that he'd memorized it. He now wore her necklace under his shirt and he touched it when he missed her the most. Michal always tried to put on a good face for his soldiers and he only allowed Joseph to see his true feelings. He understood what she'd done but had no intention of believing it would be the last time they'd ever see each other. God had brought him the love of his life and he would not let her go until the bitter end.

The sun had almost set and he looked at the sky's glorious colors. He wanted to scream at God, rant and cry that it wasn't fair, but he kept remembering the Book of Job. Michal could be angry but God had sent Aamber right when they needed her the most. Through her, God had saved his citizens, his army, his sister, and him. So, instead of being angry, he felt grateful.

He was grateful to God for saving his life and for giving him the time he had had with Aamber. Even if he never saw her again, he would be grateful to God. Michal remembered his father one evening telling him he believed Aamber would be the one to help Michal get past the anger he felt toward Cheryle. Not only had she showed him how to get past the pain but she'd also shown him how to live and love again. Instead of becoming angry at the pain she'd faced in her life, Aamber used her experiences to benefit others and lead them to Christ. She never taught with words. She taught by example.

Michal even laughed now about discovering Cheryle's deception. Looking back, he could see that the Lord had saved him. God had an extraordinary woman out there for him, one who always put others above herself. Michal's only regret was that he'd never had the courage to tell Aamber how he felt about her, but he prayed he wouldn't have to carry this regret the rest of his life. Even if he did, Michal could finally pray and mean in his heart that God's will be done.

Michal looked back out at the ocean. The wind rustled in the trees behind him, and birds chirped. It was then he noticed a small black dot on the horizon. He didn't think much about it until it began to multiply into more dots. He reached back and pulled a telescope out of his saddlebag. His heart jumped into his throat at what he saw. A whole fleet of ships was coming toward them but their flag was still too small for him to tell who they were.

"Joseph, come look at this," he called. Joseph brought his black horse up beside Buck and Michal handed him the telescope. "Is that what I think it is?"

Joseph lowered the telescope, his face mirroring the emotions Michal had on his own. "I'm not sure. Let's wait until they're close enough for us to see the flag."

Michal couldn't help worrying that it might be another clan of Vikings. It couldn't be their reinforcements, not yet. They waited an hour. Michal looked through the telescope again and was finally able to make out the flag. It had two mountains with a sun rising behind it. Then he looked at the other ships. Some had trees, some had the mountain design. He lowered the telescope, mouth open. "It's our reinforcements."

CHAPTER 11

THE BATTLE

The Lord is good, a stronghold in the day of trouble; and he knoweth them that trust in him.

Nahum 1:7 KJV

Océan, A.D. 907

Aamber lay in her cell, the rough stones digging into her side. Most prisoners were kept with one leg chained. The really dangerous ones had their arms chained. She had both legs chained, both arms chained, and a chain around her waist. It was almost comical. At least Aamber would have found humor in it if the chains weren't the only thing she wore.

Over the past several days, she had been violated in any and every possible way her brother could think of but she'd yet to give up their camps. Every time they questioned her, she tried to remember how Jesus was questioned and tortured and she only replied using Bible verses she'd memorized. One, in particular, kept running through her head, Nahum 1:7. She repeated it over and over, finding strength in the words.

Aamber even sang praises in the jail, which brought encouragement to the soldiers who had been captured and were imprisoned along with her. Jackson was included in their number, and his heart broke when he looked over at Aamber. Her being naked allowed them to see every injury. Almost every inch of her skin was either red and cut, or black and blue, or covered in dirt. Every nail she had was removed, and her beautiful hair had been cut unevenly with a knife. If she survived this ordeal, her beautiful face would be forever covered in scars. Her eyes were so swollen it was a wonder that she could see anything. She'd been skinny before but now she was all bones, and couldn't stand on just her own strength.

They often made the men watch her being tortured, thinking it would discourage them to see their leader at such a low state, but it only served to encourage them because she never gave in. They prayed, hoped, sang, and prayed some more. They were living on God's strength, and nothing else. Unsurprisingly, they had all they needed.

Chrystal stood toe-to-toe with Gideon and crossed her arms. "I am not staying on the ship! I'm going to fight for my people and you can't stop me!" she yelled. Turning, she entered her room to get her weapons. Then the door slammed behind her and she heard a board being nailed across it. "NOOOOO! NO! Gideon, please don't do this!" she called through the wood.

On the other side of the door, Gideon leaned his forehead against it, tears threatening to spill. He hated doing this to her. "I'm sorry, Chrystal. I'm not going to risk losing you. You'll be safe here and I'll come to get you as soon as I can." Gideon turned and ran, his heart breaking at her pleas to be set free.

Joseph and Michal rushed back to their camps, rallying their soldiers, telling them to meet at the rendezvous point. Lightning raced through their veins. God had sent them the help they needed when they needed it the most. They hoped the Vikings had not yet seen them coming. The element of surprise would work in their favor. They'd probably be able to take out at least half of the Vikings who were searching the forest, looking for them.

The lifeboats with the first men landed at dawn. Gideon raced to embrace Michal. "You made it! You made it! But how did you get here so soon, and with Forêt soldiers to boot?!" Michal asked.

Gideon laughed. "It was the darndest thing! They were already two weeks out at sea in our direction running training drills and having a war game with Forêt and somehow had enough supplies to last us for the whole trip back! If that isn't God's handiwork, nothing is!"

Michal sobered. "My sister?"

Gideon nodded. "She's on our ship but, I must warn you, I had to bar her into a room to keep her from swimming to shore. She's going to be powerful angry when this is all over but we at least have the security of knowing she's safe. That is, if she doesn't kill my guard and escape," he said with a chuckle.

Michal shook his head. "Well, I doubt she'd kill him, but she might give him a wallop he wouldn't soon forget."

"Where's Ruth?" Gideon asked looking over Michal's shoulder.

"She surrendered herself to the Vikings a few days ago, when her brother threatened to start killing a child for each day she waited."

Shock came over Gideon's face. "Her brother? What? Michal, you're not making any sense."

"It's a long story. All you need to know is Ruth's real name is Aamber Rose Egil."

Gideon paled. "You mean the daughter of Einar Egil, who was killed about seven years ago?"

Michal nodded. "Yes. She actually escaped the ship and came here to make a new life."

"Was she who they were looking for this whole time?" Gideon asked.

"No," Michal said shaking his head. "They didn't know she was alive until my army used their own techniques to fight against them."

Gideon whistled. "Well, I'll be darned. I never expected that. Speaking of Vikings, where are their ships? I expected some sea warfare before we made land."

"We might have sunk them. That's also a long story for another time. Right now, we need to figure out our plan of action. I still have about five thousand soldiers at my disposal, more in the prison of the castle. I would guess we've knocked the Vikings numbers down to about ten thousand."

Gideon's brows furrowed. "Then we should have a one-to-one man fight. I've got about five thousand soldiers with me. It probably would have been more if we'd made it all the way to Montagne but time was of the essence."

Nodding, Michal said, "All right. That's a lot better than we had before. I'm not sure if the Vikings know you're here yet. I think at least half of them are spread throughout the forests looking for us. We've been able to keep pretty good track of where they were."

Gideon nodded. "Then we could split the two groups up. I could lead the charge in the forest while you lead the charge in storming the castle. Will we be taking any prisoners?"

Michal considered this for a moment. "Yes. I doubt they won't be executed eventually, but at least this way we can give them a chance to turn to Jesus. Bring your men to port. I'll leave Joseph here with you in case you have any questions only a native could answer. We'll divide and conquer, literally. May God go with you, brother."

"May He be with your spirit, Michal."

Soon, Michal was racing back to his troops. His spirits were higher than they'd been in months. There was finally a light at the proverbial end of their tunnel. He prayed that Aamber would be waiting for him when he got there. Their lives would never be the same again but at least then the nightmare would be over and they could find some closure.

Suddenly, a large black horse cut him off and Buck reared, almost causing Michal to fall off. A large sword swung at this head but he managed to block the blow in the nick of time. They went back and forth a few times. Elof was strong and very skilled with a sword, but Michal reminded himself God was on his side, and God could never be defeated.

When he had his chance, Michal sliced through the throat of the other man's horse, causing the animal to crumble beneath him. A stream of horrendous curses flowed from the Viking's mouth and he swiped furiously at Michal with his sword. Buck reared again and somehow managed to kick the Viking in the head.

Elof grabbed his face where the hoof had struck, groaning in pain. Michal was shocked that the blow hadn't killed him. Elof turned and ran into the woods before Michal could take advantage of the situation. He tried to follow but Elof had disappeared and Michal couldn't waste time looking for him. He had a Viking princess to save.

When he reached his men, they were ready, eyes alert and hungry for blood. Michal couldn't help thinking that Aamber would be proud to see them now. "God has provided in our hour of need. Now our friends are here, we can take back our beautiful country from those who want to destroy it! The battle has been long, but we have persevered. Remember, men, 'All things are possible for those who believe.' Now, let's bow our heads in prayer and remember where our true help comes from! Dear Heavenly Father, we come to you before our battle. If this is not Your will, God, tell us now and we'll surrender. But, if it is Your will, give us the strength and the courage we need to face this massive enemy head-on. Give my soldiers the heart of David who defeated the giant with one smooth stone. Give them the faith of Daniel, who knew you'd shut the mouths of the lions. Please protect our families and children. No matter what our future is today, Lord, please be with them. Above all, God, please let anything we do bring glory and honor to You and only You, and in all things let Your will be done! In Jesus' most precious and holy name, I pray. Amen!"

"Amen!" his soldiers shouted back.

"All right, men! Let's prove our God is stronger than anything they can throw at us!"

Shouts began to ring out above the prison. Aamber crawled as close to Jackson as she could, and he crawled toward her as well. "Hey! What's going on up there?" their guard shouted up the stairs. While he was distracted, Jackson leaned over and tossed the dagger Aamber had managed to steal from one of the guards while he'd interrogated her. She'd given it to him to hide because she'd surely lose it.

As quickly and quietly as she could, she picked her locks. Aamber had to pretend for a few moments they were still on when the guard looked back at them. He shrugged, then climbed the stairs to holler at his comrades some more. She dragged herself over to where Jackson sat, gritting her teeth from the scrapes and wounds she was opening, and picked his locks.

Jackson then picked her up and she picked every lock that was keeping their people in. He then gently sat her down, covering her with the one ratty blanket he could find. Aamber knew Jackson wished he could hide her in the tunnel under the jail but the Vikings had filled it after they'd sprung Michal and the other soldiers. "The battle has begun. Our reinforcements must have arrived early somehow. We must help them. Stay here. I'll leave this dagger with you. We'll come back for you. You have my word."

"Go, go help Michal," was all she could get out. Picking the locks had taken all her strength.

"What the…" the guard yelled but was silenced before he could get any more out. The soldiers were weak but would fight with all the strength they had left. They rushed the stairs. All Aamber could hear was thudding overhead. She tried to think of something else she could do to help but she couldn't walk. After pulling the blanket closer around her, she held the dagger close to her chest, ready to stab anyone who came near. Before long, she couldn't help falling asleep.

Michal's troops had finally made it to the castle. They'd ended up having to fight multiple platoons of Vikings to get there. The Vikings had been closer to finding their camps than they'd realized. One more day and they probably would have found them. It wasn't long before Gideon's men were fighting side by side with his. As they fought, Gideon called over his shoulder at Michal, "So much for dividing and conquering!"

Michal laughed. "Oh, you know you just missed me and had to come find us!"

"Like a disease," Gideon shot back. Michal couldn't believe this was the conversation they were having in the heat of battle. His men fought bravely and, because of Aamber's training, they lost very few along the way. Aamber had been right about the Vikings being weak. They hadn't had much food of late and were in total chaos as to who their commander was. From what Michal could tell, the only seniority system they had in place was their leader, and then it was just whoever was the meanest. Unfortunately for the Vikings, the meanest often were the most selfish, who only looked out for their own interest.

Michal didn't dismount until they'd made it to the castle courtyard. He and Gideon had to fight back-to-back. It seemed as if the Vikings believed that, if they killed Michal the war would be over, and his men would simply surrender. Their men fought the Vikings on all sides.

After defeating his latest opponent, Michal looked around for who was next but not a single Viking showed his face. They'd been fighting all day and Michal knew it was going to be hard to get all the Vikings from the castle. He'd seen many flee into it or into the forest. They would have a heck of a time hunting them down over the next few days.

Michal pushed through the large stone castle doors, surprised that they didn't resist. The Vikings apparently had been too panicked to post a guard to try and keep them out, not that it would have worked anyway. Soldiers spread out to his left and his right. Michal headed straight for the dining room, Joseph and Gideon flanking him. Nothing could have prepared him for what he was about to find.

Aamber awoke with a start. To her utter shock, it was her brother who stomped down the prison stairs. When he was close enough, she tried to stab him, but he caught her arm easily, causing her to drop the knife. Elof wretched her blanket away and started dragging her by her hair. She tried to keep her body from scraping against the stone floors and staircase but it helped very little.

Elof dragged her to the castle dining room and, still holding her by her hair, sat at the table and began to eat the feast still laid upon it. It wasn't until then that Aamber saw his swollen black eye. She could only imagine who'd been strong enough to do that to her brother. It might be the lack of food, but it seemed to Aamber that it was shaped like a hoofprint.

Aamber heard footsteps and her brother put the dagger she'd tried to stab him with to her throat. She knew her army had come and they'd defeated the Vikings. Otherwise, why would Elof be preparing for a standoff, using her as a hostage? To Aamber's horror, Michal, Gideon, and Joseph entered through the curved doorway. *Why couldn't it be anyone else? A soldier she didn't know.* But a weight was lifted off her shoulders, knowing they hadn't been killed in the fighting.

Michal's eyes widened when he saw her bloodied, naked, and hanging by her hair with a dagger to her throat. He took a step forward and Elof jabbed the knife into her soft skin, causing her to flinch. Michal froze, a look of pure hatred on his face. "Release her."

Elof laughed sinisterly. "We both know the moment I do, I'll be dead. If you want her alive, I suggest you get me a boat I can sail out of here on."

Michal's eyes narrowed. "Fine. I'll give you whatever you want. Just let her go."

A strange expression entered Elof's eyes. "Explain this to me, Michal. You know she was a Viking. You know she cheated, lied, stole, and killed. You've proven to me your faith is genuine and, if your God is supposed to be all good, then how can you or He associate with a woman like her?"

For the first time, Michal felt compassion enter his heart for the Viking. "Jesus's closest disciples were thieves, liars, cheats, and murderers. I can only explain it to you the way Jesus did when the religious leaders back then asked the same question. He replied that it's not the healthy ones who need a doctor, but the sick. He didn't come to call righteous people to turn from their sins, he came and died to call sinners to repent. Obviously, I'm paraphrasing, but if you'd like I'd be willing to find the passage and read it to you."

The Viking contemplated Michal. "So, you're saying, even though she's done all these things, you still love and forgive her? And not only you, but this perfect God of yours, too?" Michal nodded. Elof shook his head. "I didn't ask this God to come down and pay for my sins, so I don't think I owe him anything!"

Elof began to slit Aamber's throat but, with the last of her strength, she managed to shove the knife away. Out of the corner of her eye, she saw Michal string his bow and shoot, but she pushed in front of the arrow, it hitting her in the side, and fell to the floor. Elof stood above Aamber in complete shock. "You...you saved my life?" The men then tackled Elof, who was too shocked to resist.

Michal gently pulled Aamber into his arms and rose. "Get a doctor! Quick!" he yelled behind him as he carried her toward one of the bedrooms. He laid her on the first bed he found, which was unmade and smelled of sweat. He grabbed a sheet and quickly pressed hard on the wound around the arrow trying to stop the bleeding. "Aamber, oh, Aamber my love! I'm so, so sorry! I'm so sorry! I never meant to hit you." Tears poured down his cheeks and she reached up weakly and wiped them away.

Soon the doctor arrived, pushing Michal aside. Michal handed him the supplies he asked for. Aamber had passed out from the pain and fatigue. When the doctor finished, he stepped back, bloody instruments still in hand. Aamber's breathing came in gasps and her face was flushed, while the rest of her body was pale. To Michal's surprise, Carla May pushed into the room. "All right boys, you go out there and help. I'll stay here with Aamber. If anyone's earned a rest, it's her. Now go!"

Chrystal sat on her bed with her knees pulled to her chest, crying. She hadn't heard anything all day and refused to eat anything the guard brought to her, begging him to leave and help the others. Chrystal had prayed until her voice was hoarse and cried until her head ached. She trembled with anger, fear, and sadness, planning on how she was going to kill Gideon, knowing that if he returned to her alive, she'd be too relieved to be mad at him.

Chrystal heard shouts and her door burst open. Michal stood in the doorway. Chrystal leaped off the bed into her brother's arms, hugging him with all her strength. She'd never been happier to see him. Chrystal pulled back. "Where are Mom and Dad?" The joy immediately left Michal's eyes and Chrystal's heart sunk. "You...you mean?" she said, her voice trembling. Michal pulled her close again in response as she cried.

The next month was the most miserable month Michal ever remembered living. The rest of the Vikings had been hunted and either killed or captured by nightfall the day they had stormed the castle. The battle had been bloody and they'd lost many men. After the fighting ended, Michal immediately had the army begin disposing of the Viking bodies and burying their fellow countrymen. Any dead friendly soldiers were immediately placed in their own coffins and loaded onto what became known as the funeral ship.

The people returned to their homes. To their utter shock, the Vikings had spared their fields but they had to be harvested immediately or the crop would go to waste. Out of the 20 thousand Vikings who had landed on their shores, about two hundred had been imprisoned. They were soon put to work helping bury the dead and harvest the crops.

The harvest was brought in within two weeks. After that was finished, they focused their efforts on finishing all the burials. By the third week, all the dead were buried with crosses marking their final resting places. The country held one large funeral for them all, including the king and queen, whose remains they'd not been able to find.

Through it all, Aamber barely clung to life. Infection had set in, giving her a raging fever, on top of her loss of so much blood. Chrystal had become her full-time nurse while Michal got the country back up and running. Chrystal had to constantly pour broth into Aamber's mouth, trying to give her poor body any nutrients she could, just as Aamber had done for Michal. The doctor was able to visit only about once a week. There were many wounded and Michal combined the nurses they had trained in the camps, putting Carla May over them all.

When everything had finally been put back to as normal as possible, Gideon agreed to keep most of his soldiers there for another week while Michal's army rested and grieved but sent the funeral ship ahead of them to Montagne. When everything was done, Océan had lost its king, its queen, and half its army, but citizen casualties were minimal, their crops had been spared, and, most important of all, the country had held onto its faith.

Through it all, Michal lived in fear of receiving word that Aamber had died. He spent all his spare time kneeling in the church, begging God to spare her life. The strangest part was that he couldn't bring himself to go see her for himself. He couldn't get the image out of his mind of his arrow piercing her side. Fear squeezed his heart at the mere thought of setting foot into her room.

Michal made sure all the Vikings had plenty of food, water, clothes, and blankets while in prison, trying to follow the command to love his enemy as himself. In the end, they decided to give the remaining Vikings a choice. They could either spend the rest of their lives doing manual labor for the castle under close guard or they would be executed. All except Elof. Michal hated having to kill Aamber's brother but couldn't let him live after all the horrible things he'd done. His people deserved justice, not to mention the risk that the remaining Vikings would mutiny and once again rally around their leader.

The night before Elof's execution, Michal visited him. The once-proud warrior sat chained to a wall under heavy guard. Michal stood before him and crossed his arms. "I know what you came to say," Elof began, resignation to his fate in his voice. "You want to know where your parents' bodies are. We threw them into the sea," he said, without emotion. Michal took a deep breath, trying to get the image of his wonderful parents being thrown away like that. Elof refused to meet Michal's eyes. "How's my sister?"

Michal was surprised he'd asked. "She's still fighting. I was told this morning her fever had broken. But she's still very weak and hasn't woken up."

Elof still refused to meet his eyes. After a long pause, he spoke up again. "Why'd she do it?"

Staring at the Viking, confused, Michal asked "Do what?"

Finally, Elof met his gaze. "Why did she save my life. I did horrible things to her and had literally just tried to slit her throat. Why'd she take an arrow for me?"

Michal shook his head, not believing the Viking still didn't understand. "Because she loves you, Elof. She knew if she died, she'd go to Heaven and wanted to give you the chance of having such peace when you died."

Elof shook his head, fat tears rolling down his cheeks. "I don't deserve to," he choked out.

Michal squatted down so they'd be eye level. "None of us do, Elof. That's why God had to sacrifice His one and only perfect Son for our sins. So, we'd be able to be with Him in Heaven for eternity. All we have to do is confess and repent of our sins and accept Him into our hearts and lives as our Lord and Savior, then try to live a godly life. All we have to do is be reborn."

Elof was quiet for a long time, considering the other man's words. "You claim there's one God, but then talk about three different ones. So, which is it? Is Jesus, God, or the Holy Spirit the One you serve?"

"They're a Trinity. Three that are one," Michal replied. "They're all three the same God. Think of it like a ship. One part's responsible for sailing, another part for staying afloat, and yet another part for steering. They all have different functions but they make one ship. God is the Lord and Creator over everything. He sent His Son Jesus, who was God and human, to earth to die for our sins and be raised back to life so one day we might live in Heaven with Him. Once we're born again, the Holy Spirit comes upon us and lives in our hearts. Which means God literally lives inside you, and your body becomes his temple. Through the Holy Spirit, God guides you in the ways he wants you to go. The Holy Spirit speaks softly, but if you listen for it, you'll never go wrong."

Elof shook his head. "But what happens if you sin again?"

"You repent again and try not to sin anymore. God Himself says we've all sinned and fallen short of the glory of God. Becoming a Christian doesn't mean you become perfect. It just means you have a perfect God standing by your side leading you and catching you when you fall."

Elof continued to sob. "And, ...and God would even be willing to forgive someone as bad as me?"

Michal reached out and squeezed the other man's shoulder. Michal could feel Elof's soul had been searching for Christ a long time. "Yes, Elof. He loves you and wants you to be His child."

The large man continued to cry. Finally, he said, "I...I want to be reborn. I want to accept Jesus as my Lord and Savior."

Michal smiled. With tears in his eyes, Michal asked. "Elof Egil, do you confess you are a sinner and repent of those sins?"

"I do, I really do!" Elof exclaimed.

"Do you believe Jesus is the Christ, the Son of the living God?"

Elof nodded. "Yes."

"Do you accept Him as your Lord and Savior?"

"I do."

Michal bowed his head and prayed. "Father God, we come to now, humbly asking you to forgive Elof's sins. Please, wash his heart clean, Lord, and make him your child. Lord, he wants to accept you as his Lord and Savior. In Jesus's precious and holy name we pray, Amen." When Michal opened his eyes, for the first time he saw hope in Elof's heart.

Michal spent the rest of the night talking with Elof and reading to him from God's word. He arranged for him to be baptized the next morning. Only Michal and some soldiers were in attendance, but it was enough. "Repeat after me," the priest said to Elof. "I believe."

"I believe."

"That Jesus is the Christ."

"That Jesus is the Christ."

"The Son of the living God."

"The Son of the living God."

"And I accept Him."

"And I accept Him."

"As my Lord and Savior."

"As my Lord and Savior."

Holding Elof's nose with one hand and supporting his back with the other, the priest dunked him in the water and said. "I baptize you in the name of the Father, the Son, and the Holy Spirit." When he brought Elof out of the water, he looked strange. It took Michal a minute to realize he looked strange because it was the first time he'd ever seen Elof smile.

Later that afternoon, Elof was publicly executed. "Do you have anything you want to say?" the executioner asked Elof.

Elof hung his head in shame. "I'm sorry for all the pain and suffering I've caused and pray that someday you can find it in your heart to forgive me. Please, don't let your anger at me keep you from getting into Heaven." Then it was over. But Michal wasn't sad. He knew he'd see his new brother someday in Heaven, and he couldn't wait to tell that to Elof's earthly sister.

CHAPTER 12

A NEW LIFE

For which cause we faint not; but though our outward man perish, yet the inward man is renewed day by day. For our light affliction, which is but for a moment, worketh for us a far more exceeding and eternal weight of glory;

2 Corinthians 4:16-17 KJV

Océan, A.D. 907

Aamber slowly opened her eyes. The light hurt and she started to panic, wondering where she was. "Aamber, Aamber, it's all right. It's me, Chrystal."

Aamber looked to the gentle hand that held her down in the bed, then realized it wasn't just Chrystal holding her down. Aamber was too weak even to lift her head. "Water," Aamber rasped.

Soon a cool glass of water was pressed to her lips while Chrystal held her head up. After the water, Aamber's throat felt so much better

243

and she was exhausted. Chrystal leaned over and pushed a short lock of Aamber's hair out of her eyes. "Is that better?" she asked.

Aamber smiled, trying not to cry. "Yes. What are you doing here? Is the war over?" The last Aamber remember was being in prison. Chrystal then filled her in with news from the castle, about how they'd won, and how Aamber's brother had accepted Christ before he was executed. Then she told Aamber of her own adventures, ending with Gideon locking her in a room on the ship.

Aamber shook her head. "I understand his intentions but don't necessarily agree with his methods."

Her friend's head bobbed and Aamber read the sadness in her friend's eyes. "Don't be so hard on him, Chrystal. He was just trying to protect you. Remember, men are stupid." Chrystal laughed hard at her friend's joke, the picked up the sewing she'd been working on while waiting for Aamber to wake. "Chrystal, I..."

"Don't, Aamber. Don't you dare apologize. My entire country is alive and well today because of you. I don't blame you one bit for not telling us who you are in the beginning. You are the best friend I've ever had and none of this was your fault. So, please. Don't apologize," Chrystal said and tears began running down her face.

Aamber pulled her into a hug. They cried on each other's soldiers, mourning the friends they'd lost and praising God for the friends they still had. The two women spent the next few minutes in companionable silence and Aamber finally worked up the courage to ask Chrystal the question burning in her mind. "How's Michal. Has he come to visit me?"

Chrystal glanced at Aamber, but Aamber couldn't read what her expression meant. Finally, Chrystal sighed and said. "No, he hasn't come to visit you. But I don't think it's by choice. I think he's had the image of his arrow piercing you etched into his brain, making him scared to death to see you again. I don't know if he's just so scared you will die that he's trying to distance himself or scared you'll be mad at him for shooting the arrow or for executing your brother. I've tried to convince him you wouldn't be, but I think he feels so bad he just can't face you yet. He loves you Aamber, of that I have no doubt. Just give him time to recover."

Aamber looked at the ceiling. "Did he show you the letter I wrote him?"

"Is that what he's reading all the time? He carries around a piece of paper in his breast pocket, reading it in his spare time repeatedly," Chrystal asked.

Aamber nodded. "I think he's angry at me for turning myself over to Elof and for jumping in front of the arrow."

Chrystal shook her head. "I don't think so."

Aamber looked back to the ceiling. "I guess we'll see."

Aamber Rose Egil sat in the palace garden, taking in the beautiful day. The sun shone warm on her face, while the wind carried the scent of roses and caressed her cheeks. She'd been sick for months and Chrystal had never left her side. Even now, Aamber couldn't walk long distances alone, but she was growing stronger every day.

Chrystal had told Aamber of her brother's conversion to Christianity just before his execution. He'd even been baptized. Aamber's only regret was she hadn't been there to see it. Michal had been, though. Chrystal told her he'd arranged everything and had even given her brother a proper burial.

Aamber looked down at her clasped hands, her short hair tickling her cheeks. Chrystal had cut it as evenly as she could but it would take a long time to grow back out. Aamber tried to keep it out of her face by tying cloths in bands around her head. It was strange to her, although she no longer felt the need to keep it pulled back. She wore a burgundy dress, whose long, full skirt flowed around her legs. Her old dress's skirt had been fitted because she had never felt the need to have extra fabric swishing around her legs and getting in the way of her activities.

The only thing Aamber still didn't understand was why Michal had not come to see her since he'd lain her in the bed after she was shot. She understood if he was angry with her. There was so much about herself she'd kept hidden for so long. Maybe he felt as if he could never fully trust her. Aamber just wished he would tell her what his reasons were so she could stop agonizing over it.

A shadow fell across her lap and she looked up to find the subject of her thoughts standing before her. She was surprised that she'd not heard him coming. After a moment's pause, he said, "Hello."

Aamber looked back down at her clasped hands. "Hello."

He sat on the bench next to her, seeming as nervous as she. "I owe you an apology. Actually, I owe you several apologies. My first one for accidentally shooting you."

Aamber burst out laughing, breaking the tension. "I jumped in front of the arrow, remember?"

Michal just shook his head, amused. "The second for not coming to visit you sooner. I have no excuse, but I do want to try to explain what's kept me away. You see, I have spent every waking minute since that day in fear of getting a notification you'd died. It was a miracle you hadn't died in my arms that day. Every time I tried to go visit you, I'd see you bleeding out again and I just couldn't bring myself to do it. I know it was cowardly and I'm sorry."

Aamber shook her head. "It wasn't cowardly. I can only imagine how hard it's been." He pulled something from around his neck and handed it to her. "My necklace. I didn't think I would ever see this again."

Then he pulled out the note she'd left pinned to the tree in the forest. Chrystal had told her he was carrying it around in his breast pocket, but that was two months ago. While rubbing the paper between his fingers, he asked "Did you mean what you said when you wrote this?"

She looked away, embarrassed. "I wouldn't have written it if I didn't mean it."

Michal's smile was blinding. "You see, I had another reason for not coming to see you before now."

Aamber sobered. "And what was it? Listen. Michal if you're angry at me, I wouldn't…"

Before she realized what was happening, he got off the bench and kneeled before her, opening a small box containing a ring. "Aamber Rose Egil, you are the love of my life and everything I could ever hope for in a wife. I know we've traveled a very long journey to get here but I wouldn't change a thing. I want to spend the rest of my life's journey with you by my side. I know in my inmost heart you're the woman God created for me. Please, make me the happiest man in the world and be my wife."

Aamber covered her mouth with her hands. She was completely shocked. Aamber had always known that Michal cared for her but she had believed that, when things went back to normal, he would realize it had only been because of the situation they were in, having only each other to depend on. But she knew him well enough to know he would never ask her to marry him if he didn't really love her with all his heart. A million reasons ran through her mind why she should say no. She wasn't good enough for him and wasn't royalty. But oh, how her heart wanted to scream yes!

"Oh, Michal. I'm not good enough for you," she cried.

Before she could say another word, he took her face in his hands and kissed her, and kissed her, and kissed her again. When he'd finally let her catch her breath, he whispered against her lips, "Don't you ever say that again. You are the only woman I have ever truly loved and God has made you perfect for me. Please, say you'll marry me, my Viking princess." He gave her another long kiss.

When he'd pulled back again, she looked into his beautiful blue eyes. "I love you, Michal. Yes, I will be your wife." He lifted her off the bench and began kissing her repeatedly while spinning in circles, laughing and crying at the same time.

"Thank you, God," Michal prayed, clutching Aamber to himself.

DISCUSSION QUESTIONS

1. Was it right for Aamber to tell others her name was Ruth?
2. Was it right for the citizens to steal the Vikings' weapons?
3. Should Aamber have told Michal who she was from the beginning?
4. Should Elof have been executed?
5. Should the citizens have tried to kill fewer Vikings and taken more prisoners?
6. What should the Vikings' punishment be in the end? Was their punishment appropriate?
7. Should Aamber's friends have let her brother go or killed him? Would it have saved a lot of lives?
8. Can you ever truly leave your past behind?
9. Was it right for Gideon to lock Chrystal on the ship to keep her safe?
10. Was it right for Aamber to turn herself over to her brother?
11. Should Aamber have tried to take her brother with her from the Calder?

AUTHOR'S NOTE TO READERS

Dear Readers,

I hope you enjoyed reading Michal and Aamber's story as much as I enjoyed writing it. The pair has kept me company and given me comfort many nights and I hope they can do the same for you. I did want to tell you, though, that almost all my writing is pure fiction. The only historically accurate fact in my book is that there were Vikings who sailed the Atlantic Ocean around 900 A.D.

Although my writing is entirely fiction, the trials the characters go through and the struggles they face have happened to all of us. Many of us have faced the loss of a parent or anxiety and some have even experienced the shame of being raped. All of us in our lives have faced family conflicts and felt as if God was our only friend in the world at one point.

I pray that the way Aamber and Michal handled their struggles will give you strength, and you'll stop to consider the moral questions this book raises. Remember, you will never make the wrong decision if you listen to the Holy Spirit. All of you are in my prayers, God bless.

Sincerely, Emily Martin.